ONCE BEFORE SUNSET

ONCE BEFORE SUNSET

David Deutsch

Lake Dallas, Texas

Copyright © 2021 by David Deutsch
All rights reserved
Printed in the United States of America

FIRST EDITION

ONCE BEFORE SUNSET is a work of fiction. Names, characters, places, and incidents either are the products of the author's imagination or are used fictitiously. Any resemblance to actual events, locales, businesses, companies, or persons, living or dead, is entirely coincidental.

Requests for permission to reprint material from this work should be sent to:

Permissions
Madville Publishing
P.O. Box 358
Lake Dallas, TX 75065

Author Photograph: Kirk Walter
Cover Design: Jacqueline Davis
Cover Art: "Tehura" (2012) by Doron Langberg

ISBN: 978-1-948692-56-4 paperback; 978-1-948692-57-1 ebook
Library of Congress Control Number: 2020941261

DRIFTWOOD PUBLIC LIBRARY
801 SW HWY. 101
LINCOLN CITY, OREGON 97367

For Kirk and Bella

*"Bele amie, si est de nus:
Ne vus sanz mei, ne jeo sanz vus."*

—Marie de France

Princeton, 2001
(Et in acedia ego)

Chapter One

The idea to travel had come to me, fittingly, if lazily, last New Year's Eve. Home for Christmas during my freshman year at Princeton, the holidays had proven awful. My father had reminded me, ad-nauseam—"*let me remind you once more,*" a finger shaking with a sauve savagery, "that you are the *fourth* generation of our family to attend that *self-same institution,*" notable for me because our parents had not-so-secretly doubted that I would get in— anyway, I had been home, from there, and it had been awful.

The wills of patriarchs are too often parodically prolonged but that Christmas ours had come crashing down. As with any old New England family's, it had done so quietly and with a minimum of disturbance to anyone, save myself. As the oldest son of the oldest son of a still older New England family, it had spent its remaining force on reminding me of my "responsibilities" and recalling them with all of the power of home. Our childhood and our adolescence, but praise me not our present, had, like most of our predecessors', been spent in the smallness of Carlton, New Hampshire, a town filled with large clapboard houses and all the extravagance of an early American inanity.

As a child, of course, a family history is hard to contemplate. Fortunately, we had extensive help from our father who, having shown-up his brothers by being born first, is the chairman of our family business, Belicor Publishing. Belicor is a not entirely unimportant publishing concern. It is one of the oldest and largest privately held firms of its sort in the States. Its family forerunner printed pamphlets or broadsheets for either independent-minded revolutionaries or royalists, depending on who has drunk too much Christmas punch. Regardless of its original intentions, the firm is a family one and our father, a sixty-year-old silver-haired well-groomed-but-portly control freak, insisted on taking Christmas to remind me that I am to succeed him as its chief executive: nominally of the literary arm but more imperatively of the division that controls our family profits, most of which are no longer embedded in books *per se*, but in high-end literary *accoutrements*: bookends, pens, gold bookmarks, and other such stuff.

Our mother had just left for New York to follow up her own publishing success. She had contracted elsewhere, since romance novels, my father had insisted, unironically, were not part of Belicor's portfolio. She'd gotten her own back a bit when her book hit shelves. Our father had expected, as Sean translated him, for it to sell like cockrings at an abstinence rally but she had done well. Actually, when I had read it, I had liked it.

She'd called it *An Unanticipated Affair* and instead of her heroine, Waltroud, being beautiful, busty, and well-put together, she starts off weepy, fat, and flustered. Too attentive to everyone around her, Waltroud causes so little conflict that her coworkers, her family, and her few selfish friends all ignore her. Isolated and alone she loses herself in cheap paperbacks and cries herself to sleep. Then one evening, someone's paunch interrupts her on her bus ride home. Its owner has read what she's reading and is interested, he says, in what she thinks of it. Soon they are having dinner together every week. Her life gets better and better until it gets worse, then it evens out and it ends up not so unpleasantly. The set-up is really ingenious and once you get past Waltroud's exasperating dependence on cinnamon buns and her brown paper bagging of everything, her story is worth reading, even if I'm the only one in our family that glanced past the first five pages.

Our lives though, my mother's and mine, have always been more adventurous. This is what, after all, caused the New England uproar when she'd finally taken off to New York. She'd needed, she said, to find "inspiration" for her next novel. After she's done, everyone said, though they never said with what, she'll come back. Of course it's not as though she'd need to: an unmarried uncle, who had invested well, I think, in the eighties, had left her a substantial legacy. This is good because our father would never give her one red cent. He would claim—I know him, he would—that every last penny was "wrapped up in the business." Once, and only once, I had alluded that a public separation might pique an interest in her work, boosting her already respectable sales among the Kroger crowd. She had wondered briefly, with a metallic sweetness, how some stranger's separation could possibly affect her book. All of which goes to show that she still really is one of us. Silence ... it's the perfect panacea. This is all but our family motto.

To tell the truth, I am glad that she went to New York. She is much closer to Princeton. All I have to do now is jump on a train and in an hour or so we can be having dinner, usually at some flashy restaurant that has just been "discovered" by her new agent, AJ. As of yet, of course, this has only happened twice, as they are busy trying to pitch the movie rights to Waltroud. Really, I think she wants to protect me from the vulgarity surrounding scrounging for VIP tables and talking to illiterate go-betweens and movie producers at tacky clubs. Anyway we have several outings planned for the spring. Shows, exhibitions, cultural stuff that you just can't get back in Carlton, and that she would want to do with me.

I can't imagine Sean and her going around in New York. And Donny, well ... of the three of us, I'm the only one she takes to shows. The other two take no interest. Despite Sean's alleged brilliance, he really has an anemic intelligence. He *thinks* he's smart because his whole life he has gotten good grades and sports awards, neither being too hard to *"Achieve at St. Ann's Academy!"* an unearned school motto if ever there was one, and one which only shows how poorly GPA actually attests to ability. Last month he turned eighteen but he's still totally without sense. One night, for instance, not three months ago, he passed me a note just before dinner, behind the back of our father, asking if

I liked "*cock*aegne." Then he snickered all throughout the meal. Our father *hates* private jokes, almost as much as he hates drugs and bad French.

Some people, though, shine despite their innate insipidity and Sean is worse than all St. Ann's acolytes put together. He combines inanity and effortless arrogance to be not what in any sane world he should be, a nonentity, but an "over-achiever," and recently he has just gotten worse, particularly since he found out that Princeton not only did not wait-list *him*—the year I had applied, there had been a *record* number of applicants and staggering few last year; the statistics are in the alumni newsletter—but offered him an early acceptance. People still haven't stopped congratulating the little matriculant. No matter, my philistine frère, one day incompetence will out.

Then there is Donny. Poor Donny, Donald, our youngest brother. He's not so much annoying as he is just sickly. He has never had the chance to worry about grades or school or any ordinary childhood hang-ups. Really, I feel sorry for him. He's a good kid and he always tries to smile, which must be difficult when half the time he has tubes down his throat. When even his own family waits until just before Christmas to buy him his presents.

The rest of our family, even the competing cousins, our uncles' kids, we see only on holidays, so they're pretty unimportant. Though, it was one of them who told me, struggling in her overlong Christmas Eve evening gown, that she was going to East Asia with friends for spring break and made me realize that travel, of course, was the perfect way to get out of the next family get-together.

This hadn't, though, proved as easy as I'd thought, so I'd abandoned the plan. Until, with next Christmas break rearing its horny head once more, some kids in my eating club started planning a ski trip to Aspen and gave me the perfect excuse for why I couldn't come home.

Luckily, I was able to avoid being asked, directly, to go on the trip myself. This was tricky because it quickly became *the* inane topic of conversation for the semester, where to ski, where to eat, where to drink, the answer to the latter being, of course, "everywhere."

So, I let drop halfway through last term that I had plans to travel over break with kids from Carlton. This was a deft response on my part, since the wide-ranging social status of small New Hampshire towns and the restraints of an almost hereditary snobbery prevented anyone from asking too many questions. By this point, even those who I know for a *fact* came to Jersey only because they were denied entrance elsewhere, to St. Andrews or to Oxford, say, are so unbelievably entrenched in Princetonian prejudices that afraid as they are of associating with someone from an actually impressive school and getting ridiculed, they are still more terrified of contaminating contacts with, as the resident snob of our eating club, Alan Stanton, says, pitching his voice at increasingly inaudible intervals and stretching it so as not to pronounce his r's, *"an infehiah institution."* I can only imagine what he, and everyone else, thought when I intimated that I would be traveling with guys not from St. Ann's but with three or four friends from around town. A few kids had said that this sounded adventurous, but after that, so far as I heard, the subject never again touched their Evelyn Waugh-like lips.

Anyway, my ruse worked, even though all I had known then was that by Christmas I would be tired of hanging out with any Princetonians and that there was no way in hell I would want to go back home. The flops from St. Ann's would be there and last summer I had found that their first, and obviously unedifying, year at over-ivied extensions of St. Ann's—*prickae vigent sub pecuniam*—with all of the latter's inadequacies had served simply to bring out the arrogant and willfully ignorant streaks that had been so carefully cultivated in prep school.

Besides, I knew that if I did go back, I would risk seeing Javier, the sole son of the Court Club's director.

Javier. Javier had turned up a few months after his father, who had been appointed last winter, having recently, it was rumored, divorced his wife back in Ponce, Puerto Rico. Despite such "questionable credentials," Javier was accepted into our group almost immediately. This unlikely integration, moreover, seemed an almost natural occurrence as in the summer the club pool was the one "public" place in Carlton not stultifying with pink ladies lunching, and we had encountered him there day after day. It was poolside where, after a morning shift, he would lounge around looking amazingly unencumbered, his boardshorts hanging half-idly off of his smooth slippery hips. It also hadn't hurt that he had managed to procure and then to copy his father's master key and so he had gained an almost unlimited access to the club's top-of-the-line sports equipment, to its food, and to more than a fair share of its alcohol, most of which we could have paid for but which it was more fun to have for free. He would often, in fact, egg us on, wheedling or mocking us, although most of the guys did not need too much prodding to take what was, as he pseudo-logically put it, ours already.

Subtly smart and instinctively manipulative, he was also exciting. He was a whirlwind of energy. Mornings, I think, he worked with the club's cleaning crew. I once saw him, secretly, in that uniform. But in the afternoon he'd look as fresh as if he'd been sleeping for hours. He'd meet up with us and draw us into some quasi-destructive plan he had concocted, soccer on the back nine or contact-squash in some empty basement room. He was intoxicatingly funny and often terrifying, staying underwater too long or driving golf carts off of homemade ramps. He was funnier, raunchier, and more ignited than anyone we knew.

To his father, he remained rigidly respectful, but with a secret air of anarchy. This poise appeared to right all wrongs, including his own petty tyrannies. His rippling sun-browned body, which he sported despite the conspicuous absence of any serious New England sun, made him a natural leader of minor rebellions, while it made the rest of us look sallow and weak. It also covered, I think, an intense underlying unhappiness. For when he was near us, his charismatic, almost cruel excitement would flood into others causing them to overlook his own situation, namely that his hard-working father had removed him from their hot inured home to the cold standoffishness of Carlton, almost entirely against his own will.

Javier's own employment at the club, moreover, was not a success. His father had assigned him the least liked tasks, fixing the always clogged sports facility toilets and wiping mold off of the shower walls, though early on I overheard staff members griping in soft acidic voices that he refused to work, that he sat sullenly for hours while others begrudgingly covered for him, not wanting to report him or risk antagonizing his father. I don't doubt that this was true. He had an active indolence, and even with us, I had seen him scam and weasel his way into closed-off spaces and towards restricted riches with only the least amount of effort to himself.

He was not, in truth, all that nice to anyone. Paradoxically, almost painfully, this came across most perceptibly in his interactions with those with whom, I'd have thought, he should have most sympathized. A sometime sartorial brotherhood appeared not even to give him pause when leading us into the changing rooms where club employees stored their street clothes in cubbyholes. Once, I'm ashamed to admit, we followed him into the back and removed, at random, pink and blue Goodwill polos and tattered khakis, and, at his prompting, tossed them into the showers, which he'd had one of us turn on full to cold. A week or so later, he and a few others set off stink-bombs in the back bathrooms during the dinner rush, rendering them unusable. Waiters became more watchful. Items went missing. Locks were quietly placed on doors. All to little avail. On Sunday evenings, his pockets, I am almost sure of it, were always a little fuller than they had been on Friday afternoons.

Javier himself used only the front conveniences and changed only in the members' locker rooms. He seemed fond of flaunting himself in front of the older, and even some of the younger, flabbier men, at least he did when I was there, flashing a sunsoaked grin and then purposefully pulling down his shorts. Everyone noticed him. How could they not, with his black pubic hair stark against his brown skin? Most patrons pretended not to pay him attention but a few openly gawked at him, for in all he did, he exuded a flawless, lawless charm that made his every movement seem right and almost pleasurably painful to watch.

Toward the end of that summer, however, the situation had changed. Three weeks before we all, save Javier, had to return to school, he had procured the key to one of the club's most closely-guarded cellars, one closed even to his master key. He had subsequently sequestered three cases of wine, stashing them in an unused basement storeroom. The next day, we had sat around and gotten preposterously, dionysianly drunk. At first it had been fun. We talked about our first year away and made plans for the second. Then Javier, in a rare self-revelatory mood, had talked about Puerto Rico, and about the girls there, and about what he had done with them and about what they had done with him, the over-air-conditioned room growing hotter as he had leered, at me alone it seemed, slyly. Then a couple of the others, then everyone, their lips disgustingly stained, had joined in, talking about girls, embellishing what I knew already were lies, obscenities flying, making the subject more and more sickening, until everyone, Javier included, had thrown up in an involuntary orgy of self-disgust.

The next day our hard-earned hangovers had been hellacious. Mine was at least, and I had not drunk nearly so much as the others. I had kept count. Still, these were a mere inconvenience compared to what was in store for our symposiarch. After obtaining the key, Javier had, unfortunately, gotten uncharacteristically cold feet. So he had snuck into the cellar on his own to grab what we would drink. This was a tactical error on his part. He had not anticipated a system for discerning which bottles were drinkable, which were unready, and which were irreplaceable, nor had he, I supppose, even suspected that such a system could exist. He had also, as a gracious host, insisted on pouring the first six or seven bottles himself, with the result that, despite his ceremonious announcement of each one, we had none of us any clear idea of what, exactly, it was that we were drinking, not that this necessarily would have made much of a difference. Anyhow, we had apparently consumed a few auctioned Napas the club had acquired, a few Barolos, and a fairly conspicuous amount from a case of not quite ripe "Château Margaux." When I found this out later I heard eerie echoes in my ear of *"Mār-ga,"* *"Mār-ga."*

The next night, I later learned, an assistant sommelier had gone into the club's reserve room to grab a bottle from a shelf above one of the precipitously reduced cases. By sheer bad luck she must have glanced down and noticed that a portion of the case's contents had been appropriated. After a quick peek around, she must have found several more officially complete crates partially emptied—easily recognizable, I suppose, thanks to the new director's system for marking the ordered removal of bottles—and had immediately informed the restaurant manager. He had, in turn, informed Javier's father, so as not to be blamed himself. This was probably a wise decision because when the director had found out, he had been furious. He had gotten the sales list and had visited the cellar himself. Then he'd had all of the staff lockers searched, had threatened to sack the sommelier, and had ordered cameras installed in all of the rooms storing alcohol. Finally, instead of further upsetting his staff, as this had happened on a busy Friday night, this strong silent type, who had clearly not known who it was who had cost the club a significant amount of money, and a great investment, had gone home and had beaten the shit out of his son. When I saw Javier the next Monday he would not even look at me and all the smooth tender skin around his eyes, once almond colored, had been more black and blue than even our teeth had been that sorry-sick late afternoon.

After that, everyone had decided that hanging out with Javier had not been so much fun as we had pretended and he had ignored us. Once or twice, I had tried to talk to him, but when he saw any of us, he would slip away, a look of scarcely contained fear and fury on his face. It was awful, at once a betrayal of our friendship and a relief.

What all this adds up to is that there was now no one whom I wanted to see in Carlton, and since I didn't want to end up stuck in our stifling old house, I knew that I had to find someplace where I could spend winter break, someplace where I could be on my own yet not alone, someplace surfeited with the restrained arms of anonymity. I knew also, of course, that I would go to Europe. To a capital that I could idolize idly as a comfortable pivot point between a deliciously decadent past, for in our minds we are all always aristocrats, and the glass and concrete exuberance of an ever-expanding *a-venir*. To someplace outside the everpresent immediacy of the U.S., with its contracted spotlight on no more than a few years forward from a few years back.

This sense of being stuck is why I just could not go back to Carlton. Especially after last summer, which, Javier aside even, had just been so *frustrating*.

I don't want to remember it.

But I do.

Before Javier had all but disappeared, really before we had started talking, I had started to go to the club's gym. I'd begun lifting weights and running track. I would get there at around eight or nine, a few hours before the weightroom would close, but long after those who typically use it, mainly baby-powdered old men, had left.

I'm not sure why I had started. Perhaps to avoid Gwen—Gwen, Gwendolyn, my girlfriend of the last three years. Overall Gwen was fine, and I had enjoyed spending time with her. I had simply wanted to avoid, I suppose, her increasingly inevitable inquests into when—and keep in mind that her incessant insinuations had become a strained hammering into my brain—we were going to become "*intimate*." And come on, if someone talks about it like that, using such hackneyed clichés, wouldn't anyone be cautious? Wouldn't anyone wonder if their partner was really ready?! And I wasn't going to pressure her. I wasn't even going to encourage her, I had promised myself, until she was ready, and she was not. She was simply insistent. She kept on repeating, over and over, that after a year apart she was ready to do what I had not *once* asked of her but what she now knew I wanted.... ?!?!

All she would say was that she'd had a couple of "late night chats" with her sorors, what they had called "confessions," and that she was now ready "to progress physical*ly*"—she had laid some oddly flushed, pseudo-initiated emphasis on the last syllable—*if* I could make her some sort of commitment, the "commitment" part being her sole identifiable addition to the whole script.

Needless to say, I am not a prude. It was her approach that put me off. Not her assertiveness. That was great. Or it would have been had it been her own. What had bothered me was her aggressively reactive attitude to it all. She was so forceful, and at the same time so indifferent. "To progress physica*lly*." Who could succumb to such a clinical come-on? It had sounded as if she had wanted to perform some science fair experiment at the end of which she would go back to her sorority, stand up on some stage, and announce the results, and I have never done all that well, and she *knew* it, under pressure.

Not to mention that I have no clue when we even would have found time to do what she thought she, what she thought I, what she obviously thought *someone* wanted, as she was always trying to get us to hang out with her idiotic older brother, Chad. Chad had, so far as I could tell, come home last summer for the first time in years, and, initially, I was far from happy about it.

I remembered him primarily as one of those boys who want you to feel as if they're always about to beat you up. Not that he could have. Beat me up, I mean, and he never attempted to though he did constantly try, and fail, to embarrass me. Gwen and I had been together, though not *together*, at St. Ann's since grade school and almost the entire time we had been friends. Yet whenever I'd gone over to her house Chad would ask me how Old Alexis, the local all girls school, was, slurring his x's and his s's, as if he had a lisp. This was ridiculous, and for several reasons: the first being that he was only three grades ahead of us at St. Ann's and I *know* that he had seen me in the hallways; and second *because Old Alexis is an all girls school!* and while I am not sure what precisely he was trying to imply, since for at least part of this time I was dating his sister, *and* I was on the St. Ann's soccer team, which is all boys, it was obvious that he had wanted to mock me. A pretty good reason, *I* would say, for me, and thus for my girlfriend when she was *with* me, to want to stay away from him.

Gwen had not seen it this way. She had simply said that her parents had asked her to keep an eye on him and that she had said that she would. Obviously, since she, for some inexplicable reason, adored him and he seemed to like her alright too, to the extent that he seemed to like anyone. Fine. Everyone likes Gwen. But when I suggested that perhaps they should spend some time alone together she had told me that I was being petty. The result being that, between her summer job and her after-hours brother-sitting, we were rarely alone together and what little time we did have she spent needling me about what was by then, *and by her own doing*, practically an impossibility!

Hence all my time hanging out at the club, despite the fact that I was one of the few guys with a girlfriend. Then about half-way through the summer, the situation changed. Chad and I had, I guess, somehow started, not that it was, not at first, I don't think, consciously planned, to "run into each other" in the locker room, about an hour before closing—these were—well they were not *innocent* encounters. Maybe the first one was, but not the next one or the next one or the one after that, so that for the rest of the summer, and after, I was obsessed with short sweaty scenes, with wooden benches and rubber mats, with the odors of exercised men and late-night exertions, with sweltering showers wherein an entire nakedness was, to my petrified excitement, enforced.

One benefit from these evenings was that Chad quit teasing me. Another was that he started to ask me over himself. For one week into June, some local design firm, like a *dea-ex-economica*, had hired Gwen as a paid summer intern—of course her taking the job *proved* that her "having" to watch her brother had been all in her head—and this left him to his own devices. He typically, I discovered, spent his days sleeping until noon, sometimes one, leaving him "unattended" for only about four hours until she got home; but the point remains.... Regardless, I ended up spending most of these hours hanging out at her house with him. This doubly pleased her, for I fulfilled her sisterly responsibilities, letting her off her own hook, and Chad and I were, as she saw it, becoming "friends."

As it turned out, by ourselves we got along fairly well, even outside the locker room. We both enjoy slightly sarcastic absurdities and we both like scandals, even if we have to make them up on our own. We both had, moreover, at least that summer, a desire to be athletic in a lazy sidestroke sort of way, before wanting to relax by a pool; lucky for us, his parents, who were not known for their taste, had recently had one built smack behind their kitchen in their walled-in backyard. This is, I suppose, the benefit of one's house not being historic. Sometimes we swam but most often we'd just lounge alongside it, me with an offbrand LaCroix and him with a whiskey sour.

What brought us close though, really, I think, was that we were both fellow travelers through Carlton. We could distract each other from this insipid petty town filled with its St. Ann societies and those who served them: the socialites, waiters, tattletales, and in-betweens at the Court Club whom Chad seemed to know so intimately—this is how I found out what had happened after our symposium—though once out of earshot he always scorned them, a favor, I'd wager, that was returned.

By halfway through the summer, certainly after my clubset disbanded, we were secluding ourselves at his house as if in protest every afternoon. I would go over around one by which time he was generally up and at least inclined to try to overcome his hangover, most often with what he called a "wake-me-up on the rocks." After which we would spend the rest of the afternoon, depending on how drunk he still was, swimming and sunbathing, with more or less clothes on—I can still remember how clean it felt to go gliding through the water without a suit on—or he would teach me to play tennis on the nearby public courts. He was surprisingly competent. He had played varsity at St. Ann's though he had not kept it up in college. After this we would head to his room, grabbing a refill along the way to rehydrate. He would then show me the "indie" film collection on his computer, which he would play at a terrifyingly loud volume while we lay awkwardly around, letting the liberties on screen compensate for our more timid self-touchings. This would last right up until a half-hour before we expected his sister back or his parents to come home from Concord. Then, like clockwork, he would cut off whatever it was that was on, and we would clean up—glasses, bottles, bowls—after which we would sit silently and worn-out in their hackneyed plaid and wood paneled living room, waiting for the first unwanted arrival.

I can still recall the tension of waiting in that room. His face took on a pout, just a millimeter or so off from the one I frequently saw on Gwen. I'd never noticed before how much they looked alike. How much they *were* alike. Of course he was taller and thicker and, I imagine, much better in bed, though he tended to be more moody. When we were alone, he was funny and friendly, sometimes playfully fierce and occasionally tender, sneaking me drinks, which for him *was* tender, and twice he let me beat him at tennis.

Should anyone else come around though, particularly Gwen, he'd snap abruptly back as if someone had thrown a switch. Really, it was funny that she believed we were friends. He paid me no attention in front of her save occasionally to insult me, which in some ways made him, made the whole situation still worse. He laid off the Old Alexis jokes, but he would make fun of some word I had said or of some small freckle on my arm or on my ankle, which only an hour ago his fingers had been all over.

This just made me mad at them both. It was probably this, in fact, that tore us apart. Me and Gwen. I would think he had planned it, if I was not so sure that he had been entirely indifferent to us being together … and while I am willing to admit that I was perhaps a little unfair to her during all this, she was hardly Miss Manners herself. She'd act thrilled to see me when she got home but she never once defended me when he was mean to me.

Of course, the whole mess blew over when they both went back to Vanderbilt. He had gone first then she had followed one week later. For whatever reason, he had not told me that he was leaving. We had spent his second-to-last day in Carlton together, and thirty-six hours after, he was gone. He had apparently been on academic probation and was required to attend a pre-term prep course in order to return. Gwen told me later that she had avoided the subject herself because she had thought it would be a nice surprise for me, which was either a magnificently vicious move or it shows the degree to which she'd thought that I had hated him and therefore how selfish she had been all along.

Regardless, when he left, Gwen and I came undone. I became inexplicably gray, as if a fog had diffused through my brain, and although I tried, and I really did, I just didn't feel like spending time, such an odd phrase, with her. Unfortunately, with her brother gone and the summer coming to an end, she at last stepped up the pressure. She kept on and on in a thousand little ways until I figured, what the hell? So we did … except, as it turns out, we did not. Not technically. It was awful, and then embarrassing, and then we *really* did not, and soon after we seemed to stop speaking until one day we decided mutually, as mutually as one person writing another person a *withering* letter referencing a very, *very* brief moment of whatever can be, that it was best we break up. Even then, of course, I knew it was for the best. My mind and body were working in unison to keep me from committing and that convinced me that I needed to figure out what, exactly, I wanted before … well, who knows?

I guess I sensed somehow that before settling, I should explore all my options, that I should learn what else was out there. I didn't want to wake up one morning regretting what I had missed, and had missed willingly. This is how, I suppose, my mind prepared me for the idea of Amsterdam.

The precise idea of Amsterdam, my Amsterdam, probably germinated at St. Ann's. I remember classmates sporadically spreading rumors of the encounters to be had there, that *had* been had there, in that city of sex, just off the street, waiting for anyone who wanted them. Several boys told obviously embellished stories about older brothers who had gone abroad and met girls, met women, *in absentia* of homebound hang-ups. A few older kids, the more "mature" hirsute types, outrightly claimed that they had had such adventures themselves, although when asked, their stories tended to contradict their own details. Was a certain flat by the Oude Kirk or somewhere right inside the Singel? Some produced, as promised, the occasional souvenir.

One delinquent brought in a receipt printed in Keene, but they were all, for one reason or another, suspect. Perhaps because each intrepid traveler, no matter how old they looked, pictured no matter how far outside the school, imagined surrounded by no matter how many sketchy bare-breasted women, evoked simply a puerile rule-bound boy in a crested blue blazer, as tense as a ramrod. It's hard enough for me to believe that *I* have done what I have, and I could produce far more evidence than any of them.

By the end of last August though, with first Chad gone then Gwen, I was, to put it lightly, shaken. I had been with her for the past three years, and breaking up, even though we'd hardly talked the last fall and winter and scarcely more that summer, was like discarding part of whomever I'd thought I had been, of whomever I'd thought I'd become. My expectations were uprooted. It was in the resulting emptiness that the stem of the idea of going to Amsterdam, not to force the metaphor, perked up from wherever it had been hiding, came to the forefront of my mind, and flourished.

I was grateful for this when I returned to school and in early autumn I began to daydream of going to Amsterdam. Not for vacation or to retreat but as the fulfillment of a responsibility to whomever I might one day marry. A responsibility to figure out what I want and what might just work, whether it be with someone small or tall or dark or blond or busty or rambunctious or relaxed or unexpectedly strict. Granted, this seems a shallow shopping list, but if you don't start with a spark, what will you fan into a flame? The more I thought about it, the more the idea intrigued me.

Not that I thought about it a lot. I did not. After all, I had calculus, philosophy, various histories, and our eating club's social scene, in addition to all life's daily minute demands.

Until one day, checking my e-mail in the library, I decided, on a whim, to look up "Amsterdam." I wanted just a sense of the city. Simply typing in the word, however, I felt, really gladly, a rising excitement. The search engine reported almost instantly, calling up first cafés and concert halls, then shops and museums, then hotels and historic public places of shrinking significance. The next two pages showed banks, businesses, universities, government websites, all the weights of a world-renowned city. Next I refined my search to "Amsterdam attractions" or some-such. Without warning, evidence of the city's, well, more "intimate" recreations appeared. Alarmed, I peered about me, a spritely troll twisting. Thankfully, it was a warm afternoon and my obscure corner was all but empty.

I remember clicking quickly in and out of several sites, my nerves humming, my feet tapping, my ears open for any hint of some new sound. I clicked cautiously on a few innocuous looking shops selling pot, a few touting "*safe shrooms*," one escort agency advertising women referred to as "models" and one as "modals," the malapropisms of a commercial cosmopolitanism, and then, like when you spend hours searching the web for certain purposes, glorious cycles of self-suspension, and you promise yourself just one more site, just one more, I clicked on *The Golden Eagle*. I recall this one especially because it flashed shockingly red gothic letters that spelled out "virtuelle vixens," the caption for diverse women on webcams who offered virtual and consequently oddly virtuous displays of what would, I presumed, be fleshed out in unpixelated detail once you reached the establishment. The whole idea was gut-wrenching, not just because I dreaded that someone would catch me gawking, though there was that, but more because staring felt so uncomfortably close to an impotent exploitation. Anyone could spy here for free, forever, without once affecting *them*, the women.

I x-ed out, grateful that not every site had been so specific. Specificity, however, has its own contagious currents. Several days later, researching chivalry and the politics of some thirteenth-century plague for my medieval history course, I came, by total surprise, across a site called *Galahad's Escort Service*. I had honestly not been searching for this. For the past two days I had been researching for an essay on the "kiss of peace." Then today, simply for kicks, I had typed in "chivalry," "service," and "baiser." Previously such terms had led me to genealogies, to etymologies, and to church art. Now it led me to an escort service. The unprotected edge where scholarship slides into sex.

Of course the name was tawdry, but so many more had been so much worse. *Penelope's Pornorama*, for instance, so I suppose I was relieved to find, at last, a website without wem. Abandoning for a second my restraint, I clicked on the link and ... it had not been at all what I was expecting ... I felt myself expand, my legs, my stomach, undressed, *they* were undressed! I had not actually *seen* this sort of stuff, not in the flesh, so to speak, since August and I had forgotten how inimitable it is, so many male arms, legs, and thighs disappearing and *re*appearing, at dinner, at night, stiff hips shifting at the most awkward of angles, I was aching and appalled, repelled and pulled in, nauseated with lust. Shit! I remember thinking, shitshitshit, someone could see this ...

I shot up, banging my knee. Wincing and simultaneously struggling to open a new window, I envisioned the proleptic news flash: "Local Carlton kid kicked out of Princeton for looking up—." Trying not to grimace and to ignore this new throbbing, I look around with what I hope is an air of indifference, as if I'm waiting for someone who has not yet arrived. But no one, no one notices at me. The few kids around are too far off, too bent over, and too engrossed in their own engagements.

I try to memorize their indifference, because I know that afterwards I will imagine ...

Still shaken, I lean back then lift my head to look for a clock. There it is, on the wall. Yes, it matches my watch. Good. "How disciplined he is." "Where's his friend?" I peek around once more. No one's paying attention. I've put on a show without an audience.

I return to my screen, vaguely relieved. The pain in my knee subsides. What I had seen must have been a lure, an opportunity for the agency to show off their models—and *my god*, for while I know that this will sound like a lie, the sex of these models is a surprise. I'd honestly not thought that there would be that sort of ... "entertainment" in Amsterdam.

The kid nearest me gets up and leaves.

A lacquered forest of U-shaped stacks stands behind me.

In front stretches a long broad table, an aisle, more tables then more stacks. I put in one earbud. My entire body tenses. I take a deep breath then switch windows, unmuting the speakers. The streaming images from earlier, a beautifully evoked "*éveil*," have receded into a nearly static background. All that remains are a couple of poorly pixelated twentyish-year-olds dressed up as angels, escorting angels, who every few seconds point to a not quite misused mythological icon, a spear, a lyre, a grail, that symbolize the different options offered by the establishment. Into my ear, meanwhile, floats a softly sinuous organ music, soothing and discreet.

Navigating through the icons leads to low-resolution shots of grainy rooms. I've just clicked the chalice, when behind me I hear a tap. Before I've consciously told it to, my finger has tapped the mouse to hit the "x" button at the upper edge of the screen. My heart unzips as I turn around. No one is near. My body convulses. From between two stacks, a librarian appears pushing a cart—

She peers at me, her mouth taut. She seems the type to detest students. I peer back. Through a crack in my brain I realize that her accusing eyes have slid on to the others at the opposite end of the room.

We are, none of us, to her, out of the ordinary.

Chapter Two

Leaving the library, I walk out to an afternoon that could only exist in Princeton. The air smells like white wine and corrosion, while the buildings refract a mock gothic conceit. In an hour, I have a study group for math and I have yet to prepare any of the proofs that I was assigned to explain.

Despite my workload, for the next few days then for the next few weeks, I can't bar Amsterdam from my brain. I catch myself distracted, seeing my body from disconnected perspectives rambling through seventeenth-century streets, images of images off the internet—yet even these are enough to evoke vaporous legs ambling across carved bridges, arms leaning off of arches, arches stretching archaically over canals, feeling their hard-set stones beneath my feet, sometimes moving and alive, sometimes dead and decaying; in math, in history, during dinner I hear water and footfalls slapping softly in my ears. Most frequently though I see this as if I am smearing it out in front of me: mornings in museums, afternoons in sidestreets, evenings in cheap sandwich shops, and at night … well, for that the canvas always stands empty.

Or it does, at least, during the day. Later, oversaturated, my sleeping brain steals into worlds of its own devising. More than once I have found myself searching through faintly familiar streets. Frost covers the pavement. My cheeks burn in the icy air. Inevitably, after walking for hours I find myself in an alley, then I climb and climb dark stone stairs into still darker apartments, long emptied of life. Rooms distend with heavy furniture, velvet sofas and chairs, endtables draped with brocades edged in gilt, all of which might once have been beautiful. A fusty aura hints at changes of fortune, and on most nights, the rooms feel destitute and cold, as if their contents are being swallowed, their stolidity slipping impenetrably into a mawed oblivion.

Other nights the same rooms are so hot and so humid that they disgust me. Overflowing with men and with women and with everyone in between in various arrays of evening dress, with people mingling and lounging, their faces so obscured that I can never quite see who they are. This goes on until at some clandestine cue they slip almost entirely into the shadows. This triggers the end and I start sliding away. At the last second, I see hands of different shapes and sizes, reappearing in silhouettes, inviting me, beckoning me back ... but by this time I am too far away, and I sense, faintly, that my mind suspects but refuses to contemplate what it will soon find outside of itself.

Despite all this, I make no plans until I do so almost by accident. One afternoon, when I'm pretty sure I should be in calculus class, I stray into a downtown bookstore. Sometimes I do this. I go in and, if inspired, I buy a book, go home, and devour it, shoving all "official" schoolwork aside. I've always thought an aristocratic approach to education, reading what one wants, superior to reading third-rate reflections rehashed in essays.

This time, instead of the history, philosophy, or fiction sections, I wind up with the travel books in the back. I breeze through a few books on France, Italy, and the Czech Republic, until I get to guides to Northern Europe: Norway, Denmark, Sweden, and the Netherlands. Two are on Amsterdam alone. I flip through each, select the one most devoted to the red-light district, steal it to the counter, pay for it, then take it home.

For the next few nights, before going to sleep I sneak the book from behind my bookshelf and peek through it, making sure to shut my door before I do so. Stephen, my roommate, is not often around but when he is he often bursts in on me. Irritatingly, the locks to our bedrooms don't catch. Even should he shoot through, though, he would only catch me clutching *A Concise History of Chivalric Satisfactions*, as I've used a decoy dust jacket. He's majoring in engineering and Greek and is not, I know from experience, interested enough in other people's courses to ask questions.

We'd met freshman year, and, in general, we get along. I almost, in fact, asked if he'd like to come to Amsterdam before quickly reconsidering. He'd not make the best travel companion. He's actually a bit of a loner, not that this stops him from stumbling home with some new girl every other month. It goes like clockwork. I can always tell when there's a new one, first by the calendar and second by the intensity of their noises. It must be the abs that get them going. Anyone would follow those, though it's hard to imagine him, distant and arrogant, lifting his shirt up in some bar to entice someone. But he must meet girls somehow, for he's one of the few undergrads I know who did not join an eating club. Anway, it's the same for each sequence. For the first week, I cover my head with a pillow, the plaid above me matching that beneath them. I have to, as I've always had enough of it long before they have. For the second week, the girls typically try to be restrained, out of respect, I think, for the roommate. By the end of the third week, he's inevitably sullen and they are silent, if, that is, they are still around at all. Then in the aftermath, we have the apartment to ourselves.

But he's alright, with his thick hair and thick glasses, their black plastic frames solid and square-like. Knowing him as I do, which is as well as anyone at school, I think he wears them because they make him look philosophic. A dandified Stephen Daedalus.

These days I myself try to be pragmatic. Playing with a calculator, I work out how much it would cost, realistically, to travel overseas. Estimating my present expenses, I figure that if I'm frugal, I could have about two thousand dollars left over at the end of the semester. Having overheard more about the ski-trip than anyone could possible care to, I know that with travel fares, slope fees, and food and drink—and these kids drink as though they're right out of rehab—they each expect to drown about three thousand dollars. I've a pretty good shot of getting that out of my father if I tell him that I'm going to Aspen. If he tells me to charge it, I'd say that some kid's parents already put the expenses on their card and asked everyone else to pay cash.

I'd have to be cagey about the airfare, but in the end he wouldn't care. He's always telling me and my brothers, even, and this is pretty awful, Donny, that college is the time to work out our "wildness," before we return to New Hampshire and the business. Two weeks at a ski lodge would qualify, I think, for him, as a chance to do this. And I am right. He transfers me the money, telling me only to be cautious, to behave, and to have fun. Of course, I've added this last part myself, since he has never, I can't even imagine hearing it, told any of us to "have fun."

I knew that if I told the same story to my mother she'd donate some funds too, especially since she knows how tightfisted her husband is. He had not given her one single cent when she had wanted to research her first book, before she had inherited her uncle's money, much less her second. Since I hate lying, I write that I'm going on a trip and that there *might* be skiing, which is not entirely untrue. Unfortunately, this fell a bit flat, since she had recently invested her "pocket money," as she put it, in AJ's new script. Alongside being an agent, AJ is also an aspiring "playright"—this, my mother says, is how he spells it. But if she makes a bit of fun of him, and she does to me, this just evidences her goodwill, which persists despite the incapacities or shortcomings of others. Unlike so many others whom I could name, she doesn't just pay lip service to someone whom she believes in and she even tells me, legitimately, to have "a good time" "wherever" it is that I'm going, which translates easily enough into "Amsterdam."

Once I've settled the money, all else falls into place. I find off-hour plane tickets, eight hundred and fifty-three dollars with tax, from Newark to Amsterdam and back, and a bed for eighteen dollars a night at the Hostel Royal Holland, which is supposed to be a mile from the main train station. Its website doesn't offer a stellar first impression but I suppose a tolerance for trashiness buys anonymity because it doesn't require a credit card for reservations, just a name, and for that, as it turns out, not even a real one.

I tend to inflate the benefits of waiting. The infinite possibilities expanding. Still, the blunt light seeping through my curtains on the morning following finals thrills me. It's a great awakening. It's exhilarating. It's animating. It makes me want to retch.

A tightness squats in my chest. The thin tense anticipation of yesterday, when I had turned in one last essay, perhaps a bit *too* hastily, has intensified.

I have a sudden fear that the plane won't take off.

My alarm shows 7:05. For once it can't scold me for oversleeping.

The cab should be here in a little under an hour. All I have to do is to get up, shower, and throw my toothbrush in my travel bag, which has otherwise been packed, been ready to go for a week. This leaves me plenty of time to catch the 8:30 am commuter train to Newark.

Stretching my legs I try to unclench my stomach. My brain runs wild generating an intractable tension that flows in warm waves beneath my sheet. It's for this that I leave my window open at night. At least when Stephen isn't around to complain about the bills, the wasted heat, the discomfort. I don't care. The cold creates our sharpest clearest sensation. I love its explicitness. How it creeps in and opens our apartment to the still chillier streets. How it defines the space outside the blanket. How it makes my bed that much more of a barrier, a sweated island set in a sea of ice. My body wallows in the warmth it's been cocooning in for hours. I have to get up. But for now, the temperature, my excitement, even my by now exasperated bladder balance into an exquisite equilibrium.

Mornings are the one time I'm grateful for the compactness of Princeton apartments. Having hopped to then twisted in the shower, I'm shaved and ready to go in under ten minutes. Braving the temperature, I start a pot of coffee. Returning to my room, I grab a sweater and pull pants up over my shorts.

Half an hour later, I hear honking. I make sure once more that the windows are shut and that the appliances are off. I want no images of the apartment burning down while I am in Amsterdam. Then I am actually out of our door....

The train ride into Newark is, as always, uneventful. It teases you by crawling towards and then inexplicably away from New York. Today though there's the consolation prize of watching the raindrops race on the windows before they rush off onto the tracks.

When we arrive, the airport seems gloomy and severe. People's overcoats have brought the rain in with them. The people themselves look bland and ordinary, more like profiles of people, their legs framed by the drab colored carpeting, than like select souls preparing to take to the sky.

Unsmiling faces and blank eyes are surely only an airport armor. I wonder where each one is headed, and why. I wonder who, if anyone, will meet them at the other end. It dawns on me that no one, no one *I* know, knows that I am here. No one has any idea where I am going. For the next three weeks, I will, for all intents and purposes, be utterly anonymous. Then, when all this is over, William Belicor, the name I have chosen for my only honest act of independence, need never confess his existence.

Boarding is over and the plane is half-empty. The lights dim and the seats groan. There's a high-pitched "ping" and half-hurried flight attendants stride the aisles checking seatbelts and overhead compartments. Soon we are speeding. Faster and rougher. It seems sublimely strange that all this machinery, that all these engines, that all this massive roaring to lift us should be straining so hard to take so few people so far.

Take-offs are my favorite part of flying. Leaning close to but not touching the reinforced window, I like to look at the cars as they turn into toys. As the plane gets higher and they get smaller it's comforting to watch, through the thickness of the air or through the rain, the shrinking oblongs trace tiny strips of tar that become hundreds and thousands of criss-crossing little lines leading right up to dollhouse destinations, where pixelpoints get beers with friends or get high or go, I don't know, bowling, cheating on husbands and wives, who by now are at work, with girlfriends, with friends, with rough trade ...

Presently, with the cabin lights dimmed and the plane shaking imperturbably as we soar over an earth no longer visible, I wonder what it would take to envision the world as a place for people who are, if not happy, then at least at ease.

My first five minutes in Amsterdam run so smoothly that Schiphol seems like some finely crafted Dutch clock. When you step off the plane, signs signal immediately where to get baggage, to go shopping, to find customs. There is, moreover, an overall sense of excitement, of importance, of lives being lived.

Schiphol feels every bit the world hub that it is and as amazing as it is to be here almost eight hours after leaving Newark, it's staggering to realize that from here my options for travel have expanded extraordinarily. Outside I see planes marked with names I have never seen before: *Air Algérie, Tarom, Bimon*, and others I can't even read, many in Arabic and what I guess is Cyrillic, all preparing to take off on the tarmac. Boundaries melt. It is patently plausible that I could soon be in Africa, in Asia, by the Bosphorus.

Having breathed recirculated air for too long, I feel slightly loopy. The smell of the main atrium soon jolts my system, as does a clock, surely off, reading 00:03. A steady stream of Asian businessmen rush by speaking French. Some Americans amble along in crumpled sportscoats speaking what sounds like it should be German. I wonder if anyone ever uses the showers I see advertised above me.

Exiting the atrium I glance up at the electronic boards announcing arrivals and departures, "real-time" curations of close pasts, presents, and futures. These seem off too. It strikes me, as such events generally do, gradually then suddenly within seconds, that these clocks are *not* off. Indeed, each one reads the same: 00:14. Teetering towards a bench, I realize that I have drastically miscalculated. *This is why the tickets had been so cheap.* Not because of the odd hour of take-off but because of the inconvenient hour of arrival. I had forgotten to calculate the time change!

I take a deep breath to collect myself. Okay. So, it's closer to midnight than to a dark early evening. Still, everyone around me walks on, indifferent. They are indifferent. The late hour is irrelevant to everyone else.

When traveling, people simply reset their standards.

Shaken but steadying, I recall that I still have to collect my bag and go through customs. I have fucked up enough and do *not* want to make matters worse … and I still have to take a train. If, that is, trains are still running.

They are, and twenty minutes later I'm sitting next to five Phi Alpha Gammas, loudly branded as such by their assorted Hawaiian-themed T-shirts, who inadvertently calm my worry that I have reserved a room for tomorrow but not for tonight. They seem to have similarly miscalculated the time change because four of them are loudly reassuring each other that "*thousands*" of beds can be had in Amsterdam at any hour, just like all the city's other "*freak-ee shit.*" Another shrugs and says, with an exaggerated nonchalance, "well, if worse comes to worst, we can always hole up with some—" the others interrupt him by snickering then getting uncomfortably quiet.

I try meanwhile to maintain the respectful train-traveler stupor, staring at the slightly stained seat in front of me and ignoring everyone else. These guys though soon start up again so loudly that it's impossible not to pay them attention. I listen as their voices rise and half-fall asynchronously, one drowning out the others, as if they were at home, egging each other on:

"no man, *ev-ree-one* wants American money—"

"They'll open up when we let them know who it is—"

"knock, knock—"

"get to the hotel, drop our shit off and hit—"

"should we leave our passports?"

"*Hell* no. I ain't leavin mine to get stole," spouts one who with his radiant white face and bushy brown curls looks the youngest, "fuck." This pretty prodigal is dressed like an out-of-work angel. Slouching in his seat, his absurdly comfortable looking white sweatpants have slipped slightly, such that they would be so easy to pull off entirely, and out of them stems, pathetically, a slender almost immaculate looking waist, while his torso is engulfed in an overstuffed unzipped and hence oddly *décolletage*-like ski-coat. This all creates a no-doubt unintendedly enticing fragility, and I imagine my tongue on his Adam's apple.

Despite or perhaps in spite of his delicacy, he is, out of all of them, the loudest. His dense distaste of even the *idea* of his passport getting stolen is half, I think, pitifully funny, and he is so adamant, so fiercely ready to indict all of Amsterdam that his intensity, though I look away, makes him available to everyone. A man in a dark suit across the train, I can sense it, is dying to tell him that *should* he lose his passport, he will always, with that waist, have a way to make money.

"Calm down," interposes the sole quiet one, his tone lightly but commandingly mocking the other's excesses, his brown skin contrasting coolly with the wild boy's pink whiteness.

"I just don't want some shitass stoner stealin my *shi-*"

"Woah," the calm one cuts in, "we're still on the train—rein it in …. Now, when we get to the hostel," he pitches his voice low so that his friends have to soften their howling to hear it, "we will see if it has a safe. If it does, we will *all* put our passports into it. If it does *not*, we will *all* take them with us. Every Gamma's goin' home."

He exudes the comfort that floats instinctively from those who temper their tone to their environment. His symmetry, moreover, radiates order. Unlike the pale idiot or the broad-shouldered boy in the "Seoul Brother" hat sitting next to him, he conveys an easy self control. It's in his prudent pupils, in the smooth V of his spread legs, in the way his lips recreate words. He frequently, I'd guess, leads others without effort.

After this, their conversation tends toward the practical, not leaving much for the one in the skicoat to say, save to announce at one point that he's going to get "so high … bone so many bit-" at this the calm one kicks him and orders him outright not to swear so much. Still, I can tell by the way that the others twitch and shake that he only vaunts what they're thinking as their isolated thoughts strip ahead towards pot, more pot, and prostitutes.

Ten minutes later, we all jostle out to the platform. Stairs lead up and into the open. Coldness floods around us sloughing off the stale warmth of the underground air. Ahead I see the trackpants of the fraternal frontman. Vapor puffs from his mouth, evidence of the heat in his chest, in his stomach, by his balls. I shiver and, for an instant, our eyes lock. I break away, disconcerted. I've the distinct impression that he has been aware of my attention, and that he is not sure that he likes it. He, too, has turned away and, shooting a few indiscernible words to his friends (my stomach stumbles), he steers them off, laughing, tumbling into the crowd (no, no looking back), with chants of "coff-ee shop, coff-ee shop" hanging in the air. Traffic intervenes. This is the last, I think, that I will see of them. Ours will be different Amsterdams.

Damrak Station and its throngs soon take over. Its fore-plaza presents a dense obstacle course with diverging half-rings and zipperlines for rattling trollies and trams. Everyday travelers, adulterers, druggists, diamond dealers, and generally perverse people dodge efficiently on to these spines of the city, homeward bound. Others bumble confusedly, knocking across the tracks into belts of taxis, buses, cars, and hordes of still more harried people.

Beyond this is Damrak Straat, in all its glory. The Straat itself is a sensual overload, bursting so precipitously that no one could hear or smell or imagine much less contemplate any idea outside its onslaught. Every step forward throws new lights and shouts and brash "ding-ding-dings," like slot-machines relentlessly and angrily paying out. All around the aromas of elephant ears and decomposing people mix ceaselessly, engulfing potential pickpockets and perverts, so many shoulders and arms rubbing incessantly that it's hard to believe that it's after one a.m. For me, I suppose, it's hours earlier. I can't tell. Time here gets swept up in the inscrutability of the current, past noisy shops layered with neon, past shiny signs flashing red-white-gold-red-white-gold, past pinwheels of purple-pink-black; several kiosks emit some off-sounding rap which is not quite English yet not quite not; many sell bumper stickers reading "Amsterdam=High-Heaven," "Amsterdam is for Amours," even "Amsterdam is for Anal," I see these repeatedly until I ignore them to watch a bearded unicyclist, a half-dressed older woman, two young women in knitted caftans, three teenage boys in stonewashed jeans so tight it is a miracle that they can move. They rush past, screaming, talking, laughing. There's a near lawlessness of languages, including scraps of English which irritate me until I realize that they carry a heavy sloshing accent, one rasped by vendors, by genders of indeterminate age, from eight to eighty, thrusting cheap souvenirs onto anyone whose eye they can catch, and by greasy paunchy men in sideshow tuxedos enticing people into casinos. This amusement-park atmosphere first excites then disappoints then comforts me. This is exactly what I had wanted. People who so covet your cash that they could not care less about *you*.

Looking up my eye catches a sign announcing, in neither bright nor bold letters, the *Ho el Royal Holland*. It's sheer luck that I saw it, but this must be my hostel. My bed was booked for tomorrow but under the sign a wizened old man gesticulates, which must mean that they still have vacancies.

Seeing that he has my attention, he catcalls his tributes towards me: "Is verrrry cheap, man, is safe, is *clean* ..."

I stand for a minute and listen to him, to be polite. When he starts, however, in a loud and in an oddly lecherous voice to praise the hygiene of the sheets, I hurry in, embarrassed. I hear him calling behind me, his accent thickening as he works stupidly harder, nearly killing his case, "is right next *red-light district*! Two minute, get good hea—"

The hostel door blockades, mercifully, the last of whatever it is he is shouting.

Holding my breath, I walk through a tunnel-like hallway and am soon delivered into a cramped and too brightly lit yellow lobby. To my left I see an uninvitingly rough wooden counter. Baring traces of polish and gilt, it's now made mostly of splinters. Behind it stand two spiney and equally unappealing old men. Each wears a threadbare red livery, the indoor equivalent of their outdoor compatriot's overcoat. To their side sits a small sign covered in dust on which I can just make out the word "informition," next to a poorly printed picture of the British flag.

To my right sit two "antique" armchairs. These have canary colored cushions and chipped gilt volutes. A corresponding canapé squats at the not-so-far end of the room. These are visibly on their last spindly legs.

"You want room?" A grumble limps from one of the cadavers behind the counter.

"Yes," I say, my own voice sounding unexpectedly croaky. "I do. Well, a bed." I clear my throat. "In fact I'm scheduled to stay here. This is the Hostel Royal Holland, isn't it?"

"No," he retorts, sounding relieved, "is *Ho*tel Royal Holland."

Incredibly he looks down, as if he expects me to leave.

For a second, there is silence. From the dust and the decay I had guessed that customer service is not this place's forte. Still, without wanting myself to be rude, I am not done asking him questions.

"Well," I raise my voice, "I wonder if you could tell me where to find the Ho*stel* Royal Holland." I pull out the confirmation email I had printed and set it on the counter. Unfortunately, I had not actually looked at this until I was on the plane. It has the name of the hostel, but not, as I had anticipated, its address. It does have, however, a telephone number, to which I now point. His eyes move, as if despite himself, down the sheet.

He clearly wants to send me away yet for some reason he does not. "Hold," he snaps, as if we are on the phone. He nudges his cohort who looks barely aware of us. He shrugs, perhaps confused, perhaps illiterate, but entirely indifferent.

I should have expected that it would be too much for one of them just to call the hostel.

Directly I think this, the first one picks up a receiver.

His right hand makes four swift punches. Too few to have actually dialed the number.

I start to say "forget it," for there is no point in his *pretending* to call, when he holds up a finger. This simultaneously communicates "do not speak" and "wait." All the while he keeps his eyes on the paper. His face straightens. The other end must have answered. Still, he waits, then he speaks rapidly in a foreign language. Not, I think, Dutch. I hear him sound out "Hos-*tel Roy*-al Holl-land," twice. Pausing, presumably to listen, he soon repeats, somewhat whinily, whatever it was he had already said. His brow furrows. He offers a brusque, placatory word, perhaps "akkordte." Then, with an exaggerated importance, he replaces the receiver in its cradle, as if, having been chastised, he now wants to puff himself up.

It won't work.

Turning, he announces, as if no response could be more plausible, "*Ho*-tel Royal Holland is *Hos*tel Royal Holland. Is same. Different wing. Different room."

But," he adds, as if recalling some charge, "you prefer hotel room, yes? You are a-lone? Is good deal—"

I start to refute this but he interrupts, "Special deal for travel all-lone nice boy. Room just for you. Forty *euro* per night. Is more clean. More nice …"

"More clean?" I ask. "Is the other room not clean?"

"Of course is clean." He sounds annoyed. "Fifty American dollar per night … is good deal."

"No. No, I'll just take the bed, a *hostel* bed."

He caves and I pay him for the first and the last night. I get a key, which alone feels a little like a triumph.

Soon I'm making my way to the hostel "wing." The establishment does actually have two sides, each accessible through their own jib-style doors in the lobby. Once through the door to the left, I find myself on a dark narrow staircase. Going up, I actually have to concentrate so I don't trip on the ripped brown carpet, all pockmocked with cigarette burns and stains, I don't even want to imagine from what. I recall the yellow and "gold" lacquered lobby. It's frustrating when a place intentionally raises expectations then refuses even to try to meet them.

Atop the all too obviously unvacuumed dead-end half-hallway, I remember that I had expected imperfections and that this is an adventure. So, time to adventure through one of these two doors. The left one has a faded number nine that matches the marking on my key. Jiggling this into a rusted catch, I make enough noise to let anyone, if there *is* anyone, inside know that I am about to enter but not enough to wake anyone up if they are asleep. All I need, I remind myself, is a place to store my stuff safely and to rest.

No matter how scary/it's only temporary.

Once in, I am relieved. It's not that bad. I had half-expected it to be dark, on account of the hour. But the lights are on and, like those in the lobby, they are bright. Too bright, actually, as on closer inspection this room makes the lobby look clean. This excessive wattage discloses dust and dirt and, gross, dead bugs ground into the carpet.

I'm not, though, going to sleep on the floor. I feel a bit better about this, so I start to examine the beds, cots really, twelve too-tiny-to-be-twin-size cots hunkering half a foot off the floor. These are spread equally across the left and the right sides of the room. Between each is a foot and a half or so and a roughly four foot aisle offers a straight shot down the middle.

Glamorous.

Really, it's not that bad. The cots even have sheets—my god, what if they hadn't? No, no hostel, even this one, could be that ill-equipped. Four cots are unmade and look as though they had recently been used. Three have sleeping bags, a luxury that I had not thought to bring. The rest have tucked-in, tough-looking linens and coarse, grey blankets folded at their feet. This is more than enough considering how hot it is in here.

Luckily, there's one bed left by the lone window at the far end of the stifling room. I take it, wondering whether the other guests have come alone or together. Regardless, they must all be out exploring the city. Looking out the round window pane, so thin that I can hear faint noises from outside, I can feel Damrak Straat. It's calling me, too. I am *here* ... and out *there* ... I close my eyes. I try to breathe in some of the smells, some of the palpable excitement that I had seen on the streets. I hold my breath, exploring it, tasting it, testing it, until I have to exhale. Mostly I'd got the mal-lingering odors of the attic. A fly, I notice, dust covering its corpse, lies callously on the sill.

Back out on the street, I'm glad that I decided to do some exploring myself. Despite all I've done today, my body feels energized and I know that I'd not be able to sleep. Alone in that room, sensing the city outside, I'd be stuck awake with a tired traveler's euphoria.

Not wanting to abandon my passport, I stuff it in my front pocket, along with my wallet, and the room key. I leave my guidebook. For the first night, I'll be an intrepid adventurer not a tourist in prepared territory.

Immersed in the lights, whatever traces of melancholy I had absorbed from the room, from the whole hotel, dissipate. Being outside and on my own is revitalizing. The cold air incites spurts of adrenaline and my faint sense of my passport in my pocket feels excitingly unsettling.

Nudging all fears to the back of my mind, I start up Damrak Straat, away from the station. The drag still has its exigent excitement and I don't want to stray too far tonight. I am, I admit, eager to see the red-light district, but I don't need to act like the typical American tourist, chasing after pros- and pot the second he steps out, ignoring all else that Amsterdam has on offer.

After several blocks of the main thoroughfair though, I find that the straat offers little more than the same sensations laid out *in perpetuum*. At first these feel appealing, if not too attractive, with their noisy lights and gaudy sounds. But this ostentatious atmosphere dulls as I realize that despite their hype, the shops are fairly formulaic, selling the same shoddy souvenirs with the result that every booth blurs into an interminable tedium. Repeatedly I see the same pizzas, burgers, and french fries, exhausted under heatlamps. Even the casinos, which litter the sidestreets with their flashings and clangings, morph into insignificant stars that refuse to vary their alignments.

Thankfully the carnival ends at last and at a point that re-energizes me. I see a small sign announcing the "*Dam Square*" and I laugh out loud, a result I'm sure of my own slaphappy exhaustion and my own ignorance. What square? The *Dam* Square! Oh, the Dutch. Anyway, I'd been considering returning to the hostel and this convinces me not to go back quite yet. I don't want to get lost but I also don't want to fall asleep without seeing one really worthwhile, perhaps more picturesque area of Amsterdam and the square will give me a landmark to guide my way back.

So I wind my way down the adjacent Hoog Straat, thinking that I won't forget that name either, and then down one narrow side street after another. I am chasing, I know, the fool's fantasy of finding in an ancient city an authenticity untainted by tourists. But after four months of dreaming of "Amsterdam," I am hungry for new images. So I turn first round one corner and then round another until the groups walking past seem sparse to the degree that if I am no longer inundated, I also don't feel isolated or exposed. I have read stories of tourists caught alone late at night.

I turn off again, this time not quite catching the name of the street. This one, like so many others, follows a canal. It meanders, lined by intermittently lit street lamps, hitting the right notes of safety and solitude. These notes lengthen and deepen as standing on one of the bowed bridges I look over and into the water. It must be like ice down there, despite all its electric eyes blinking.

I walk on, glancing from the water to the buildings and back. Their recursive reflections look so thick that had I not read that most edifices here are seventeenth century, I might have thought that they were medieval. Funny, right as I think "medieval," I come across my first red light, dead ahead. First one, then too many to count, little red blossoms shining like so many midnight suns. Of course I had known that they were out here. But seeing them in fact is surreal.

My mind reaches out with a cold lucid caprice.

This feels … no, don't confuse fate with subconscious calculations.

I start closer and my ambivalence unfurls into I don't know what. I had, I suppose, expected a shock of immorality. But this is so prolifically puerile. Green and gold stoners, faded flowerchildren with salvation soldiers and fratboy freaks, blowjob bongs and bibles with beergoggles, plastic pot-plants, and finally I have reached some sort of center. I see what I think is the Oude Kerk outcast before me, a futile fortress locked against its enemies yet forced to reflect their signs which flicker across its walls, the most recent fruits of an emptied out enlightenment. I see now why it's called the *red-light district* as opposed, say, to the *Oude Kerk district*. It's not a case of *church* over *prostitutes*. It's simply that, when you see the red lights lining the windows, the sacerdotal spaces become half-hidden dumbshows, sideshows self-sequestered into affectedly sanctimonious shadows, muted testaments to a never innocent now infamous age, outdone by electric forthrightness and cheap techno.

The red lights especially though draw one in, like some bloody bodybait. Flowers of infertility. From afar, of course, each flushed frame attracts you, much more so than those that are next to you. Their ardent red inundates you, barring you, almost, from being bored, while never quite succeeding in exciting you. Navigating the district offers a paradoxical awareness, for although you want—and everyone–admit it or not–*thinks* that they want—to peep at the women, the closer you get to them, the closer you also get to all that surrounds them, so that the lights, which are unmoving to steady your stare, remain crassly vulnerable to one more spark sliding into view and enticing you away again, and again and again, so that there's no chance to stare at any one of the windows since each new illumination forces some unexpected incentive, some fresh new excuse to seek out some old empty temptation.

I consider the scene as the Kerk might. Stuck in this funfair of sin with its vicarious debaucheries, its smells of beer and elephant ears and sick, its walls buffeted by the cries of tired jam-packed people with scant interest in its hard stifling seats.

Suddenly I catch sight of a woman in lingerie pointing at me. I turn quickly to walk off. Seconds after I risk glancing back. She's now gesturing to someone else.

Spinning back, the world looks for a moment as if someone has taken an oilbrush and smeared it across everything. Then noises break in with short static-y bursts. Rastafarians duke it out with rap and day-glo dollar signs, shops call to supplicants, half-baked already, touting plastic pot leaves and t-shirts proclaiming "I didn't xxx-hale."

Next I know I'm following a canal away from the mayhem, the confused confines of commercial libertinism that come only to the edge of any promise. I soon encounter an intersection. A sign announces the "*Oudezijds Achterburgwal*." Whatever this is and wherever it goes, I don't stay on it long but turn right then half-left then veer right again and again.

Off the main road the scenery shifts. It's a little less septic. There are fewer clusters of red lights and the wares on offer look, well, less calloused. Occasional whiffs of pot linger but not like by the Oude Kerk. What surprises me is how several "coffee shops" sit impeccably tucked in between darkened stores stocked with books and whiskies and string instruments. The coffee shops' lights twinkle dully, outward signs of self-restraint nestled into blackened brick buildings, so much so that there's a reassuring charm to the decay of them. These shops must cater to the city's more *discerning* smokers, those who don't fetishize our fetal nature or want revolutions without work. With names like *Le Verre Vert* or *Le Divertissement*, they look suited for those practicing a pragmatic intellectualism or seeking some fleeting exquisiteness, whether the flowers of their own failure or an atonement for letting the weight of the world settle within them.

This is more deftly sophisticated than back home. Tons of kids from St. Ann's and Princeton get high. Mostly, I think, to offset the tedium of being themselves. They smoke then play video games. Personally, if I smoked I'd take the train to New York and go to concerts or to art shows. But pot makes me paranoid. It makes my mouth dry, and I get tongue-tied and feel weird.

This is what happened the few times I tried it over the summer. Chad usually had weed and I got tired of saying "no" each time he offered it. At least with him there was little risk of getting caught. Not in their backyard. Not in Carlton. He was so blasé about it that once he even got me to smoke in front of Gwendolyn. Each of us tried to inhale more than the other. He must have known it would piss her off. Royally. He laughed and laughed, blowing smoke at her until she left the room, then he had blown it at me.

For two days after she'd refused to talk to me, which was actually a relief because when she'd "relented," and I had known it would go like this, it was to lecture me. *Obviously* I didn't care about my future. If I kept on like this, I'd end up in the gutter. She sure shut up though when I'd suggested she save the sermon for someone else.

Here no one will nag and pot is not illegal. I hear him coax, in his mocking football-field voice, "come on, *man*," I had loved it when he'd call me "man," "I can *pur*sonally guar-ron-*tee*," here he'd grab his cock, "that you will *not* end up with cotton mouth," then he'd laugh and laugh. Later, with a softer sadder tone, with neither of us quite touching the other, he'd whisper, "Will, come on, Will, a little fun won't hurt us." I remember how he'd say my name, indifferent or taunting in front of others, teasing or searing when we were alone, so that anger and aching scored the whole monotony of our too chaste summer.

Across the street I spot a small coffee shop, the *Café Beatrix*, and with his voice in my ears, I step towards it.

Chapter Three

Opening the door to the café, I slip into an oppressively warm room. Long but not wide it exudes both coziness and enormity. A strong piney scent washes over me so that the world feels too top heavy, like a philosopher's workshop. The walls have time-worn plank paneling and gnarled floorboards peep between tattered red rugs. Paintings hang in unornamented splintering frames. Incongruously in-line with the place, a supple-sounding trance curls around the air.

To my right stands a counter. A long lanky blond boy sits reading behind it. Acting casually, as if I feel utterly at home, I walk over and reach for a menu. The front side alone lists twenty different "varietals" of what, I realize, must be weed. The back advertises pastries, I think, and coffee, tea, bier, and jenever, all cheaper than the pot. The front side has several stains. The back side looks virtuosly untouched.

The café is all but empty yet, still slouching, the boy has just barely bothered to peek at me. I examine my options, choose one, then put down the menu. No movement. I shift. At last, pushing back his bangs, he looks up.

Suddenly unsure, I hesitate then point at a moderately priced varietal. I have no idea what it is. It doesn't matter. It will, I've no doubt, get me stoned.

At last standing up, the boy starts fussing indifferently over one of thirty or so little drawers fashioned like an old apothecary's cabinet in the wall behind him. He wears, I notice, three hemp necklaces, a yellowish threadbare button-down shirt, which matches his skin, and loose brown pants. I glance at what he was reading. *Saussure*. Haha, everyone is "so sure" of something. I must be nervous. I look at him. He has long greasy hair and is the type of guy whose stomach is tapered and tight but who has a flat old-manish ass.

After fiddling for a while with whatever is in the drawer, he comes back and holds out one perfect joint. He looks at me, expectantly. It's his first full expression but I am stunned. I'm not sure what I'd expected, but I know that for twenty euros it was more than one stupid joint.

"Twenty euros for *one*?"

"Ja, een spliff, mate." He replies slowly, with a twisted broken English, his blankness restored.

He holds up the joint, his hand entirely steady.

I tense up. There's no way twenty euros buys just one finger's worth of weed. My face grows hot. My arms tighten. Someone has walked in behind me. I don't want to cause a scene, so I force my fingers out. None of this matters. I'd have trashed most of a bag anyway. I shove the American equivalent of twenty euros across to him. My first, and last, payment of a tourist tax. He has taken my money, meanwhile, and is looking at it as if it's strange, which to be fair, though he is a jerk, I guess it would be to him. Pulling out a piece of paper, he punches a calculator morosely, chings open a drawer, and comes back. With one hand he hands me a pile of change, with his other he pushes—a tiny see-through sack! It's half-full with what must be the rest of my weed.

"One spliff." He had *rolled* one spliff. The hotness in my face changes temperature. I smile absurdly and stammer "*danke*," the one Dutch word I remember, then I move off with the temporary taste of relief.

I retreat to a table by a window. This must sit separate to bear the brunt of winter, for the frail panes offer little insulation. Fresh breaths and tiny frost tongues sneak in to temper the otherwise overwhelming warmth.

The couple who came in after me, I notice, make their

purchase more swiftly then head towards the fire at the opposite end of the room.

Shivering off a reverie, I examine my bag, my fingertips tapping incriminatingly all over it. I am nonetheless relieved to be acting outside of myself as I admire the lawn-like hue of the weed. Tiny purple and gold furs offset its brownish-green angles. I hold some to my nose. It's fresh and fragrant with only a hint of the fetidness I associate with pot. Perhaps I wouldn't have been hustled even if I had just gotten the joint, which now lies lengthwise on the table, tight and narrow, not at all like the misshapen cylinders I've seen kids smoking at school.

Still, I want to roll one myself. Like Chad had shown me. Fortunately, the kid at the bar had passed me matches and papers along with my change. Really, that transaction had gone as well as it could have.

My first attempt is not so good. It comes out half overstuffed and half limp. From experience I know that this will melt the moment I put it to my lips. I try again. The flame catches and … success! I take my first mouthful in months and instantly the taste takes me back to Chad—

Then I'm coughing and I'm recalling, gratefully, those kids at school who claim to have weed that tastes like raspberries or blueberries, like some sort of fruit. This really does have the faintest flavor of an orchard. I suck in slowly and, instead of drowning, I feel like I've found a heavier, faintly acrid air. This time I gag only a little before the pain subsides.

I recollect myself, pretending to look at the paintings nearby. Most depict antique sailing ships, a tribute, perhaps, to what some guidebook I'd read called Amsterdam's "first source of affluence." These canvases though carry such enervating colors that they scarcely suggest opulence. Leaning towards one then another, I peer into hazy flat-planed perspectives and unwavering monochrome waters into which for any sailor to enter he would have to be skewed into two dimensions. At least these exist, almost assuredly, as their own originals rather than the reprints I've seen in the shops, the reprints of reprints of van Goghs and

Rembrandts, of blue and black-bonneted bourgeois Protestants peeping out at patrons.

I take another hit. I won't think of him. The shop is so warm that the windows have fogged over completely. I try not to cough and I fail.

This stuff is strong. Stronger than I had expected. I shake my head. It feels as if someone has wrapped it in soft gauze. I breathe in again. The air's thickness increases, not unpleasantly. I smoke subtly. Savoring it. Just, I imagine, as some Regency gentleman must have done in some seventeenth-century drug club.

I look again at the ships. My eyes land first on one detail then on another until they have all blurred together, the paintings, the walls, the people, flowing now with the trance until the whole distending shop reorders itself. It's harmoniously long yet intimate in its immensities.

For a second, for who knows how long, I try slow ing all of this d o w n, m y s m o k i n g, m y v i s i o n. The music seeps into the walls, until I can't see but I can *sense* it growing, until anyone, if they wanted to, could reach out and touch it, coming down in curls, sliding across ships, slipping into surfaces, making them move, slowly at first then faster. Ineffectually imagined seas heave in ways that their artists could never have imagined. One ship sets sail, another blows towards an island, still another plows towards the inflamed orb bleeding through at its edge.

Is it morning? Is it evening?

The question itself is irrelevant. Why should I care that I am alone in a strange city smoking pot. The infinitesimal sailors, half-clothed, tiny chests heaving, don't care, why should anyone else? The café is utterly indifferent to my existence, its aura conducive to those in nonchalant knots and to those more intimately on their own.

"More intimately on their own," I think, and giggle. How ridiculous. Still, oddly enough, I am exhilarated. Here and now I could meet anyone, *many* anyones, any âme at all! All the patrons provide routes for reaching or retreating. Within seconds I could be back in the crowd, scattered, spread into so many arms and legs, into this free-for-all, which allows me to smile even as I try to stop. How *farfetched* this all is. I am laughing and I couldn't stop now even if I wanted to and for some reason this isn't unnerving. I add on to it, I exasperate it, exponentially, thinking of those kids skiing or shopping or some, such as Stephen, still studying, only now for *next* year's exams! Sturdy sexy saint Stephen still in your boxer shorts studying, the savant, ha! a half-sexy celebrant, living up to your eponymous ancestors. Such a snob. I bet they were not so abdominably, I mean so *abominably* anal about their apartments! God, when I get high I always think about—

Now is not the time. Still I consider that flap—never open enough to reveal even a hint of hair. My eyes jump back to the here and now, away from the picture I've been staring at for who knows how long. Who cares? These pale hoary haired men, wily women, guys my age strutting, they're all too preoccupied to pay any attention to me.

I try to connect my thoughts as they jump through my mind. And I *can* connect them, if only for an instant, as I remember that just outside these doors whatever you want is on offer, if you can offer an offer back. A few months ago *bodyboy22* had typed in a New York chatroom "tight bod for tight bod. I ask only for what I offer" and I had read this as an ultimate morality. Now I'm laughing again at contradictions that feed false fantasies because here *all* is on offer to anyone who can account for it. The exigencies of Amsterdam have dispanded into a carnal carnival of mayhem and money all along those canals, alleys, and overpasses, up those stone staircases leading to places I can't presently picture but where someone, finally someone preys you will want what they—

Someone, I realize, is grabbing my arm.

I turn and hear, "do you?"

He sounds annoyed, as if he's repeating himself.

"Do you have a *maatch*, maan?"

Drawing his hand from my arm he points, as if for an excuse, to the counter. This is now absurdly crowded. He shakes his head. Shocked out of myself, I reach for a match—*do* I have one?—and steal a look. He's roughly my age and wears tight black jeans and a shiny ivory shirt. He's vaguely sexy, in an unbalanced, tired sort of way. I want desperately to talk to him but I don't know what to say. I force my eyes to his. They are opaque and offer no help. Before I can stop him, he's off again, into the crowd. Without the match.

Still, his touch remains and with a watershed after-effect as I find myself in conversations, perhaps I have been for hours, half-comprehended and spurred on by the wave of someone's wrist—"non, *non*, parce-que j'en*tends* la peau du jeu," someone gurgles, "ou, si vous m'entendissiez—" a baritone surges to discuss the merits(!?), I think, of "*l'*abstinence," or perhaps "*l'absint*," I can't tell which because someone turns and all I can discern is a man announcing in a high-pitched German, tinged with the slightest slur of simpering, odd with its so adamant "ich," "ich habe eine *sehr* hoffnungsvoll Hotel auf—" "right off of Damrak, I'm sure. We have abandoned our gildter for the vulgar excess of your euro," everyone laughs as an older man sweeps me into his train, "mais j'ai *peur* que nous n'avons peu soucieux des disputations des jeunes. Et nous, *nous* ne voulons pas devenir des vieillards, des *Gides*, qui j'admire," he grins leeringly, "bien sûr, mais—" his neighbor interrupts to make some quick pedagogic-sounding reproof, "*le Chanson de Putain* marque," the meaning of which I miss but which prompts another primed conversant to interject, "mais oui, *oui*, mais ça c'est pas la *pointe*," he draws out the "*nte*," impaling it in his mouth, before adding "au moins, c'est pas *ma* pointe," and he chuckles self-ingratiatingly.

"Alors—il y a toujours M. Hollinghurst," a younger man tries to slip in by saying something exquisite, "qui est hon—" almost by instinct I identify the previous speaker, the chuckler, as an American, and I temporarily lose interest in anyone else. He exudes the aura, with his cravat, his brown-checked jacket, his easy unidiomatic professions, of the still landed English gentry. A counterfeit cultural caché. Sure enough, spotting me, he refrains from braying one more word and I soon see him wandering elsewhere in the crowd.

Despite his flight, or perhaps on account of it, I detect a tacit understanding, a certain silent intimacy that props the unarticulated tumescence through which these men talk. They leap freely from topic to topic as if they are old friends who, having lived for a long time apart, have reunited without quite recalling one another's names. These they dance politely around, "mon ami," "mein leiber," "mijn lieverd," cutting in and out of refined subjects with an urbane impersonality. No one mentions any occupation or asks why anyone else is in Amsterdam, idenitifying details are kept carefully undisclosed.

Initially I'd supposed that this café was dedicated to locals. I'm in the midst though of a fair amount of foreigners. Mostly men. Many appear overripe and their tweeds and silks cannot quite hide their sagging skin. Of course there are some about my age but we have all ended up in our own diaspora. Off in a corner I see the one who had asked me for a match. I spot one single drop of sweat dripping down his cheek. One man comes up to me and sputters "*tool, tool*," in an odd accent. I smile and shake my head. He must likewise want some sort of lighter. By now I've been asked so many times for matches and papers and pot that I have offered them all away. "Desolé," I say, "je n'ai rien." Several generous people have tried, with a shy shrug or an open hand, to share whatever they happen to have. Everyone is generous.

I'm enjoying myself but itinerant eyes wander. In the depths, I see a bearded man with model good looks slipping one hand into an older man's pocket. Someone much younger, much slimmer leans into a troll walking out. And it's around now that I first really lay eyes on *her*. She's laughing when she looks up and our eyes meet. I am instantly enthralled. She's slender and darkly luminous, like some standoffish medieval Madonna, and I can't stop staring.

She stares back but the crowd, already swollen, crests. Someone shoves between us, stretching the energy in the air so that, by the time he has passed, our connection is cut. Perhaps some friend had claimed her, perhaps she had been swept around, perhaps she hadn't seen me at all.

Then someone is clutching my arm and everyone is off again and the whole shop is swirling. A hand is at my elbow, a voice is whispering in my ear. It's her. The crowd is at its apex, flickering flattering voices echo everywhere, and her fetid breath floats into me, "*see you soon~*"

A minute, an hour, surely less than a day later, I'm once again outside. The sharp air and the silence of the city fight the fatigue that had crept over me. That woman, her voice tinged with a rich guttural accent all its own, "*see you soon—*," what had she meant? She had whispered, I think, other words in my ear that I couldn't catch though I had caught her sharp contradictory odors: smoke, lavender, sweat. I'd had glimpses of her only, of her cheek, her ear, her nose set indolently to the left, all looking like porcelain. Her hair a savage slapdash sallow, save for its roots. Her eyes, flaming blue, would burn you if you came too close. Her mouth had as it had flushed against my ear.

The cold has revitalized me. Stonily sober, I long to learn all about her. What she likes, where she lives, what she does when she is alone, and why she had chosen me, out of everyone. I picture her typing at twilight, fantastically fast, composing radical tracts on providential stars and stoned angels. She works late in cold caves, in forest cottages, in bare rented rooms, filling them all with ink smeared manuscripts, and when she writes the world alters, minutely, in its most intimate aspects.

I might have followed her, save right when I could have a man in a tweed jacket and a brown tie had taken hold of my hand. Had I talked to him earlier? Someone had laughed, hysterically, and he had looked with revulsion at the source of the cackling. A good-looking middle-aged man was needling an oily adolescent, himself verging on old age. Borders were breaking.

I had moved and the tweed man had, very gently, restrained me. "My dear," he had purred, "you are leaving now? Is too soon … you will hurt yourself hurrying out your '*porte etroite*.'" His words had come out viscously, "more narrow than what after our friend chases, no?" I remember him now, we had joked about Gide.

"Excuse me," he had said, courteously, "but you must try this cig-a-rette. You would be so upset if you missed it." He had sucked in his breath, as if genuinely fretful at this loss. "It's tabak mixed with *very* rare Algerian hash. It is exquisite. You would like to try." His right hand had produced a slight white cylinder. His nails shone. They were preternaturally even. His whole demeanor had an unreal hygiene, a too-well-cared-for physicality that instead of exciting, deadened. He had placed the slender roll in my hand. His gestures, I had noticed, had they not been so refined, would have been frighteningly forceful.

I had puffed on the cigarette ... but to no effect.

"I have got to go."

"*Muss es sein*? Well, *es muss sein*," he had mused. Then he had receded back into the crowd.

Walking now in the open air, I'm somehow higher than I have ever been before. Still, I'm thinking sensibly, fantastically, and with an inexorable honesty. The past twenty-four hours unfurl before me. I stop and stare at a canal. Its stone walls jut out arrogantly into the water, the wet darkness of which rubs impassively alongside them.

My fingers tap along a balustrade. My nerves recall her hand on my arm. A minor euphoria resurges. It disappears and I walk and walk until, by chance, I hear the ding-ding-ding of a casino. Turning towards it, I see what must be a byway of Damrak Straat.

A shiver shoots through me. I realize how tired I am. Lost and exhausted within its sidestreets, the city's allusiveness would have quickly lost its charm. Even here, I sense the hazards waiting for the disoriented, the perils lurking along unlit lanes and obscured dead ends.

Not for me, though. Not tonight. I surrender to the harsh hospitality of the main drag. Dregs of safety and revulsion half-awake with the dirty clanging. Following the darkness, this garishness is sickening. It's exhausting even to imagine the energy required to run all this, hour after hour, day after day, until all that's left are squeaks and groans, scarcely trying to fain freshness, shoving the same stale overpriced pizzas, the same fusty funnel cakes after everchanging and hence homogeneous tourists. A consequentially crass cosmopolitanism.

I slip past sporadic packs of people, herds of college kids by now so smashed that they could scarcely conceive of a "consequence." I wonder briefly if the frat boy I'd rode in with is among them. Then I spot the *Royal Holland* and the thought of my bed, of any bed consumes me.

Once inside, I am struck by the silence. Wanting only to lie down, I hurry through to the lobby. Passing the counter I half-note that a young man with a goatee has replaced the ornery old men.

Twitching up with a quickness that would have broken their bones, he jerks down a book.

"Where going?"

"I have a room here."

"Which, please." He has an inquisitorial alacrity.

I stop short and report, "nine."

"*You* then are one who took key," he snaps, as if releasing in one spurt an epoch's worth of anger. "*You* have caused *many* problems. Is *one* key for *one* room. Bring *here* before you leave."

His tone makes me mad, dulling my exhaustion. What hotel, what hostel wouldn't have an extra key? He is purposefully being obstinate.

"Look," I hold up the key, "I'll bring this back … when I am done with it."

"*No!!*"

He stops. Even he seems shocked by his vehemence. He repeats himself, a little less forcefully. "*No*. You will leave it here. Door is unlocked. Room *stays* unlocked when patrons are in it."

Yes, that makes sense. Leave the door *un*locked in this shithole hotel so that when I'm asleep in my cot someone can come in and slit my throat.

Who cares. I'm too tired to fight and he's too mad for this truly to be about me. He's so angry that he is actually trembling. His face stays impassive but his sparse facial hair quivers like a spider caught in its own web. It must itch the tan smoothness of his skin. Up close, he looks younger than me. It's only his ingrained indignation that makes him look older.

Briefly, I consider inviting him up to discuss this. I imagine his only intermittently hirsute body twitching. But this might push him over the edge and I am done. He can sit here and stew if he likes.

I hand him the key and leave him to his miserable self.

Once in the room, I'm enclosed in stillness. At first, I find this soothing. The altercation downstairs had unsettled me. It's unnerving to be attacked unexpectedly. Here it's quiet and dark. Someone must have covered the window, leaving me to feel my way towards my bed. The last one on the left. There.

To make sure, I reach for what should be the wall. It feels like sticky burlap. I shudder. This must be what's stuck over the window. So this bed must be mine. Deciding not to get undressed, partly to hold my passport, partly to not have the sheets against my skin, I take off only my shoes, then–holy hell!!!–my hand thrusts into the pliant rigidity–it's not linen–it's the hard hairy flesh of someone's stomach! In my bed! For an instant I revel in the heat, in the beer-tinged breath, in the tension of *touching another boy's body*. Time expands until this firmness unforgivingly gives way ...

A rough hand shoves away mine. Someone gasps, jerks up, and sucks in his breath.

"*What the–?!*"

Its intensity covers its alarm, a dazed Endymion warning off intruders.

I'm pushed and I fall. Hard. I'm stoned. I'm *stunned*. Wrong bed. Wrong—? Of course you idiot or you wouldn't be on the floor!

"What the *'ell* are you *doin'*?" A noticeably English voice shouts out louder this time. I'm thankful that I can understand it, but it's surreal hearing what should be an elegant accent attacking.

"Bloody fairy!" it spews, ruining any hope for reason. "Oi! someone flip the fuckin' lights."

Voices protest, sounding variously slurred and sluggish, not wanting to be woken, much less blinded, for someone else's scrap.

On the floor, my head ringing, I search for my bag.

Bits of debris, *disgusting*, stick to my fingers. Has he moved it?! No, thank god! Here it is. He must have kicked it under the cot.

Kneeling, I offer a fetid resistance, "you *moved* my bag."

No response.

"You moved my bag ... this is my bed—" *asshole*, I want to add, but my whisper is already unreal.

"Psst, not what you want *mon ami*. I've been 'ere three days. This is *my* bed, this," still coarse, his voice sounds less disoriented, and it has intensified perilously, "so you can piss off, cause you can't jump in 'ere wiff me."

Someone, somewhere, laughs.

My eyes at last detect an outline. He has a youngish, stubbly face and is shirtless. His torso lurks squat and lean.

"Look mate, it's 'is bed," someone sighs, tired but objective. For an indebted moment, I have found a friend.

"'e's 'ad it all week. I seen an extra bed up front— 'op in it or piss off so we can get back to sleep."

This is not right, yet everyone starts settling back in, so I grab my bag, which had *clearly* been kicked, and, for amity's sake, I return inward. The other asshole was right. The cot opposite the door is empty. Probably because while it's warm everywhere, here it is *sweltering*. It smells like an overripe oven. The cot has cocooned this in and I can't help wondering, as I slip between the sheets, how often they have been soaked with some other guy's sweat.

Tucked into this cot, I can still hear that first nasty grunt from that taught working boy's body. Hot drops of humiliation, of fatigue, of an unwarranted wrong scald my eyes. I force them back. I imagine biting his nipples, the rough black hairs crawling up his legs, to his abdomen, punching his gut. It would be hard, and if he were to hit me? His skin would trace mine and first would come tenderness, and pain, fading, would become ...

Chapter Four

Fantastically, the sole change in Damrak Straat from last night is the snappish natural light and the myriad middle-aged sightseers. Women in skirts either too long or too short who cling, generally, to older men overdosed in cologne. They mix in and out of the bandana'd and dreadlocked crowd, flooding the shops and the casinos, too old or too self-restrained to last until midnight yet compelled to take in all the trashy glitz that they can before they retreat to their hotel rooms.

I myself feel too refreshed to be where I am. I had woken up sluggish but with the coarse sheets reminding me almost instantly that *I am in Amsterdam*. Hues of auburn and brown had pervaded the room, the Dutch sun not quite able to break through the shade. Remembering the onslaught of yesterday, the fuzzy light had made the situation seem as ridiculous as perhaps it actually was, and already that day was distancing itself from this and succeeding into the next. I had lain back lazily, giving in to the vague, indistinct details drawn against the room's burlap reredos. Then I had sat up clearly and soberly and wanted with a jolting intensity to get up before anyone else.

The heat of the shower in the green communal bathroom had made me lightheaded. The stall was grimy and dank but the hot water had washed off the airport air, the smoke, and even the stale sweat of last night. My body had felt tight and smooth and clean and really, I think, I am not embarrassed. They are the ones who were assholes. Having had too much to drink or to smoke. They probably wouldn't even remember what had happened. I had gotten out, dried off, and got dressed, my fresh shirt and jeans sitting heavy from the steam. Both exuding that tinny not altogether unpleasant odor of clothes trapped in luggage too long. Relieved to see that everyone was still asleep, I had stuffed a few books in my knapsack, grapped my coat, and got out.

Now I want to avoid crowds completely so I head right, turning again to meander on to Kalver Straat. Seeking to avoid tourist traps and to find local shops, I happen upon an unfortunate fusion of both. Kalver Straat is an enormous open-air mall catering to Amsterdamians and to assorted Eurotrash. Even at 10 a.m. shoppers hunt ravenously for clothes, for accessories, for any of the junk that they want to need for so long as it takes to swipe a credit card.

The shops here actually swarm with people, some boasting only a hair's breadth more clothing than the working women had had on last night. They scream and shove as if at a parvenu amusement park. I have no interest in this, so when the current I'm in shifts, I veer off. Soon I'm alongside a neo-gothic Gap, complete with a crenelated storefront and a cardboard statue of a knight advertising a new winter armor, a peacoat. Fleeing this soldier of poor fortune, I escape, at the next opportunity, to a less crowded sidestreet.

It's no longer mid-morning and my stomach is growling. I see a Burger King, but I refuse to eat fast food in Amsterdam. Soon I spot a bakery filling the curved ground floor of a corner building. A weathered sign reads *"L'Aigle Dorée."* This looks as if it's hung here for centuries with the same sugary smells wafting out from underneath it.

Inside, the shop exudes an old-world charm. A steel-and-glass display case scarcely challenges this as it reveals dozens of precisely shaped pastries. I admire how ripe red berries all but overflow oozing underbellies of custard, how meringues boast wan pastel pinks and greens, how round brown babycakes sweat honey and nuts, and petit fours laced with thick fondant and white webbings and immaculately shaped madeleines and macaroons tinted cherry or plum glisten with feverishly soft spots of sugar, all atop the crispest of white linens.

Through a service window I see white-haired men blurring the boundary between artisanship and art. An old canary-colored woman takes people's money. A blackboard serves as a menu. The writing is foreign but the prices are unambiguous. The shop grows a little less inviting.

When it's my turn, I order a "koffie" and "un croissant" from a glass covered cake stand. Affixed to this is a "3" and Europe's everpresent calligraphic "€." The woman frowns and I reconsider. This is my first morning, which is an excuse I'll have only once. I add, "et un des tartlets des fraises, s'il vous plaît." She smiles thickly, her lips coated in pink, a cunningly mindful Midas.

Reaching a table I set down a croissant that dwarfs the plate under it, a tartlet that can barely contain itself, and coffee. True this all cost twelve euros, but recalling prices in Princeton, I can congratulate myself on my frugality.

Putting my change in my wallet, I find a paper stuck to its leather exterior. Not thinking much of it, I peel it off the casing and examine it. Neither a receipt nor a part of my plane ticket, it's folded tightly and it comes apart only reluctantly to reveal a strange skeletal handwriting.

Sitting down, I flatten the note out in front of me. Then coffee in hand I focus on the sunlight streaming through the window directly next to me. Excited, I stretch into this strangeness, forcing myself to relax to a state of inattentive contentment. This lasts until my stomach rumbles, bringing me back to the present. I push the tartlet aside. Complex satisfactions should come at the end, thus simpler ones aren't preordained disappointments.

Biting into the croissant, I look at the mechanically made lace and the definitely faux delft set all around me. On the whole, the croissant is rather bland. Chewing it, I slip into the apathetic state that we, most of us, live in for most of our lives. It's a mindset that protects us, generally, from the flaws that surround us, from that nick on the plate, from that run in the linen, from that crack in the glass. No matter how miniscule, there's forever some flaw, some unforeseen errancy that waits to be made relevant. We adapt to ignore these, peremptorily, and we thereby disarm them.

Inevitably, my thoughts return to the note. I smooth it out. My handwriting is untidy, but this is illegible:

> *beatifulboycome soonandvisitme. 1127 Jenever Strcome 2.00 tomorow. —Gretta*

My mind anarchically recalls Gwen whose handwriting looks like an old-fashioned sans-serif type. The only vaguely intelligible part here is what looks like a date, one from almost a week ago: "1127" could be "11-27" with "Str"=Satr=Saturday? and what looks like "tomorow"—Dutch for "tomorrow"?—scribbled after it.

I look out the window. This bakery can't be too far from the main train station and it's only two blocks from Kalver Straat. Yet these buildings must be much older. They look, actually, like those in the rld, save exceedingly staid and prosperous. Their bricks and stones look flush, their façades clean. Sylvan sentinals stand before them. Well-cared-for men in overcoats, gloves, scarves, and fedoras hustle along the sidewalks. Women, too, in cashmere coats and medium-high heels, several carrying attaché cases, rush severely into the wind.

I like that I can sit here, warmed and removed from the workaday world. Absentmindedly I examine the note, incoherent and crinkled. I must have had it for a while. Had I picked it up inadvertently at the airport? On the train? Could someone have put it in my pocket? Had that frat guy ... no, too good to be true, and he was never close enough. At the coffee shop? Any one of those men ...

Playfully, I try to sound out some of the scribbles. Dutch, after all, is not *too* different from German nor German from English. German was almost our national language and a few words do look like familiar. Actually ... I grab a pen from my

54

bag. Soon I'm rewriting the Cyrillic-looking cursive letters into Latin block ones. Separated out like this, it's almost intelligible. Minus the mistakes and the atrocious handwriting, this seems to be in English, and to be some sort of invitation.

Creepy is what it is. Particularly as I now suspect, though I've no idea how I got it, that it's meant for me. Unnerved, I push it aside.

My mind flashes to the woman from last night. A heat floods through me. *She* could have slipped this to me when she had whispered into my ear. I pull the paper back to me. Its solidity makes her that much more real. It brings back her scent. Smoke and lavender. Making sure that no one is looking, I sniff the note. It smells like my wallet, like decaying leather. I feel creepier than ever sitting amongst the proper presence of doilies sniffing a ratty old piece of paper.

I stare back out the window. This theory makes sense. The men I'd met, with their moist manicured hands, could never have scratched out such an artless guileless letter, such an indifferent invitation.

Outside the weather has grown gray. People appear more bundled. I glance back down. This would explain why she had said *"see you soon"*—though–*oh!* "Str." is *Straat*. "1127 Jenever Str" is an *address*! The note snaps together. Tomorrow at 2:00, which is *today*! So is this her home? Or a café? Or somewhere else altogether?

Outside a sedately sophisticated woman, swathed in black, her blonde hair swept up brilliantly into a beret, walks stridently on, no doubt towards some financial firm, some bastion of grave taste and middle-class morality. Inside the bakery, faux delft squats on spotless shelves.

Before I know it, I've made up my mind. I will meet her. She obviously knows her way around the rld. Perhaps I could ask her about … an electric charge shoots through me. Not that anyone is looking. What would happen if these inoperative hausfraus knew what I was thinking? No doubt they'd throw me out in disgust.

I grow light-headed at the thought of this.

I cut into my tart, this falsely consecrated ring so ready to be ravished. Thanks to its flawlessness, I'd been unwilling to breach it. Now half of it caves in and the other half slithers out obscenely. After all, it tastes rather rotten.

Chapter Five

Once again on Kalver Straat, I look for a bookstore. My guidebook, albeit fairly complete, had not listed Jenever Straat. Her apartment, I guess, is not a major tourist attraction. So I want to find a proper map. But rather than cartography, the majority of shops around me boast a ubiquitous eurotrash attire with mannequins modeling shiny shirts and tight-fitting jeans. These, I'll admit, have a certain sexy *je ne sais quoi* but seeing the same crap-copied couture over and over gets depressing. The majority of it, I'd bet, gets made for two cents in Asia and sells here for roughly sixty euros an item. It's a racket.

At last, down one sidestreet and across and through another, the crowd gets older and sparser and I see a small café, an antique-ish oddity store then ... a window brimming with books! Culture kissing commerce. Inside, I find guides in Dutch, in English, in Arabic, in French, in several Asian languages to almost anywhere that anyone might want to visit within or around Amsterdam. I page through an atlas optimistically entitled *The Complete Street Guide to Amsterdam*. One hundred plus pages filled with numbers and grids. I turn to its index. No "Jenever," "Jennifer," or "Jenifer" Straat. Perhaps I've mistaken "J" for "I"? No luck. I pull out a bright yellow volume, the *Overall Street Guide to Amsterdam*. I turn to its index. My finger slides past "Jansen," "Janus," "Jenever"!—section C-4.

Flipping to C-4, I half-tease myself, wondering where she might live. No doubt somewhere near the center of the city. And sure enough, I'm right, though I had *not* expected C-4 to be smack in the middle of the rld! Her neighbors not exiled intellects but whor—I recall her porcelain skin and her cigarettes. I had envisioned her ensconced in elegant squalor with shut-off chandeliers or in a tenement crammed with exotic émigrés. Now I wonder, perhaps for the first time, what she's really like. I can't picture her cleaning up after a husband or baking cookies all day for kids.

Regardless, I quickly jot down the relevant street names and jump up. I'd come here for a reason and it feels good to have accomplished my goal.

Next I browse towards the back. It's struck me that since I'm here, I might search out one or two other useful guidebooks. Wandering into a section marked "Geschiedenis/History," I find tomes specializing in the city itself. Those in the first case, nearest the open aisle, pertain to topics of more conventional interests, such as *Amsterdam and the Dutch Crusades* or *The Haven van Amsterdam and the Golden Age of Dutch Shipping*. The more sparsely stacked top shelves hold slimmer volumes on more specific subjects, *Amsterdam in the 1880s* and *Tulip: the Life of a Seventeenth-Century Horticulturalist*. The middle shelves offer photography collections, several in cadmium bromide and borax. Opening one at random, I find painstakingly framed, tenderly taken shots displaying intricately cut canals and churches. In another, I page through beautiful out-of-the-way banks and bridges, all enhanced by immaculate young men, half-naked and sprawling on balustrades or lounging under archways.

One volume has an antique sepia tint to it. The effect is haunting. Turning pages I stare at stately, adoringly, yet almost warily captured Adonises. One in particular shows an intrepid young man preparing to dive into a canal in the cold cordiality of winter. It's an intimate act of evasion in a treacherous bewildering world. At once frozen and tender, he has been caught in a moment of absorption, bathed in the late-afternoon light, his stomach taut above his high cut black bathing suit, the contour of his cock and balls bulging softly. The fifties-style coloring and the forlorn ochre of his skin stand out against the obscurity of the water, imbuing him with an impenetrable iconic hue.

The next bookcase holds flimsy paperbacks, erotic anthologies, and "best of" collections, all designed to be disposable. On a shelf amongst these, I find precisely what I'm looking for, a select few "blue" guides that provide more than just phone numbers and addresses to private businesses but also reports on specialities, safeguards, even costs. Themselves cheaply constructed, intended for shortlived lifespans, they nonetheless offer a priceless practicality. Rather than just access, these provide actual options, a true if paradoxically impersonal sense of what's on offer in small cubicles and in obscure apartments across Amsterdam. I browse through a few of these, their flimy newsprint paper and throwaway objectivity making me queasy, until a nearby set of books catches my eye. These are analogous to the blue guides and yet markedly different, so different in quality in fact as to become different in kind, as a casual phrasebook is to a concordance or an index to a compendium. They manifest an entirely different respect for their subject. Heavy and encyclopedic, they have first-class leather covers stamped with gilt and they look like heirlooms. One series with beautifully banded spines is entitled *A History of Prostitution: Profanity and Profundity, 1AD to 1967.* It runs through twelve volumes and includes a stand-alone intro. Other specimens, if less ambitious, are equally meticulous. Some are registries so thick that they must list all of the past and present brothels of Amsterdam, including many marked "not open to the public." Several series must have taken years, if not decades, to compile, with fantastically high overheads. Hence the expense, for discreet tags reveal prices running to what, for some, must be a month's income. Their completeness, however, suggests that they had been labors of love, for which such scholars (for really what else could you call their compilers?) ought not to lose out, ought in fact to be rewarded, and for some earnest amateur, the charge would without a doubt be worth it.

As a student of history, it's wonderful to browse through these, to hold them, to weigh them as authorizations of so many intents. Stealthily, I lean forward and sniff the one I hold in my hand. It smells musty and clean all at once, like between

Chad's—I notice some pale man circling this aisle for at least the third time. Looking down, I see how filthy the carpet is.

Looking up, I see that such pasty middle-aged men are skulking by more frequently and are lingering longer. One nearby, looking at a magazine, actually readjusts himself. Each is a doughy döppelganger of the others. All have wide white foreheads and fat faces with necks pressing indelicately into their collars. Almost all have pleated paunches. These aged adolescents look as though they should be at home, half-tucked under tables in stiflingly stunted kitchens as they stuff themselves with food. Fare that they have bought but that others serve spiced up with scorn. Few families admit utter failure but all are quick to criticize, until such husbands and fathers creep here, scanning the lower shelves with downcast eyes and half-upturned heads.

Not that I mind middle-aged men, if they take care of themselves. There's this one man back home who—but why am I thinking of this? I pull out a small mixed guide that should do the trick. I laugh nervously at this thought and someone stares. Fronting its pink-and-blue back, I abandon these "history" buffs and head toward the counter. There I pay and take a bag with my book, all the while making as little eye contact as I can with anyone.

Once again on the street, I try to shake off my queasiness. Paying for the book, my head, for an instant, had gotten so hot that I'd thought I was swimming through sweat. Now I slip into the crowd, just one more shopper, just one more paradox of the people, as an accomodating current sweeps me up, our speed fluctuating as we reach the next H&M or TopMan or forgettable "haute-couture" quickie-mart.

With relief, I find myself trailing, yielding to the ardor of so many aspiring emptors. Flashy and noisy, they dominate the street. I welcome them since I myself must be discreet. It was a condition of my coming and it strikes me—"*pardon, pardon,*" a woman runs into my arm—that perhaps I am hypocrisy's handmaiden. I too enjoy watching others not watch me until the satisfaction of my secret grows warm. But I am different from those men. I don't *know* what I want and *that* is why I am here, so that in twenty years I won't be skulking round the backs of bookstores. I see my future self having not taken this trip. At best, I'm surrounded by beautiful bindings, a bottle of scotch, and ineffective anti-depressants. At worst, I've twisted the trust of a bitter, once-faithful wife. So how, overall, can what I am doing be wrong? It is time, I think, to remind myself of this. Unlike some people—my father, Gwen, that girl who caught me picking my nose in the fourth grade—I hate to focus on my moral failings, but to fixate on what hurts is helpful. It helps to linger over each possible problem, be it shame or discomfort or guilt, until even those that are excruciating are not only refined but are eroded, until you are less bothered than you are just bored.

I dodge two tourists pouring over a map.

Take, for instance, my buying this book. What harm can really come from it? I have hurt no one. I have, in fact, helped some clerk by keeping that bookstore in business. I have helped the store. I will help those businesses that the book advertises, enabling them to offer employment, not to mention help the women that they employ to stay safe, for the book I bought offers sanitary suggestions. I have not hurt myself, for I can afford it. I have not even suffered in my own moral standing, for what I did was not wrong! Buying a book isn't immoral and the suggestion that it is is absurd. And if it is, the clerk and the store and the authors are all my accomplices. No one exists on their own. I made sure, moreover, to pay cash, so I am untraceable, and those men who stared at me by the shelves will tonight let their imaginations run so wild that "I" will not even be me.

Now I feel exon–I am exhilarated. Even being back on Kalver, I feel a facile fondness for everyone, for the lurching women with huge bags, for the bottle-blonds in cheap gautier sunglasses, even for the uniformed schoolchildren who weave quickly through the currents, their fiercely benignant voices hovering above us.

In their wake I spot the Gap that I'd seen earlier, with its castle-like façade. The poor pasteboard knight still stands before it holding his sign, *"Gawain says: Guard yourself ... against Winter!"* I walk past, and see *"Gawain zegt: Bewaak uzelf ... tegen Winter!"* What an ad. A passionate adventurer put out to pasture, weighted down with a cheap cardboard overcoat, deaf, dumb, and defeated. The just cosmic joust of a long suffering and a long-suffered chivalry, one that's outlived its shattered standards and its subsequent service to the absurd cravings and the perverse pleasures of limp lieges, rampant women, and too many self-serving hallucinations of heaven.

Thankfully, I suppose, despite setbacks, false starts, and savage mentors, science, our new creed, still supersedes chivalry. Experiments supplement tournaments. Yet with this new system, errant explorers can still contest, defend, elevate, even transubstantiate our world, leading us to be more accurate, more complexly flexible. Think, for instance, of all our transformings of Xs and Ys into Is, allegories being only algebra with a little leeway, turning our world into *le pays des fees*, to let us recall I, if it's ugly. Religions ruined their authority when they started to transubstantiate gods into goods and us into evil, ignoring the almighty I. *Caveat redemptor.* Too rigidly cruel rules of an immaterial creed that could not be condoned.

Spread by pagans at sea to chapels in Kalver Straat to clapboard hell houses in New Hampshire. Man-made mythologies. Granted, this from one who not five minutes ago was dredging the mire of his embarrassment for a newfound mathmythtisticism. Still, there can be reason in ritual. Confession, Mass, lit candles, all evidence of humanity's taste for investigation, creation, extrapolation.

A cold drizzle falls. The same once trickled into thatched huts and cold cottages. I hope that the unmonied monastics, huddling together for warmth, rubbed their cold young bodies, despite their lice and their faeces, and got off, having not entirely understood their insurance system for the next world, because in this one, their prelates were wrapping themselves in unearned ermines and hoarding their spiritual indigence amidst incense.

Gwen had been a conventional Catholic and I had supported this, largely because religion tended to reinvigorate her romantic "restraint." I had once even, towards our end, as a service to her, went to Mass. I had been disappointed. If in Europe churches evidence human ingenuity, in the U.S. they are monuments to mediocrity. Hers was a garish structure with an overly lit apse and what the well-fed congregation no doubt dubbed a "judicious" use of gold. The whole shop seemed designed to assuage the conscience of its congregants. There were no indications of unrepentant sins, and modern Michaelangelos had simply replaced exquisitely harassing art with apathy. The clergy, in turn, had given up garbling the good word in its originary languages and had taken to slurring sermons through cheap microphones, dangling the unwanted reward of an anodyne eternity; although, the eye of a needle aside, tithing entrepreneurs couldn't have had any trouble wandering through the vestibule with ample room to discover their names in it. The gelding of guilt.

Of course there had been some benefits. Chad had still been home and we two had drifted in behind Gwen, prim and proper in her Sunday suit, and then their parents, conformist yet mostly uninterested. The result had been, as I had anticipated, awful. He'd been hungover and bored, his tie choking him until, ignoring the protests of his *mater dolorosa*, he had loosened it to hang low in his lap. I'd sat close enough to him to smell his sweat. He'd have done better in the Middle Ages, starved then fed beer, bread, and abstract ecstasies designed to trick him into abandoning earth, all in mourning for some uncertain eden.

This too though would have been an immoral reworking of old rituals. Of psychological escorts to existence. I prefer rites more athletically intellectual than slyly somnolescent. Say oral joustings or textual tournaments. A training to face the multitudinous causes of consequence, the consequence of causes, in so many secret scarlet synapses, the unseen ripples of responsibility, altercations become altared actions, the pains in pleasure and the pleasures in pain, revising what's gone wrong and perpetuating what's gone right. If you prick someone for one reason, isn't there agony, and if for another, elation? Grins turn to grimaces turn to groans and we have to determine which leads to which and why.

Take chivalry, for instance, everyday knights errant. When the curb collapses and we find ourselves face to face with an unintended glimpse, an uncertain smile. When cruising becomes a quest. A contemplative courtoisie.

Take that guy in the jean jacket, his arm on some girl's shoulder. At most he's a year, maybe two older than I am, and she's peering through a window at rings. Her dry brown hair streaks down her purple-jacketed back. He has an easy, almost indolent beauty. His rite each morning must be to shower, to dry off idly, then to slip into jeans, straining them over his half-wet, just-thick-enough thighs, right up to his oh-so-smooth stomach before reluctantly grabbing some shirt. Sensual and dangerous, oh my sexy chevalier.

In fact, he looks uncannily like an older version of Hans, the well-groomed jock from my high-school *Achtung, German!* textbook. *Achtung* followed a group of "friends" who acted out everyday activities: going to class, eating in cafés, meeting exchange students to whom they'd explain Berlin. Hans was clearly the bridge character, the one who always got along with everyone, the intellectuals, the athletes, the German version of cheerleaders. His arm was always across someone else's shoulder. He smiled sincerely as the group did homework or went walking along laughing. "Oh Hans, ho, ho ..." When their soccer team won a trophy, he was the guy who got to hold it.

Hans was impressive. Now this guy's impressive. His face, his hands, his half-cocked hip, his unruffled ease despite that girl's primordially prehensile groping as she gawks awkwardly into that window.

He acts blissfully unaware of the ritual closing in on him.

Yet! this same overtly apathetic advantage, this quietly conceited complacency, draws attention, makes him susceptible to unexpected advances.

He stares coolly, thoughtlessly, into the street and, for an instant, our eyes meet:—:

Then his have moved on....

Still, he has seen me, and if only he can imagine what *I'm* imagining, he wouldn't look so certain, or so disinterested. Hans all tied up. Hans all oiled, all glistening. All his simplicity, all his disdain for everyone, inverts itself. Our eyes have overlapped and now, if only in the back of his brain, he'll start to wonder why I had stared at him rather than at anyone else. All his confidence, all his invulnerability will be shaken and he may get mad. Hot and unhappy, he'll go home, and in his room, his madness might reshape itself into some splendid scarlet shoot. He'll consider that we alone, that he and I and no one else are privy to our private thoughts. Consequently he won't, in his heart of hearts, mind our meeting. Stripped and without armor, he might even find that he enjoyed it. Slowly and surely, yet not so slowly and not so suspiciously as one might think, the small smile, that self-assured sinecure will re-flicker across his lips. My staring, he'll decide, was an act of homage. I was reassuring him of his rights. For what he wants, above all, is to be wanted. His hand will slide down ... and in this way I have enlightened him. I have helped him to come to new conclusions. I have been a curious squire for his coarse jousts and for his spiritous expenses.

Thus I have compromised us both, one look, one connexion diffused through so many desiring dendrites, until we are none of us so innocent. Of course there's a tyranny inherent in the truth of this, a mental maginot line that we ought not to cross. For we all engage in unwanted, unwarranted incursions, supposedly innocuous but that work our will, no matter how weakly, on to others. Unjustly. Still, if I've expanded his horizons, if I've facilitated some empathetic understanding, even if I won't be the one to benefit from it, then this has all been for the better.

So with the nacreous sky hanging over us, I walk on alone, past one more Gawain, dumb, damp, and delinquent, my yellow bag thudding against my leg and cutting, without effort, through the air.

* * *

Much, much later, I'm back on Jenever Straat, the sorriest street I've ever seen. It's dark and I'm grateful that I'd been here before or I'd never have found it.

Hours earlier, I had passed the train station, its two tall towers standing like robustly august governesses surveying a school, moving into a landscape that had quickly decayed. Last night the rld's promiscuous freedom and its coarseness had seemed exciting, even edifying. During the day it had just seemed sordid. Making my way toward Jenever, I'd passed through Zeedijk Straat, which had been bad enough. Its streetsign had been half-hidden by wires and by advertisements marring what must have once been fine eighteenth-century apartments, tributes to the domestic pride of the port. When I had turned on to Jenever, however, the stench had been truly appalling.

Still, I'd found her door, right at two, as her note had requested, and before I could contemplate the consequence, I'd rung the buzzer next to her name, with no response. I'd waited a bit, suffocating in what was really an alley, where the buildings were set so close together that what little light came through seemed primarily to reheat the refuse: trash bags, rotten fruit, broken ashtrays, torn condoms. The smell of tenants past, present, and a few who could have been from the future, felt like they were tendriling up my nostrils and into my brain. It was beyond rank. I'd rung again and waited, wanting to leave but feeling pulled down now by the power of the place's own abjection, by its very dead-endedness.

After a minute or so, I'd heard a cracking noise. Looking up, I'd seen a miniscule miserable face framed in a high window. It had looked, without exaggerating, obscenely wrinkled, as if a thousand and one tiny cords had whipped across it. One for each of her life's incurable calamities. This old hag had acted, moreover, as if she was glaring at *me*. Was she afraid that I was a thief?

Hearing sirens, I had taken off. Who knows, the old woman could have been crazy enough to call the cops, although the chances that they'd rush off to that straat were minimal. Better safe though than horribly sorry.

The rest of the afternoon I'd spent walking round the canals. I'd been disappointed and angry. I had been stood up. As a consolation I'd reminded myself that I am here as an investment in my future. I am not here to have fun.

Some excitement had nonetheless re-entered the air. Neon lights touted joints and gold lamé jockstraps, and hummed along to rap, reggae, and bits of Beethoven's Fifth transformed into a Far Eastern-y semi-tonal trance. A shop hawking leather and lace had a plastic Victorian-looking tea set with an electric clock reading "17:00" and the slogan "*it's HIGH time for tea*" set in its window. Military time and high time. A catholic convergence. Next door a store called Marakesh sold brightly colored caftans and books in Arabic. A coffee-colored boy had stood scowling out in front. I had stepped aside to think. 17:00 military time would be 5pm.

What if Gretta had meant *2am* not *2pm*?

What if I had just been too early?

Yes! So she *hadn't* stood me up.

Knowing that I'd return to Jenever Straat offered a surprisingly reinvigorating relief. Under its influence, I'd enjoyed the remaining afternoon and early evening while wandering around the urbane Jordaan district. Its crowded cafés had looked welcoming and warm. Lights blinked from the quasi-congenial bulbs attached to blue and black peeling houseboats, wavering constants in a cold-hearted picaresque cosmos. Passing elegantly narrow, brightly lit townhouses, I'd heard laughter and the *clinking* of crystal. So chic and so refined, I'd wondered what all goes on in there after those soirées are over. Last month I'd met a guy online with a townhouse in Brooklyn. He'd worked once, incredibly enough, for Belicor, an attractive sandy-haired director in his mid-forties who had been headhunted. I'd remembered him because my father had been both angry and impressed by his defection, which had incited various tirades against him at home. I had been anonymous but the man had been self-assuredly open and he had invited me to a party that might have been, I imagine, just like these. Smart and cultured, with just a whisper of ruthlessness. He'd wondered, for instance, if I'd known his assistant, Stuart Smallpeter, a recent Princeton grad. The party, he had said, would be black tie, but Stuart liked to stay late, to strip to his boxers, then to get pissed on as he was picking up glasses and plates. ("Champagne piss," he had typed, "lol"). I had declined his invitation.

But tonight I have a new one, and that then is how I ended up back on Jenever Straat, in Amsterdam, at 2 in the morning.

Amsterdam

Chapter Six

So once again I find myself up on her stoop. The only difference is that it's now covered by darkness and by the few faint snowflakes that have finally started to fall. They make the alley look no cleaner, only differently decrepit.

Before I can stop myself, I've reached out and rung.

And,

"Yes—"

A voice spurts out from an angle, complete with a short sharp accent. It's the gracefully gutteral *vox voluptatis* that I had remembered.

"It's William." My voice grows louder then trails off at the end, waiting for recognition. I'm always afraid that I'm someone who people won't really remember.

Will she remember me? Of course she couldn't know my name, so I add, "from last night. From the *Café Beatrix*."

There is, on her part, a long pause.

I look at the source of the sound. It's an undersized icon, an eastern orthodox *staritsa* set adjacent to the buzzer. The voice emanates from a miniature mesh grate set in its mouth. Really, it's rather clever.

Leaning towards it, I offer, "You, um, slippedyournameandaddressintomypocket."

Still no response. For an intense second, I wonder if I have again misinterpreted her invitation.

What *am* I doing? Why am I *here*?

Just then, I hear an anemic "*urenhhh*" emanating from the door, as if the building itself groans at the prospect of one more occupant.

Seconds later I'm tripping up a rusted staircase towards the sound of a door that's just been unbolted.

My mind is a mess. I've never had the sensation of so much, so suddenly. When I reach the fourth floor, a second, still more disorienting smell invades the first. An intimate decaying disaffection.

My head swims so I lean on the landing. I see a cracked aperture at the end of the hallway from which the hunkered outline of an old woman—the one I'd seen earlier, it has to be—squints into the corridor.

"Up."

Jerking my eyes away, I move up, until there she is, grimacing and at once swiftly and without urgency gesturing me in to her apartment.

In its brown light, I can see her straightforwardly, for the first time. She looks more serious than I'd remember, and more haggard, as if she hasn't slept well … for ages.

"Gretta?" I ask, regretting, as my voice leaves my mouth, the indefensible inanity of this first question.

A flicker of pity passes over her.

She looks me up and then down and then sighs.

I myself, meanwhile, am mesmorized.

Inside, her apartment presents a perhaps soviet-style severity. A burlap couch, a sagging armchair, a thin stand with an ashtray and a plate with tattered tea bags sit protected by unkempt curtains, all in shades of brown.

Hearing a thud, I turn around. She's shut the door and is examining me. Her eyes have a hard deep-seated intelligence that makes me try to stand taller. Once again, she unabashedly grabs my elbow, this time to turn me around roughly and thrust me towards her couch. My arm is on fire from where her fingers had caught me. I'm not sure whether it's from pain or from excitement.

She sits down and takes out a cigarette. Despite her disconcerting air of fierce perceptiveness, she exudes an utter carelessness. She wears, for instance, a light blue housecoat, with two front pockets at her hips. She withdraws a lighter from one. I wonder if she had, in fact, forgotten she'd invited me.

"I," I start, hoping to break through this silence, "I hope I'm not interrupting …" only I'm not sure what there might be to interrupt.

I sense again that she's making some sort of decision.

It's unnerving.

"No, I have been busy," she reports, "*but*—a pro*duc*tive eve-ening," she stops to light her cigarette.

"That's great—" I start, then stop. Better ask a question than affect to know its answer. "What exactly went so well?"

Her face falls blank.

"Is no-matter. Is—"

"No, really, I'd like to know," I interrupt, hoping that my interest in her will revive her interest in me.

"Is no-matter," she repeats. "You would be bored."

Her accent is hard to catch, though it's clearer here than through the intercom. She sounds Slavic, with an echo of the Bel-Ami boys. But she also exudes an indistinct *internationalité*. At times she has a Germanic precision, the French sophistication of swallowing certain consonants, and the suggestion of an English *à l'Anglaise*, as if she'd learned this last.

"Well " she waves her hand, "surely you came here with… expectations?"

I had? *She* had been the one to invite *me*. Why would *I* have expectations? If I'd had any, I guess I'd expected her to be in some ways more, and in other ways less, aggressive. I'd expected some much more instantaneous psychic connection.

Yet here I am sitting uncomfortably, even as she leans back, exhaling smoke, showing no concern at all at the awkward intervals in our conversation.

"Yes?" she prods, drawing out the "s" before taking a drag off her cigarette. She switches her smock up higher. The tip of the ash burns. *My* god! an apprehension weasels its way through my brain. *Is she trying to seduce me?!*

My face fires up unpleasantly. My arm hair prickles.

I blurt, "do you go to that café every night?"

With a severely scornful simplicity, she says, "no."

It's impossible now to imagine that she wants to entice me, though every move she makes, her skin, her smell, even her hair reeks of a rough sensuality.

"I do not go out very often at all. Anymore. When I do, I go there. Is change from work here—" her shoulders shrug, like a razored parabola, answering yet avoiding my questions.

She laughs. "And you were, how would you say, '*funny*.'"

Funny, odd? Funny, amusing?

"I was 'new,' you mean."

"No, I mean you were not like the other boys there. *Your* hunger, it was not *their* hunger."

My brain burns and I feel myself flushing. What does she think that I had been doing there?

"So, I thought that perhaps you might have made a mistake, and that tonight, we might meet." She says this with the hint of an accomplishment, until she adds, "this is what I *had* thought because you are, in your own way, 'attractive'"—she breaks off to grin, or possibly to grimace, it's surprisingly hard to tell which, and I recall one of Stephen's sophisticatedly darkhaired girlfriends telling me, "you are a beautifully awkward boy," and feeling as if she was talking to a toy or a pet.

"So you thought I was looking—"

She lets my last word linger, then asks bluntly, "tell me why you are here, in *Am*sterdam. I would like to know. Last night you seemed," her hand seesaws, from side-to-side, "confused."

She rests her hands on her knees, her cigarette still smoking.

"Well," I long to offer the real reason I am here, but taking her cue, I'll be inexplicitly honest. I'll be glib, "it's an *enchaînement évolutif*."

"Ahh," she says, her tone implying that she is not impressed but also that she has confirmed some assumption, and that, though self-satisfied that she is right, she is, all the same, a little disappointed.

"Many men come here for this," she waves her cigarette in front of her, "and some come here," she points it at me, "for that." She brings her hand up and inhales, then exhales. The acrid smell of smoke hangs between us. For a moment, I have flickers of insight that could explain her if only I could put them together.

Meanwhile, she seems to have seen right through me. But how could she? Had anyone else? A fear of revealing what I have been thinking without having refined it first or worse without realizing that I have revealed it at all lurks constantly as a substream in my brain. I think back, fighting the feeling that someone has sat on my chest.

She inhales, then blows smoke out of her tobacco- and tea-stained teeth.

"So this is off. I am having music then and-" she waves her hand, as if she were an unseated aristocrat contemptiously maintaining her manners. Without even asking what I want to listen to, which is rude, even if this is her apartment, she walks to the cabinet and puts on a record. The scratchy strains of a Szymanowski quartet, one I recall faintly from a St. Ann's fundraiser last year, spurt out as she disappears into another room.

When she returns, she carries two tumblers and shoves one my way. Wafting out from it is the acrid odor of what has to be the most unrefined, the most unadulterated vodka that I have ever come into contact with, the sort I imagine, perhaps inaccurately, that the poorest proletariat in some Soviet backwater must swill in incalculable quantities.

"Right," she declares, as if cutting through to some quick, "so you come here from the *States-*" again she waves her hand at me, "looking like-" I look down and see my faultlessly ochre loafers and my perhaps too-tailored khakis—"inexperienced and looking for some *aventure sexuelle*." Funny how her English is, at times, all but perfect. Holding her back are only her own clichés, her using French, for instance, to refer to amourous exchanges, and her own affected aesceticism.

So fine. She's guessed. So much the better. I'd met her in a coffee shop. She'd invited me to her home hours after midnight. She has to have a good idea of, maybe even an intimate experience with, what goes on in the rld. If only my fear and adrenaline could carry out, as if in an overflow, the questions that I ache to ask her.

I take a sip from my tumbler. It's absurdly strong and I gag. She gets up, disappears, then comes back with a cobalt blue cordial glass. Handing it to me, she gestures that I should drink from it. It holds a prunish sort of port. Its sweetness is deceptive and it grows noticeable stronger as it slides down my throat. When it hits my stomach I find myself making a concerted effort not to be sick.

She meanwhile has emptied half of her tumbler and looks ready to move on to mine.

"Okay," I say soberly, and I explain exactly why I am in Amsterdam. Incredibly, all that I've been trying to set aside since I left the U. S. takes only two minutes to tell. By the time I've finished, she's only a few sips into my abandoned vodka. The music still rages softly, shooting out a thickly layered sort of scherzo. Annoyingly, she seems scarcely surprised. She'd already deduced the generalities, so I don't expect her to look astounded. But here I am actually *admitting* it, actually *saying* it. Out loud. And all she offers is a sustained indifference.

She continues to sit there, putting away enough alcohol to kill an army—I want to say this, to hurt her, but it won't, I know, and I don't want another short shot.

At last she starts asking questions, dispassionately, disinterestedly probing what I have been turning over for days, for weeks, for months on end in my mind. Could I find some woman who might unlock, permanently, secret synapses or a man who might seal some shut? For me, it's an uneasy relief. For her, it's background noise, an obscurely irrelevant experiment to which no one is or was or ever will be paying too much attention.

"You *do* realize, don't you, that you are one of, what? two point four out of five *moral* Americans who are here for this. The rest of you—" "Come on—" "What?" "How can you know *that*—" "Know what?" "That statistic, 'two point four out of five.'"

When anxious I, like anyone else, tend to swideswipe at otiose details. It just feels deflating to fly so far, to reveal so much, only to be made to feel that I am first, insignificant, and second, derivative, especially when I know it already. For I do. It's for that reason precisely that I am here as opposed to anywhere else. Here I will not be recalled. Here I will be unexceptional. Here I can slip into a routine that has been practiced prudently and proficiently for centuries.

Still, being stuck into some statistic makes me mad.

I am always, moreover, suspicious of numbers tossed out off-the-cuff. So I go after this. "Your calculation sounds a bit too simplistic to be true." I say this a bit nastily, while simultaneously hoping that my appeal for precision will impress her.

"Of course is not *exact!* But is *accurate*—is as *close* to '*ex*act' as one can get, and much closer than *you* could get. I give also a two point three percent margin for error." Her eyes flash defiantly, as if daring me to argue with her.

I will not.

I will.

"But how can you even *guess* at that? How could you get an accurate estimation, much less a 'margin of error'? People don't declare that they are coming here … for … *that* on their customs forms."

"But *I* know." She says this summarily.

Yes, but "how?"

She sighs, exasperated. But she obviously has no respect for those who back down.

"Because these numbers are calculated from clients. Perhaps this 'pool' might be off, mais *voi*la," her English breaks down when she gets angry, "but the *madth*, this is *flaw*less." She jabs with her cigarette for emphasis.

"But how do you know that, well, these 'client' numbers aren't forged?" Her eyes blaze and I backtrack. I hadn't meant to accuse her of dishonesty, I just—"I mean, how do you know that your margin of error is not … erroneous?"

I smile my inanest golden-boy St. Ann's smile to remind her how silly a serious subject can turn. After all, I don't want to be rude, but if she's going to stab people with her standard of intellectual acuity she should have to stand up to it herself.

"Because," she snarls, "these clients are of friends and of *mine* ... and *I* am one course away from doctorate in statistics from Čiastkový Technike University *and I did all these calculations myself!*"

My face must have fallen because she's suddenly smirking and her voice, which had been rising, sinks.

"Anyway," she says, sounding much more throaty, "what does this matter, when you are here and are not *only* a statistic, no? So for now," she says bemusedly, practically *purring* this last word until it fills the room with a bizarrely deceptive sort of sexiness, "perhaps I *could* help. You are not, you know, *really* what I like, and you are a bit *petit* for 'un Americain,' *n'est-ce pas?*" once again, her signature shrug, "but for tonight, for *you*, who are so pretty, I might make, as I had hoped, an exception."

A sweltering surge flushes through me and my head feels heightened. It's not just her calling me "petit," I am not muscly, I know, but I am tall, nor is it her calling me pretty, others have told me as much, nor is it the abrasive bouquet of vodka on her breath, rather it's that someone who is so quick and so acerbic, who is on the verge of earning a doctorate, and is sitting right here in front of me, is—she's made it too clear to miss—someone who touches men for money.

Oddly enough, my light-headedness comes not from her admission, I know, of course, that this is not so extraordinary, though at Princeton prostitution tends to be much more metaphorical, but from a mixture of jealousy and revulsion.

She reaches out and I shudder.

"So," she says, staring until I feel as if I am the one who is exposed, "I am not your 'type' either. No matter. It would have been good for us each, no? *Tous les doux*. But if you do not want, is not much in it for me. When not making money, I want someone involved—"

She shrugs, gets up and walks into the kitchen, then reappears carrying, unabashedly, a half-full bottle, clear save for its red-and-gold crest, an ostentation that cannot distract from the inferiority of the product behind it.

"So, I am done with business in all senses, ehh? and as I am not tired and you are not—" she gestures up and I blush, "we might as well have another drink."

She doesn't seem bothered at all and somehow I am the one who can't help feeling insulted. Why hadn't she tried harder? "You gave up a bit quickly, didn't you?"

Draining what has to be her third or fourth glass of the night, she looks up and laughs. Incredibly, she shows no sign of inebriation, unless of course you count her increased willingness to be indecent.

"Well tonight, you see, I was not in it for the money, and I'm not actually sure, you know, that you could have afforded it if I was," she pauses and stares at me, "although perhaps you could. Anyway, once I did this *predominantly* for the money, for almost any money at any time, and I had wigs, such cheap wigs, to make more, and I would *work* and *work* and *work*. Now I see *who* I want, *when* I want … I still take their *euro*s, of course," she smiles mischievously and with the same aplomb as any businessman who is resolutely sure of his success. "But now I keep my clients select, five or six Frenchmen, nine Germans, three Nigerians, two Kenyans, two South Africans, several Swiss, one Lüxemberger, and a very few, very rich Nederlanders, and every now and again someone new. For fun. For *chance*. Rest are older, more 'mature' men, and these I keep mainly who keep ability to satisfy *me*—" I can't help but wonder where she had met these very rich and very potent "older men." Not, I suspect, at the Café Beatrix.

Still more unaccountably than what she does or where, is the sense I get—it's a singularity that wraps itself around all the others, like a prophylatic—that she actually *enjoys* being, actually enjoys making money as a—and it's as if, for her own protection, I have to hold the term for her employment apart from her, like a dirtying detail that could ruin all else that is, in every far-flung sense of the word, wonderful about her. Crude, crass, and inexplicably elegant, she is unlike anyone I have ever met and I am mesmerized by her.

"But, I have talked too much already. So tell me, you do—what, exactly? You are too young to be here alone, no?"

"No," I say, "I'm in college."

"Ahzo, and you study what?"

"History—"

"History." She says the word as if she's stuffed it into quotation marks, as if she wants to hold it apart from her with a hygienic, inflected sort of tweezers.

"and philosophy. Really though I read whatever I want. Books on feudalism, on courtly rituals, on Nietzsche and morality," yet as I say this, I hate how here with her it sounds more amateurish than aristocratic, especially since, for reasons I can't even imagine, I want to impress her. I don't mention that I'll probably pass calculus with a C+, at best.

I can see her tasting the word "dilettante," "and your family—surely they have decided at what they work?"

My family, I inform her, produce books, philosophy, classics, current affairs. I emphasize, not *exactly* dishonestly, our intellectual enterprises. She wouldn't, I suspect, be enthralled by our gold-plated fountain pens.

To my surprise, she seems unusually interested. She asks about journals, pamphlets, bindings, her eyes narrow, her head tilting forward ever so slightly then just as suddenly she abandons the subject and starts on a tangent.

"Your family has business, so why do you not study accounting, or finance? Is not this what most young, mediocre businessmen do?"

For a second I'm struck by the incongruous fact that, were she not a middle-aged Amsterdamian immigrant with an accent, a faded housefrock, and a gap between her two front teeth, she'd be exactly the sort of woman who my father would want me to marry.

"We also sell marble bookends and gold-inlaid fountain pens."

Her face twists abruptly and reddens.

"This sort of *personal property* is *obscenity*," she spits.

This is precisely the response that I'd hoped for, and a chance to change the subject. "What about *your* family? What do they do?"

Her expression shifts, but not for the better. She looks at me as if I had just vomited on her. I can't help but wonder how, after all her prying and intimate questions, I had stumbled upon the one innocuous inquiry that, for her, is apparently inappropriate.

"They too 'produced books' … but the insides. They wrote them."

She sounds sullen but this is wonderful. I envision bearded and fur-clad, murderously moralizing Tolstoys running around with her features writ large and her erotic aggression.

Wanting to keep her going, I ask "well, what did they write? Novels? Poetry?"

She glares witheringly and snorts, her flimsy nostrils flaring, as if at some irony that only she can catch. "No. My father did not waste his time with such nonsense. He wrote for 'people.' He was a public scholar."

"Where at?" I prod. She is as unwilling to give up particulars as I am.

"In Čiastkový he had what in English you call '*fellowship*.'" She laughs. I think at the idiom.

"So that's why you went—"

"*Notatall*," she snaps, then recollects herself, as if knowing she had overreacted. "No, I was always a very good student. I was invited on my own merit, at sixteen." She chuckles, and then, as if reminiscing, she says, "Second year of doctorate, I even got state scholarship to Moscow."

"But before I could take it," she says, looking away, her voice colder and harder than ever, "we had to leave. My father, no, really *we* were exiled."

Chapter Seven

Gretta's revelation, her coldly unemotional exclamation, "we were exiled," lingers in the air. I find myself much more uncomfortable but also much more excited than I have been all evening. At last we have landed on hallow ground. On ground that she must let lie fallow, as if she has forced far under it some sacred subject.

Rarely do I disinter details from people's pasts. When Javier, Chad, even Gwen had flashed spare fragments of their lives lived elsewhere I'd rarely responded. I rebuff the burden of knowing someone when they aren't around me. But this situation offers an exception. There's some timbre to her voice, some hesitation in her face that suggests that an audience, an anonymous audience is exactly what she wants, what she needs. As if unpleasant intimacies recounted in front of some stranger might make them seem somehow safer, less volatile. I'm having, meanwhile, one of those emptying yet self-inflating out-of-body insights. The universe has placed me here, for this moment, for someone else.

Her eyes flash back towards me as if locking me into some internally masochistic remembering. I promise myself I'll be a worthy witness.

—"we were exiled." Melodramatic as this statement is, it's scarcely the sole charge of her story. The word "exiled" subsists, on its own, as little more than a fuse. Or a conduit. The rest of the evening, she sits habitually sipping, though she's never less than half sober, and spinning out what that word actually entails. At times she is eloquent, at times she is ambiguous, and at times her story is as tempestuous as the quartet that she gets up to replay over and over. It rings, if this is possible, with a clearcut indistinctness, its details so strange and so remote that they are difficult to reconcile with the woman who had told me, not a half hour ago, how much she likes, "*fund*amentally, to fuck men for money."

Starting from as close to her infancy as she can, her conciliatory concession to her meticulousness, she outlines her life. She recalls a childhood in a small Slavic village, which, she says, had exuded the vigorous air of an eastern rurality, filled with a pre-industrial amiability and an all but blood-born hatred for everywhere else. When she was eight, her father, an economist specializing in inchoate communist economies under tzarist regimes, had uprooted his wife and his daughter to Sedliakobek, the nearby provincial capital where he had been working. After a year or two more of outpublishing his local colleagues he had been called to the faculty at the still larger, still more foreign city of Gradz. Eventually he was offered a special fellowship at the national university in Čiastkový.

Here, she remembers, was where her father had really begun to thrive. In an age of extortion he'd been an only superficially institutionalized academic who had flourished amongst libraries at last adequate to his intelligence, amongst colleagues who were at least close to it, and amidst dense conversations about economics and incipient forms of proletariat ideologies, his contributions to the latter occasionally causing a stir. Here he had come home most energized and, later, most pained. His family, meanwhile, had subsisted under the gray gloom of an alien architecture and alongside a hungry and oppressed populace, all of which, as her father was taking great pains to point out, had the potential to create a substantial agricultural sustenance were it not drenched in anguish. This state, he argued, could be allieviated only by the red of Soviet sickles and by farming scientifically without fear.

For living in the capital, she recalls, had gradually shifted her father's research and writing. Hurrying through soiled streets, his mind had wandered from statistics of farm labor under the tzars or the cost of repairing sixteenth-century plows as he had glanced at the putrescent markets around him. Such scenes had sparked a series of slowly emergent shocks and his dawning recognition of a more current economic crisis, one obvious to everyone else subsisting in it. He had begun to publish, intermittently, articles on the unfulfilled potential of the city. These indicated a shift still further from the political quietism of his superiors. Still, when he was invited to stay on after his two-year fellowship had ended, as a full member of the faculty and with a token increase in his stipend, he had determined resolutely to do so.

He decided this definitively because shortly before this invitation to stay her mother had gotten seriously sick. His assumption had been that along with a proximity to archives and libraries, his position at the heart of Čiastkový would give her more immediate access to healthcare. This assumption was a sound one, or it should have been for someone who had at least tried to connect to the right branches of the party, albeit on his own terms. Unfortunately for him, and still more unfortunately for his wife, outside of the academic circles in which he moved and outside those of the government's intellectual elite—"in which he was *very* well known," she insists, "if not always very well *liked*"—he was almost unheard of and the urgent medical care that he had so honestly expected his position at the university to ensure— and perhaps it might have, she reflects, for him—for her mother, it was all but absent.

She shrugs, as if to say, "such is life." Then she says, "she would have been better off had he *not* tried to claim 'priority.'" But he had and so instead of going to the public hospital, "which is where he would have gone for himself," where cases were handled according to their severity, his feeble string-pulling had gotten his wife into a lower-level room in a "specialized" hospital that had the benefit of being said to be antiseptic but that was in a system where access to care was so dutifully "ranked" according to official hierarchies that each time a more "imperative" person came in her "unimperative" mother, who when well had organized impoverished artisans' account books, had gotten pushed just a bit farther back. She had twice, she says, watched orderlies abandon her to help some overfed, be-furred wife of a politburo member who had drunk herself into a stupor. I think instantly of Wealthy Rodney, one of the more "distinguished" members of our eating society whom we have twice taken to the hospital because he had downed more bottles of wine in one sitting, each coming in at well over a hundred dollars a pop, than some studious inner-city school kid would have shots at taking a four-year college course.

Yet as distressing as this experience had been for her mother physically, she reports, for her father it had been devasting morally. He had long believed zealously in what he had called the "*Potentiality* of the People," in the inherent tendency for societies to support, physically and intellectually, individuals in their times of need, since the whole of society benefited by aiding the unfortunate to climb to their feet calmly, orderly, and with dignity.

Although of course, she observes, in an oddly off-hand manner, latent within this philosophy lies the propensity for a society to reorganize *purely*, she sneers here, along lines that are benevolently utilitarian, a doctrine that when taken to extremes, albeit ones hinted at only obliquely and deep within the core of her father's writings, encouraged "the Potential for the People" to override any authority of the governing body after it had clearly and consistently abrogated its responsibility to the greater good, having long disregarded its duty to assuage the material and mental pain of its people, in favor of some self-serving stasis. Still more problematic were the potential connotations, the variously vague, even unstated corollaries, that the ultimate willingness to, that the ultimate *necessity* of allowing an educated people to even imagine the need for a new government and to advance a system where everyone could have access to a rigorous, not wholly unindividuated education, combined with the requirement that every *body* work at some task for some time, was a perpetual right and one insisted on by the sheer physiological constitution of our human natures. Hard work, healthcare, education, and a series of small federated alternative societies, he had hinted, were the four essentials to achieving a state that came even close to utopia, one based *not* upon the outmoded foundations of money but upon the indications of the basic equivalent *needs* of its members and to the sustainability of a compassionate collectivism.

Most problematic though were her father's later papers published in popular presses in which he had insinuated, she shifts ever so slightly, a need to reorganize the paradigms that channel any society's dispersal of goods, proposing that any distribution of services be based upon individuals' immediate needs coupled with their willingness, if able, to provide the public with concrete returns: producing food for the hungry, medicine for the sick, an education for those ill-informed, so that each individual might return to work and benefit everyone else, enabling society to assist them once again when they turned elderly or infirm. Such "cyclical redistributions" and "diminishments of need" he argued, would bring about—and here she stands and actually starts walking about, gesticulating jerkily, growing more and more agitated with each word—a new "Potential," an "Aptitude," she declaims, and in such a frenetic way that I can't tell if she's doing it ironically or feverishly, that "would pave the way for a revolutionary reassessment of the *ex*-change of value itself!!!" Her eyes flash then she snorts, exhaling heavily—it's unclear whether in agreement or in annoyance with the, for me, all too ambiguous valiencies of her father's force.

Of course, she continues with abrupt apathy, any overt insistence on this—really, I think, not so original—doctrine came later. At her mother's first hospitalization, she says, it was still in the background, still incubating within the qualifying clauses of her father's longest sentences. Internal rupture, however, followed internal rupture and after touring first the hospital his wife lay in, then a neighboring one, then one miles from either, his style had grown starker. At once more and less cautious, he had dissected, like a scientist, how the inequalities and the disparities between the working, the really working, and the inheriting or overpaid administrative ranks were thriving, not in historical statistics but in actuality, right in front of him.

This kept on for months until he began to alternate between

hospitals and schools, admitting some intrinsic connection. He went from one almost unfunded institution to another, watching as doctors worked for days and teachers for weeks, forbidden or simply unable, due to a lack of equipment or time, to perform unpaid-for procedures or to give obviously required assistance. Patients and pupils alike, meanwhile, all too many, hardly knew how to help themselves. Too often their temporary caretakers had to start at so basic a level that it hardly seemed worthwhile to advance beyond recommending "exercise" or "to sound that word out phonetically; no, that's an 'r,'" knowing all the while that their hard work would be undone at home.

At his home, he typed firm facts with short objective analyses. He reported how from his wife's room or from the windows of wealthier classrooms, he had seen the wide array of spin doctors and over-insulated military manufacturers and the students of shaded executives, of outsourced drug firm officials or of the comptrollers rumoured to run the inadequate healthcare systems and the deflated budgets that the patients at other hospitals and the students at other schools had saved and scrounged to satisfy, carelessly demanding and ignoring the same tests or books or tools that were so desperately needed by, and so dispassionately denied to, those who enabled their existence.

Night after night and day after day he saw this and what had once been only an embryonic idea, one even a little restrained perhaps out of respect for his repeatedly promoted position, began to mutate and to mature. His articles, and she has traced them, she says, became no less factual but now focused on advancing correctives, remedies that would immediately redress the government's refusal, from the perspective of anyone but the very well-connected, to fulfill its responsibility to keep the newly entrenched elite from running roughshod over the perenially underprivileged poor: from the old man who could not return to work as a carpenter because he needed a knee replacement, which was too expensive; to the young woman who could not return to her lab because she needed migraine medicine, which was too expensive; to the toddler who, to the infant who …

In his classrooms then, with cold clinical logic, and with varying degrees of explicitness, he forced his students to re-examine assumptions regarding the eventuality of the state apparatus ever "withering away" or of any but the very lucky "working their way to the top" and he indicated that any government, that any *society* that failed not only to protect but to improve upon such basic human rights as the right to work in fair circumstances, to be educated in adequate institutions, and to do more than just simply subsist should be considered now not just with a wavering irreverence but with a downright disrespect.

Still worse, for him, was how these hospitals and schools became so many test cases or indicators of all the ills plaguing both his homeland and abroad. He doubted whether any real revolution could redeem itself where one family, where one class, where now one corporation was allowed and even encouraged to accumulate wealth beyond one generation. Whereever, he insisted, people remained rich without a continual redistribution of resources, there would rot a hereditary poverty, classes kept too exhausted, too perpetually unaware of even *how* to work beyond basic brute labor. Of course every now and then an individual with an uncommon intelligence and an overwhelming will, such as her father, would rise up virtually unaided. But, she insists, "are far fewer geniuses than most people would like to admit, and even in these cases, most use the bodies of others as stepping stones."

When her father had first been promoted, she reports, it had been for what he had written while he was a young semi-radical professor at a relatively irrelevant and provincial university, and back then, she explains, he had maintained the pragmatic faith that for the revolution to work the people must maintain an exacting, almost absolute, loyalty in both body and psyche to the state, which in turn would provide them with their requirements. He had revised these ideas considerably, if subtly, as he had read more and thought more and once he had actually lived in a city. But he had done so in articles published in journals that were technically hermetic and that, frankly, had remained unread by almost anyone outside of economics departments, unread by even the lazier so-called scholars within them.

Now he was overhauling his earlier innocence. In both classes and papers for popular presses, he promoted a more truly radical socialism, one that would evolve from feudalism to communism to a limited form of anarchy, in a factional, fractional sense. This is to say, if I understand her description of it, that individual villages or cities would work independently of each other with regards to their social and cultural customs but that their combined wealths would be reallocated, as needed, among them. When one individual or when one village or when one city began to accrue more food or more medicine or more industry—for of course, she says, some will always work harder, and so should be rewarded, without overwhelming the opportunities of the children of the indolent—than they had either earned on their own or, more importantly, than they could possibly need, when someone young and able for instance had "inherited" an amount that would allow them to live long after they had abandoned any form of labour, this wealth would then have to be rendered up to a small overarching entity, this surplus to be sent where it was needed most and reinvested into healthcare and education. This process could create opportunities without withholding individual incentives, and certain laws, the now middle-aged professor argued, could be set up to enact all such transferences and occasions for advancement peacefully, so that the nucleus, the warmhearted core of such societies could exist in mutually advantageous interactions. Her father called this an "eager and altruistic alimentary exchange," a form of trade, including knowledge trade, based not upon greed or upon principles of self-sufficiency but upon a mutual good will and an understanding of the larger advantages for the beneficial health, self-rule, and pain-free-as-possible existence of every individual and city-state.

"Yes. Fine. But what happens when your *best* minds defect for more money?" She glares at me accusingly, as if *I* should have the answer. "How to compete with courtiers to corporate cosmopolitanism?" She snorts, "what happens with the Russian Trade System? This was never considered—" again she cackles, "and instead of subsidizing to banks, to military, in his system *those* resources would be assigned to universities!" she bursts out into a louder, still harsher hilarity, "Can you imagine? With those committees after committees? Is almost medieval save that instead of advancements of *souls*, advancements in chemistry, in physics, would be made by state schools and there would be no surplus profits unless marked for more research—"

She takes a sip then goes on with yet another of her sudden shifts, more calmly and with much more decorum. "At first, when those outside his classroom heard this, no one said much—for what," she leans towards me, "*what*," with a sudden ear-piercing spit, "could someone say to this? To this ridiculooseness?! Especially as *he* was saying what at least *half* of them were *thinking*." She shakes her finger at me, as if I had been thinking but not promoting this exact same proposition myself. She sips.

"Anyway, some student told their father or their uncle, or some stupid party official or some military officer read the wrong article. Do not speak against the government, he was warned. Do *not* speak against the military. Of course *everyone* knew he would go on and so they 'planted,' everyone knew this, *he* must have known this, someone in his lectures, and when they had *more* than enough 'evidence,' they rejected his proposed courses." She stops and sips. How she must have hated her father, and how she must have adored him. "He was assigned to teach rudementary economics, to teach, really, party dogmatics to first-year students, not that he could teach them much they were such ignorants—the future commissars of Čiastkový!—

"His graduate students, meanwhile, his disciples dispersed, and then—" for a second she looks as if she is steeling herself, "since he would not teach their doctrine, not without forcing it through his own ideas, it was recommended to him 'quietly' and for his 'own safety' that he stop teaching. That he stop writing. Not that by this time any press would touch what he wrote, not with his name on it. Then even anonymity became too dangerous. There were rumors. There were suspicions. No one would hire him. No one would pay him one ruble. No one would even *visit* him." The acid in her voice is unmistakable.

"Of course he kept writing, locked away in his bedroom, seeing no one, even if they *would* come, letting in only mother and only very late at night." Her mother, she recounts, had recovered enough to come home, had then taken a sudden, albeit expected, turn for the worse, and had once more revisited the hospital before returning home to die on her own couch. This was sad, but it was not a conclusion. So soon after, a continued, more intensified phase of composition had begun, for her father was no longer distracted by someone retching at night in the bed next to him.

In this situation, and only sixteen, Gretta was effectively left on her own. On the bright side, she smiles, this had allowed her to apply to Čiastkový's math faculty without her father's aid, so she had managed to appear ignorant of, or at the very least uninterested in, the more "problematic" heresies of her father's recent "philosophy," without offending him. Hers was a first round acceptance, although perhaps, she supposes, some within the university's upper ranks had hoped that the institution could recoup its reputation with party leaders if it could reindoctrinate the brilliant daughter of the still more brilliant, and, from at least one perspective, pettily dangerous dissident whom some fools had once actually invited to work within their walls.

After several days of classes, she says, she had jumped three levels ahead. This caused her to meet a slender, young, and oddly attractive "associate academic director" named Yuri Sadinov, whom she'd almost immediately started "fucking." "I was lucky," she drawls, "that he was good at it, because he was my first." Hence, I gather, her affection for all things "amorous." For she goes on and on about him, "he was handsome and strong and smart, not analytical," she qualifies, "but instinctive, and good at *physical* pleasures. He was perhaps better still at his job though, which was not at all academic." She snorts, as if at some obscure irony, even as I notice how mixed in with her ridicule is some tiny hint of terror.

Perhaps this was because, as she soon found out, she says he took no pains to hide it, his actual role was not so much to "associate direct" academics as it was to enforce the party line by rooting out from the student body any active or even any future nonconformists.

The expulsion of her father from the university had been for what were, as opposed to what were to come or to what had obviously already occurred, relatively minor dissident actions. His treatment had served as officials had intended it to, as a warning to others. It had nonetheless made the particular position, so to speak, of the relatively young Yuri precarious. If he had kept on with her he was bound to have faced one of two critical outcomes: he could have been seen as himself having "converted" the dissident's daughter and so reap the rewards of proving a remarkably effective "administrator" or he could have been branded by his rivals as a co-conspirator. She, meanwhile, was forced to appear as unaware as she had first claimed to be regarding her father and his work. The two were thus constantly "straining," as she puts it, in a balancing act, the tensions of which she suggests with a leer, one that considering their situation is vaguely revolting, appeared only to have increased his vigor.

The self-same attributes, however, she recalls, that had made him so energetic in bed, his exuberance, his ambition, his intense *awareness* of all that slipped subtly around him, were, she soon discovered, the exact traits of egotism that had earned him such a distinguishing job at the university. There he had used them as dexterously and as eagerly to impose his authority in one arena as he had risked undermining it with her in another.

—She would later learn, she says, that his penchant for self-destruction was stronger than even she had suspected. A classmate had written her, years after she had left, and had recounted how Yuri had seduced another student two weeks after her departure, the daughter of an up-and-coming if then still minor party officer who was soon put in charge of all Čiastkový's academic institutions. This explains, she says, how quickly Yuri had become one of the most feared and dangerous men at the university, even as his amorous intentions had stayed not with the second girl, whom he had ended up marrying, but had wandered on to a few of the daughters and even to some of the sons of still more powerful men, one of whom had ended up having him shot, or whom perhaps had shot him himself. The details of the situation remain, for obvious reasons, I suppose, unclear.—

But long before she had understood the extent of Yuri's fixated craving for control, she had loved his pale lean body, his obsessive attention to detail, and his dark jabbing cock. In this midst of her own fascination, and her first semester of school, she'd also met a scrawny, obviously underfed doctoral student named Ivan with whom she'd had several statistics courses in common. Occasionally after a class they had eaten together or had gone out for coffee to discuss the application of stochastic or probabilistic theories to economics generally and to communism in particular.

Six months into their friendship, Ivan had disappeared. No note, no reason, no warning. A few days earlier Yuri had come upon them laughing and, in what was, between them, a rare gesture of physical affection, Ivan had put his hand on her arm. She had seen in the director's eyes that he had misinterpreted the situation. Drastically. Not wanting to add weight to his reaction, she had ignored it.

The day after, Yuri had quietly entered the Economics Department and had accused the sharply intelligent but painfully shy Ivan of plotting to acquire the tainted professor's papers. Instead of denying this—and she swears that, although an admirer of her father, Ivan had rarely mentioned him—Ivan had pushed up his old taped-together glasses and had responded by defending, for the first time in public since his dismissal, her father. Standing tall, even as he had tripped, she had heard, over his words, he had called her father a "prophet of the people" and had declared, fatally she supposes, to Yuri, who was always so carefully groomed in crisp khakis, that "uniforms have no place in universities." Before anyone else could react, two men whom Yuri had brought with him had grabbed the up-till-then restrainedly high-strung student, who desperately raised his already high voice to stammer out, despite his torso being bent backwards as he had been hauled hysterically away, "*Di*versity not *Uni*versity, *Di*versity not *Uni*versity"—or whatever the equivalent was in their language—until one of the guards had gagged him.

Previously, she says, overt intimidation had been reserved for student activists, for idiots who had printed anti-state essays, or for creative types who had vomited up thinly thought-out allegories protesting politics, bad art that time would have censored on its own. Now officials had gagged a gifted math student. As if to forestall criticism, Yuri let slip that the dissident was simply being questioned and warned. Ivan would be released that evening, though Yuri lamented that such suspects, namely the guilty pusillanimous ones, all too often ran away.

Sure enough, as if according to schedule, although no one said this, Ivan had missed his next day's classes and a study group. Gretta had learned later from one of his roommates, whom she herself had had to threaten to get to talk to her, how he had come home late the previous evening and had not even bothered to undress. Then at four am the roommates had been woken by four or five young men in uniform and Ivan had once more been gagged and hauled off. The informant had whispered all this standing roughly five feet away from her. She had hardly been able to hear him.

At that time, Yuri's influence had not yet reached capital proportions. But, so far as she knows, Ivan has not been seen since. "His health," she says, "had been weak and life there was already not easy."

"After that ... well—"

She seems tired. It's hard to speak, and for so long, in a language that isn't one's own. But it's more than that: her tone, her expressions, the uneasy suspensions of sound, followed by so many fast-flowing explanations, all suggest considerations repeated over and over in one's head, but rarely, if ever, uttered out loud.

I wait and the silence distends itself, as if along a razor's edge.

"Well," she says, startling me, "by this time, the Supreme Soviet—" exhausted myself, and still caught up in the tension, I giggle.Before the "Supreme" Soviet, I wonder, had there ever been an only "So-So" Soviet? It's like laughing at a funeral or the insane urge to kiss a roommate who's interested in anyone else. Only she's not really talking to me and she probably hasn't even been aware of me, not really, for some time. "—and by this time had started *glasnost*. A mess. A beautiful, beatific mess. Papers reporting corruption everywhere and vague accusations against everyone."

She extorts another shot from her all-but-empty bottle.

The upshot of glasnost was that her father managed to publish a furious diatribe against the government. Not wanting to risk statewide attention by arresting him, the local party had his arm broken then suggested, for the last time they said, that he rethink how to use his liberties.

"A few months before," Gretta tells me, "he had mailed, under a false name, his most important writings, embedded in party propaganda, to a friend exiled in Austria. He had heard that this friend afterward moved to Amsterdam. The same day he was talked to for the 'last time,' he mailed off more packages. Later that night, we got what we could carry ... and we left.

"At the border they took our money and, of course not knowing who we were, who *he* was, they let us out." She smiles a bit madly, as if Yuri and his ilk were, after all this time, still following her and still getting outfoxed. As if we all were.

She pauses, her eyes awash in vodka and recollections, looking slightly stunned.

So, I gather, they had left behind many books, a few papers, Yuri and Ivan, and all else of only sentimental importance. By the end, she says, they had not had much anyway. Her father had no family and her mother's only sister was a fool. Her mother's only and much older brother was himself in Amsterdam, giving them one more reason to flee here rather than to anywhere else.

Once in Amsterdam, they had rented an apartment from her long absent uncle, who had grown, they then learned, into an unexpectedly successful businessman, which had only exacerbated his carefully cultivated miserliness. So much so that at their first meeting, he had reiterated, he had *insisted* upon his need to have the rent by the first of each month. This in itself was absurd. He had to have known that they could not have left Čiastkový, much less the State, with any substantial amount of money ... and all the while he had never once asked after anyone back home, not after people whom he had grown up with, not after his fellow citizens, and he had never once, then or at any other time, asked after his sisters.

Maybe, I suggest, her father had written earlier, so he wouldn't have to discuss the painful subject face to face. She dismisses this. "No. Forgetting is simply how one survives here, and he survives better than most." He had shed memories like zealots shed weight, though, she muses, it was "oddly admirable" how like the epitome of an avaritic he himself had stayed so stick thin, denying himself even the most fundamental of alimentary pleasures, as if he were subconsciously stuck fearing some famine.

Anyway, after angry negotiations, they had moved in having signed to pay double the second month or be out. *"Alors,"* she says, jabbing her finger, "I did what I had to do. I did what made *sense*, without anyone telling me yes or no. What was logical. What here was easy! What was my *right*. *Right* and *right*, for here, these words, with all their imports, were aligned ... and," she hisses, "I *enjoyed* it—"

She pauses, as if to let this sink in,

"I *enjoyed* it—"

She repeats this softly and assuredly, as if what she had done was not at all out of the ordinary, as if she were some Girl Scout who had gone out to sell shortbread. "These men, you know, were not un-often handsome and some were even young, although unlike him," she must mean Yuri, "even these, they were only ever *eager*, not ravenous. They were, *most* of them, old and some were *rich*, and some were not, and some were intelligent, but most were stupid, oh so stupid, so that they would do, without protest, whatever I told them to. Some even had nice bodies, nice hands, nice nails that smelt clean, sometimes too clean. Then when they were done, they would get up and wash, getting still cleaner, to go home, just like I wanted them to, to their wives, so that I was alone....

"After, alone and with peace, and in those days almost *everyone* *wanted* safe. They *would* be safe. For them, this was only for fantasy. They wanted no lingering traces, and for the rest, if you told them to, most of them would and if they would not ... well, were eternally others—and no," she must see the look on my face, "was not perfect. There were some nights," she shows me, for a second, a scar on her left leg and one on her arm, "in particular, but the men here, most of them, are not violent. The violent are usually i-dealists, no? and this defeat of i-dealism is, in itself, for some, a type of u-topia.

"My experience, of course, is not everyone's. I speak five languages, I have read ex-tense-ively, I know of the world. *Alors, I* did not stay on the street but one month. I got a 'broker,' I called him, and soon I had an apartment right across the hall." She gestures, as if to say *right* across the hall. "At night, we would both of us work," her eyes well up, as if with nostalgia, "*and at least I enjoyed it.*"

I must have grimaced because she now exclaims, "achh, what, I should have sold my brain? My mind? For eight guilters an hour? This is better? Why? To help businessmen make more money? I should have tutored undergraduates at pennies per student? If a brain, if a soul is more sacred than a body, why abuse it? No, are equal. What happens to one influences the other. I chose the best option for each, all together."

To calm tensions, we both take sips, listening to the music swirl round us.

She nods tipsily, nobly, almost beatifically. Her upper lip has taken on a sheen of perspiration, caused, no doubt, by memories of long-over evenings and the miracles of her own anatomy.

For a moment, and as if from above, I see the two of us sitting here, with all our dissentiences.

"Well," I echo her, "at least you enjoyed it."

She looks at me queerly and with more than a hint of disdain.

"I *did*—and I *still* do." She gets up and restarts her record. Together they start again and she sounds suddenly not sober but close to it, "but *this* is your problem: is half-*nat*ural, this *sex*, and you cannot even say the *word* for it! Of course you cannot, because you do not even know yet what it means. You do not even know yet, I think, what you *want* it to mean. You are what? eighteen? nineteen? and you do not even know yet what you want for yourself! This is why with older men is so much easier: *most know what they want.*" I want to protest that I *do* know what I want, but this ipso facto isn't true. To find this out is why I am here, and right now I want only to leave.

Once more rich sounds soar over us, and underneath she exhorts, more and more triumphantly, as if some rough prophetess of sex, "you must, you know, be able to *speak* of *flesh* and of *fucking*. Nobody I know," she says, as I shiver, "wants silent sex. You must take *plea*sure from it, if you want it to work!" Agitated, I swallow the rest of my port. This conversation has at last become too uncomfortable.

"Ahzo" she pronounces, proclaiming between the beats of the music, "you will come tomorrow. Yes? Come in the evening," she commands as she ushers me off of her couch. "When I am finished working—no, not with men—same time, and we will discuss what you must do. I have decided," she says, directing me to her door, "that I will help you. But *remember*," she pushes me and she is, though tiny, incredibly strong, "tonight, tomorrow, always: you must *not* build sex up and up like some godless cathedral! Is natural and nature must be shaped and altered with a strong mind. It must also be indulged to progress," and with that she shoves me through her door, a cello climbing behind me, and without me, on its own.

Chapter Eight

My morning and afternoon pass like trains stuck in traffic. She'd told me to come over again, earlier this time, at eleven, but that before then she would be working. But doing what? Crocheting cigarette packs, perhaps, or knitting baby booties for vodka bottles.

Her promise, however, "I will help," holds a lure and towards the appointed hour, I head back to her apartment.

Leaving early, I give myself time to bypass the hemorrhaging heart of the old rld and to walk instead around its outskirts. I walk down the Singelgracht and turn from there on to the Nieuwe Doelenstraat. As it gets darker, I get closer and I see twice, and in close succession, three men walking hand in hand—a thrupling that seems natural save for the radius of a perhaps self-imposed lovers' isolation around them. Up ahead I see one couple and then another clad in some sort of onyx-colored outfits, leather and lace, the second two walking arms intertwined and looking as if, out of all of us, they alone are at ease in the world around them.

This path should have taken me on a straight shot on to the Kloveniersburgwal. But it hasn't. Somewhere a sign must have fallen off. *Kapel* kaput. Or have been stolen. It'd be the perfect start to an adventure story save that the sun has set and the stars are hidden and I am now, I'll admit, a little uneasy. Everywhere here seems to have sunk into an unrecoverable decay, worse even than Gretta's alley. It's moved past the sights, past the sounds, past even the rank smells that signal at least *some* passage of time, and hence hope.

Here is only a quiet eternity, an anti-apocalyptic passivity.

Even the rare people that I pass appear to be only the forms of human beings rather than anyone whom one might meet. Barren bodies with limbs standing still, faces expressionless, looking like they've slackened to stare out everlastingly. Even were one to slide behind you and slit your throat, it would be done utterly without interest. I think of my ouvrieatic angel, undoubtedly long since holed up in some touristy pub. Here might be the only place in Amsterdam that, for better or worse, we could help each other out, his need to beat, to not be beaten, becoming a beatitude.

When even this phrase fails to make me smile I realize that I am afraid. I'd retreat but by this point it has to be better to keep going than to turn back. In either direction, before me and behind me, most of the streetlamps are out. They have burned out on their own or they have been knocked out. Either way, no one has replaced them. Those that remain are set so far apart that for swaths of space they are all but useless.

Close stone chapels must have once experienced a like environment when late at night and in the dead of winter the votives lit by wizened women or by monks with the benumbed hopes of saving the unrepentant souls of lovers had flickered out, one by one. Here, instead of Latin chanting, men in overcoats offer a trawling invocation, one picking up where another has left off, "*coca, ecstasy*; *coca, ecstasy*," a soft insane litany.

Eventually, and with a thawing relief, I see someone else. He's walking fast. Not as if frightened but as if a franticness had been buried deep within a calm cold resolve. A perverted paradox. He's handsome-ish, with a long face, and he looks only a couple years older than I am. With his peacoat, khaki slacks, and loafers, he could be a New England aristocrat. I watch him and I wonder if anyone will approach him when he, on his own accord, walks right up to one of these men!

I turn my head instantly and walk past. This is not an encounter that someone outside it should watch. I walk on more quickly but with less fear. To the wraiths gliding in and out of the darkness, my presence must be an utter and, in the end, an irrelevant accident.

Now a woman appears, tall, thin, and blonde. I must, I think, be near the edge of this district. Though a certain … incongruity in her outline, in her way of walking, strikes me. Her gait is off. She appears stunned, as people do when they walk out of light into darkness. Indeed, and I am filled with an unadulterated relief, I bet that the faint haze behind her is the Oudezijds Achterburgwal, which would explain the frazzled look on her face. She must have been harassed. How relieved she must be to be out of the rld's hecticness. For a second, with a willful naïveté, I move to warn her that she's headed towards worse. But as we lurch forward, her face startles me into silence. Her hair looks so stringy that it couldn't have been washed for weeks, maybe months. Her eyes meanwhile are wide open and static, her entire face looking as if it had, at some indeterminate stage of her life, just stopped. Making it ageless, as if she has not seen time pass. Or worse, as if she has seen time pass, and pass on without her, leaving her high and dry. Time however had not torn those clothes, which from a distance had looked fine. Even fashionable. But from here I can tell that they are tattered, black and blue, ripped through, revealing rough red blotches such as no one should have the right to see. Still, she takes no notice of me. She staggers past, not five feet next to me, and she does not turn her head once. She just jerks idly by, as if she has all the time in the world.

Once we've passed, I imagine her reaction when she walks up to one of those men. Then her eyes, which I'd thought to be vacant, to be the worn-out organs of a long-addled addict, will not be empty at all but will be fired with unseen obscenities, and her ears filled with the soft siren-calls from the sides of the street. To her, I suppose, they are all that is audible. There's no way, I realize, that I could help her, and any word that I might offer could only be a pyrrhic apology. What's more, a moment later I see a sign and shortly after I've walked into the full welcoming radiance of the Oudezijds Achterburgwal.

Letting her slip from my mind, I arrive where I have been headed all along. Once again, it's the rld as I've imagined it. Tourists and colours and souvenir head shops. Harmless. Picturesque. Pot and porn here are innocuous. Even if its roads are compact it must take more than a week to get to its extremities. If I am careful and calm and if I dip just once or twice into what it offers, it will be an experience not an existence. Not a subsistence. I am not an addict.

No. I am simply someone who wants to find out what will work for *me*. Tensions will fade and relief will come with an unending epilogue, when the stock of what's been done is safe and sound and is ready to be retrieved, *in and ex memoria*, whenever it's needed, for whatever uplifting, self-serving, or self-sadistic purpose.

This city, moreover, doesn't force one to extremes. It's amenable even to the most anodyne of endeavors. It welcomes them. I glance across the canal. Take, for instance, the sign for one of two publicly sanctioned *musées d'amour*. The museum just sits there on the western embankment of the Oudezijds Achterburgwal, one of the city's most central canals, snuggled in between two nondescript sex shops. I look casually for the nearest bridge. Crossing it, I see that the museum has, of course, a window. Sauntering by this, I see three mannequins arranged in positions and dressed up to foreshadow, no doubt, some of what you'd see should you pay your admission. Two of the dummies are bound, looking as though they've been that way forever, in black leather and lace. The third wears an unironically ivory Victorianesque latex negligee. This latter lounges on top of a red velvet blanket by a picnic basket, with plastic grapes and bread. The latex is futuristic but the rest evokes a past such as some only slightly more eccentric Renoir would have wanted it.

Whether orgy or outing or both all at once, this window is a theatre of the sexual absurd. It's all unrealistically artistic, as most sex, I suspect, is not. Still, what's truly bizarre is how this whole scenario seems set up with the intention that it could be recreated, that it could be sold, that each patron could aquire, from the surrounding stores, each one of these items. Stepping back, I can *see* them in the shops on either side of the "exhibit."

Art, sex, "half-off" (?!) sales on jockstraps. It's an interactive aesthetic in a crudely commercialized "exxxcess," and I walk away from it half-queasy and half-titillated, with neither sense quite overriding the other.

Such uneasiness floats through through my thoughts until I meet Gretta again.

"We will meet 'friends,'" she says as I walk through her door, "so we must hurry." Still, she takes time to pour us drinks and to quiz me on my day, mocking my choices of museums, before she pushes us out and off to some coffeehouse. When we enter, a group already seated around a rough-hewn wood table stands up to greet her. There's a flurry of kissing on pale cheeks and inebriated embracing, including from a young blondish man in a suit whose lips barely hide his tongue tasting her skin.

This ritual over, they turn to stare at me uncertainly, even antagonistically, as if I might be some undercover agent, someone sent to listen to and then to sell their secrets, for which I'm fairly sure the market is infinitesimal. The blond one in particular glares at me, a lock of hair hanging over his forehead as she sits in a chair next to him, which he had so clearly reserved just for her.

I find myself next to a slightly perspiring bald man who has made room for me by shoving aside two unkempt women on either side of him—"are *commune-ists*," he mock whispers, "so they won't mind sharing." He grins as they scowl at him and look away. "So what," he shifts closer, his accent clearing, "brings *you* to Amsterdam, and how do you know our Gret-*ta*? Or perhaps," he grins conspiratorily, "one should not ask."

Luckily, a waitress steps in and interrupts us. I'd seen Gretta at the far end of the table speaking to her and pointing at me and to avoid ending up with whatever abominable alcohol she had ordered for us, I say, "witte wijn, bedankt, just witte wijn."

The bald man winks at the waitress condescendingly, orders a refill for himself, then shifts back to me, his sleek black sweater stretching around his gently burgeoning belly.

"So," he caughs, "let us start softly. You must be a visitor, yes? So, what did you see today?"

"I went to the Rembrandt House and the Foam Museum. Tomorrow, I hope—"

"To see a better one, no doubt. I joke. But what, I wonder, did you think of them."

I hate this cloying kind of playfulness but it's catching and I find myself saying, not entirely dishonestly, "they were a beautiful disappointment."

He laughs outright and across the table, with a coy yet masculine cooing, he calls loudly to Gretta, "*oh ma chère, quel pêche!*"

"*My* name," he takes up again before I can turn to anyone else, "is Charléus," he pronounces this Sharles, "like '*le baron*.'" He chuckles then starts pointing around the table, talking delicately under the din, "this is Antoinine, that is Tasha, that old man there is Sergei, although here he calls himself 'Serge,' this is *El*oise, her parents read too many English novels, and that over there trying to get into Gretta's not-too-tight knickers is Steffen. All of them, save of course for Steffen, are unabashed, if inactive, communists, although," he assures me, "they won't hold 'the counterclockwise twist of fate,' as *they* would call it, of being an American against you."

Our drinks arrive and he pushes aside his empty glass and continues on in this vein, gossiping about this one's work on Kandinsky's "inner necessity" and that one's "history" of Ivan Ivonovich, his accent starting to slip as he sips one jenever after another.

By this point several more people have come in, mostly a few faux "pretty" girls with way too much makeup on who stoop to kiss Steffen, in particular, on the cheek. These ladies carefully avoid looking at *her* and she herself ignores them. Professional rivalry, I wonder? One woman confirms this, squealing, "why Gretta!" She looks Gretta up and down then smiles, revealing a crooked array of incisors smeared with pink, like some dangerously tempting if orally-disfigured fairy. "I never expect to see you here ... of course I know, with your age, you can only come when you can."

Gretta leers and retorts, "Vash, how clever of you to paint your teeth. It helps to distract from your having so few of them." She then raises her own upper lip in an ostensible endearment, one that shows off her own tea-stained yet more or less intact fangs.

Vash, who with her greasy hair embodies a rotting of the word "wash," turns her head and seems to spit, then walks around the table and sits right beside me, leaning across to sneer "*Charles*," before flagging down the waitress. This accomplished, she turns to me and first quietly then with an aggressive flirtatiousness bombards me with questions, "so why, darling, are you in *our* Amsterdam? Oh, I ask *everyone* this. Is for business, or for *pleasure*? Or maybe your business is pleasure. *Is mine!*" She cackles wildly then continues on in a broken English that I can't quite understand.

The woman working on Kandinsky whispers loudly and markedly in my direction, "do not worry about her. She cannot even speak the Slovenian she was raised with."

"My dear," Charléus murmurs to Vash, "you really are a *mistress*—or should I say a *mons*ter?—of subtlety." At the same time I see his eyes light up. He's as interested in my answer as she is. Across her grainy aura of alcohol and plagiarized perfume, I smell the soft extravagance of his soap. The two of them, so utterly incompatible, are so seamlessly complementary.

"I've come," I tell her and Charles, "for the museums and the theatres and the—"

"*Excellent*," Vash interrupts, "I *adore* Amsterdam for all of this. Is really *too* much here. Theatres, museums, opera houses." She waves her hand as if to imply that she herself has visited all of these just this evening.

"Really, my dear," Charléus sighs, "there is only one *real* opera house in Amsterdam and you have never once, I'd wager, tapped one tiny toe inside of it." He leans in again, having backed up to avoid her arm, to tell me, "if you really *are* here for art, you should see the *Van Prostans* house. Is *splendid*. Is an old 'canal house,' you know, still owned by the *original* family, with their collection of very good second and third rate masters. I know them. Their son is an old—is a good friend of mine. A forty-year-old 'queen in jest' bending forever for hardtbought peers, ha-ah! The family so *generously* allow the public into their home, for a small fee. I could take you, if you like. Of course there is also the *Allard Pierson*, which is not quite so *authentic* ... no, but you must see their Etruscan selections, which I am *sure* you would enjoy. The *bas reliefs* alone are outstanding!" He smiles, self-amused.

"Yes, *all excellent*, as *I* said," Vash sneers. "But is more to this city than these statues and paintings, which really are all so '*schmutzig*,'—old rijk people's porn."

Halfway down this drink I notice that I could not, not honestly, call Vash *entirely* unattractive, she's certainly welcoming, in part because she seems so interested in others, if only to be angry with them or to lure them in, and her complexion, really, is both cloudy and clear.

"Well, at least there is *one* word you have learned—"

"yes, 'schmutzig' and 'oude flikker'—meaning men that visit museums!"

"Psica," he snaps, briefly abandoning his softness.

She grins at him then turns back to me. "No, no, you must see the *other-*" another wave of her hand, "*sights!*" she pronounces this with an awkward attempt at an American accent.

He snorts derisively but her hand is on my arm and she is ignoring him. It's indecorous but there is a part of me that finds her breath on my earlobe entrancing, and by now it's late, it's very late, and I look over and see that Gretta has a whole host of empty tumblers in front of her and a cold aureate expression. Steffen, meanwhile, has uttery divested himself of his aloofness and is presently *lapping*, like a dog, some cloudy yellow liquid out of her hand.

I recall someone having said, "is a very well-known *jurist*."

The handsome addict I'd seen earlier comes to mind. I recount, I don't know why, what I had seen to Charléus and to Vash.

"Why *darling*," he says, "you must have wandered onto our Kapel Gevaarlijkstraat, off of Warmoesstraat. But how did you get *there*, I wonder? You were in the midst—unknowingly, I *assume*—of the worst, though perhaps not too *truly* dangerous narcotics dealers in Amsterdam. I will admit, to be fair, that some of those side streets are at times 'interesting,' if you want a modern Malbulgia—"

"Yesss. Malebulgias, you know all about *those*, don't you, Charles," interrupts Vash.

Charléus again breaks, but just barely, his careful suave courteousness to snarl at her, before resoldering it to say, "still, is best to avoid all this, unless you know *exactly* where you are going, or you have an excellent guide." He pauses, offering a compelling nonchalance, "because, as one of our more poetic, Pim-esque politicians has said—is amazing, no? how a politician can construct phrases that are, at times, so elegant—'such streets,' I translate, 'are the unwanted afterbirth of our too pregnant extravagances.'"

"Charlé*oose*," a voice calls to him from the other side, "you are waxing romantic. Too much so, I think, for how often it is that you go there yourself." I need not turn around. I can tell by the slow rolling rocks in the voice who it is. A drunk, disheveled, slightly disintegrating but still strikingly precise porcelain doll. An exquisite orphan of an intellectual excess.

"Tut, tut, my dear," he says, eyeing Steffen, "not *this* evening."

Not hearing or perhaps just overriding his warning, she continues, "why, Charles, don't you write some *belle-chose* phrase of you own?"

"Well, my dear," he jeers sweetly, "if it comes to that, why don't *you*?"

The room starts to turn. She lunges at him but almost instantly thinks better of it and settles back down, laughing.

He chuckles himself.

"Nach, *how*," Vash shouts, I think at Gretta, "is *Janêk?*"

Charléus wipes his right hand nervously, yet elegantly, over his tonsure and smiles, as if no one has ever been unpleasant.

As the night flows on, I deftly parry his insinuating invitations to "abscond ourselves" to go to his place for champagne or to see his "rare photograph of St. Oscar of Oxfort's funeral," to hear his recording of Gide reading, and after a while he grows understandably bored or disenchanted. The impotence of being an urning. He allows Vash to take over and moments later he is murmuring to a pale young man, with a face a little like a jackal, but superlatively slim in black jeans and a long-sleeved silk T-shirt. I see him slip the man ... I'm not sure what. Not long after, there's no sign of either of them.

When I look back, Gretta has gone too. I panic. Her coat is not on her chair. Steffen is not around either.

A man with hazel eyes, a sour but sensual face, and what looks like a short, adamant body appears next to us.

"Go a-*way*, Alexey," I hear Vash hiss.

They murmur a bit and he sulks off.

To steady myself I swallow a lot of the very hard fruit infusion in front of me.

The next morning I wake with my mind in an iron maiden. In fact, I hurt all over, an unfair totality considering that clips and fragments are all that I can recollect of last night. Vash rubbing my thigh. Gretta gone. Our bill sitting soaking in front of me. Cackling hysterically as my father, certainly asleep, pays for some "*anarchist*" in Amsterdam to get shit-faced. Now I am too sick to be more than just a bit mad. I recall Vash and myself outside. A closed, low-rise food mart. A concrete playground. "Is far," Vash had said, "but I am not Gretta. I do not live in two shitty rooms like animal." She'd spat then burped. "Is owned by uncle. She *says* she pays but is too spensive." A brownish compound and her telling me that her roommate was "out."

It'd been clear instantly that they had not been expecting "visitors." Used-looking lingerie and cigarette ash lay everywhere. Brushing off a coffee table, she'd surreptitiously picked up a butt before making a show of pulling it out of her purse. Relighting it, she'd sat on a sofa, a gross reddish-brown mess, claustrophobically cattycornered to a small double bed. I'd tried not to glance at that but couldn't not notice its greasy grey pillows and its sheets stained with, well, I'd refused to guess what.

She'd pulled me toward it and I'd remembered that one cannot will an erection. Striking out at random, my mind had landed, gratefully, upon Alexey, dark, half hairy, tough, from the train, from the hostel, here he is melting out of his shirt, his shorts—it was not violent; it was understandable—we were so obviously not into each other—she'd no doubt had him which helped me to have her—there'd been a desperate—thank god I'd remembered to remember this—unwrapping then a re-wrapping, of arms, of legs. I had been so grateful to be up for it and so grateful—not eight minutes after—when it was over.

"Thank god! Thank god we were safe!" A timeless pacifying prayer. I had pulled the latex off then flushed it through the sewers. Without asking, I had staggered into her stomach-churning shower.

When I had staggered out she was setting up two oversized smudged glass goblets.

"You know," she said, "she not so little crazy."

I'd nodded automatically. I'd just assumed she meant Gretta. It'd seemed obvious somehow that she should come up.

"She sits all alone, you know, the whole day doing god knows what. She writes! Ha! *I* never read one *word* she wrote! Not even *wrote*, you know, but *copied* in those crazy words no one but her more crazy father under," she hiccups, "-stands."

That Vash could have read even one letter that Gretta had written *or* copied sounds, even now, so absurd as to be out of the question. Still, the over-assured tone of the half-informed had come across as bizarrely expert and as my stomach was still feeling sick and my legs were too weak to walk, I'd found myself reluctantly content just to sit there as she had prattled on ad nauseum about her.

"You know," she'd said suddenly, reaching for her wine, smiling her coy cloying smile, the one that evidenced how stiflingly sultry she can be, "what really surprises me is … you are not even her type!" and how formulaically malicious. "But then you are not *my* type either, you know. *She is not the only one who can choose*!" she'd spat out this last bit with a high-pitched peal, looking surprised at herself after, as if it had come out involuntarily. She'd made a visible effort to control herself. "Too *pret-ty* … Really you remind me a bit of—" and again there was the high-pitched peal, "her *brother!*"

Then she was cackling again and looking as ugly as ever. I could not believe I'd—I'd had to get out of there. She—suddenly she'd shouted, more to herself than to me, "*she* went home with *him* but *I* went home with her *brother*!"

I'd jumped up, knocking over the bottle, now empty. She was still drunk. Maybe be more than drunk. Moving frantically, I'd thrown money out onto her table, well over the amount I'd read that average places ask for, then I'd grabbed my coat and fled to the sound of her screeching.

Lying in my cot now, here in this overheated room, I recall running cold down her street until at last my stomach had emptied itself in some gutter. It makes all this easier, I suppose, that she had tricked me into going home with her to get back at Gretta. Perhaps for making fun of her. What I have to remember, though, is how clearly I was a meaningless variable in her emotional equation.

Now all that's left in my head is ... not regret, but apathy and a desire to ask Gretta about what Vash had said. For not once had she mentioned to me a brother.

Late that night I knock on Gretta's door. She opens it, looking elegantly austere. "Come," she says, "I have one more paragraph, then I am done. If you sit *silently*, you may stay."

After about ten minutes she reappears, with a beer for me and with whatever it is she that drinks at home for her.

"So," she says, "you had good time last night?"

"Did you?" I counter.

Our voices sound harsh and falsely indifferent. Had there been time for her to learn that I'd gone with Vash?

"You never told me that you have a brother."

From the look on her face, I can only guess that we must both be surprised.

"What is your 'work'?"

"Translating, editing, preparing."

"Preparing what?"

"Writings."

She sighs, as if she realizes that she's being short and that there's no reason not to tell me. "My father's writings. His uncollected work, what we smuggled into Amsterdam, what I could collect from libraries, from his friends, from here. Hundreds, thousands now of papers and notes."

"So this is what you do here all day? Work on your father's work?" I picture her hunched over some desk for hours on end, working over already worked out ideas, which will no doubt *not* revolutionize society.

"Dostoevsky is useless for re-spiritualizing society but you can read his books to discover how not to waste your time trying."

The shear absurdity of this response startles me, so I switch tactics. "Why don't you ask your brother to help?"

"Because," she says sounding unabashedly derisive, "he cannot read Russian. He can barely read Dutch. He could not translate into German or into English, which he only half understands, and as for the math," she laughs, "he scarcely went to school and our father never had time to teach him. And when have I time to explain to him surplus values, compound interest, and exchange rates?"

I try not to look surprised. But hearing that she has an all but illiterate brother is a little like learning that Einstein had a sibling who could not tell time.

I want to ask her what he *can* do, but given her history I am afraid to and I dislike that I find this fear exciting.

Looking at me mockingly, as if to confirm what I so selfishly hope to hear, she says, "so he does *ex*actly what *I* did. What I *do*. Although he, of course, has not had my advantages."

Following this, there is silence.

Her cold eyes bore into mine and with no more discomfort, on her end, than I would expect after a recitation of her grocery list.

I notice how a fine strand of her hair curls around her right ear. Looking at it, I am struck by the likelihood that, in my whole life, I have never met anyone so callous.

She moves and once more my blood boils.

"Good," she says, "is nice you were here. But now you must go. I have 'colleague' arriving at twelve"—she, I note, would never be romantic enough to say "midnight"—"I will occupy with him all tonight and with work all tomorrow. In the mean time, why don't you," she grabs a pen and paper and scribbles in her all but illegible chicken scratch, "go here. Tell him," him who?, "that *I* sent you. If you do, he will let you in, I think. Then come back Wednesday, when I am free."

Le Sacre du Prince

Chapter Nine

Outside it's now snowing. Flakes fall softly and just thickly enough so that their grey-green ash half-sticks to the streets. Torn between wanting to catch a glimpse of her "colleague" and an odd fear of seeing some gaunt greatcoated ghoul, I walk off towards a distant streetlight.

Pulling out her note, I shield it with my hand and examine it. Now that I know what I'm looking at her writing is a *bit* less difficult to decipher. 88 Avernusteeg. I take out my guidebook and discover that this is on the edge of the rld. Off of Warmoesstraat. Wonderful.

A half hour later, I've walked over six blocks. The street is much farther than it had appeared on the map. Once I almost slip but I end up awkwardly keeping my balance. Two half-dressed women stubbing out cigarettes see me and laugh then fade through leather flaps, no doubt eager to escape the cold and no doubt loathe to lose money. Despite the clearly dangerous conditions, business in the district is booming. By the time I've walked a few blocks east, however, the crowds have disbanded. Once again I almost slip and as I right myself I see that the street is empty. What, I wonder, would have happened if I'd hit my head here? It's useless to conjecture and only a few seconds after I see a streetsign for Warmoesstraat.

The snow continues to drift and it powders the few scattered shoulders still intoning into the night. Where on earth has she sent me? I see a street name Waarachtigheil lit by one unburnt-out lamp and shortly after I see a tiny steel sign that says *Avernusteeg*.

Turning right, I'm relieved to see that Avernusteeg is cleaner, its snow less tainted than from where I've just come. Its white-dusted brick buildings appear almost elegant save for their intermittently boarded up windows and the occasional sagging stoop. Above all, it is quiet. As if in a vacuum.

Then there it is. I feel flush, despite the cold, despite the ubiquitous emptiness. 88 Avernusteeg. It's a tall old townhouse that blends in imperceptibly with those around it. Like its neighbors, it eschews the rld's seventeenth-century extravagances, its volutes and gables, for a seventh-century austerity. This townhouse though, if rundown, has an air of exclusivity, perhaps because its bricks have become barriers not for empty corridors or for undead tenants but for discrete old men, *timerentur mundum*, with or perhaps now without much money who cannot bring themselves to patronize (to be kind) the more common locations. I imagine these men congealed, ensconced already in reserved rooms, replete with degenerated, if aristocratically reimbursed, refinements.

The only evidence, however, that 88 still transacts with this world are the few sets of footprints crisscrossed in front of its stoop, and now my oxfords indelicately disturb those that preceded them.

When I reach the front door I see a covert plaque by the bell that reads: "*Beaumont House*." I ring and it's an act so simple that, though I'd initiated it, it's over before I can account for it.

Inside, a soft chime sounds and a drop of sweat drips from my armpit to my underwear. Seconds pass then the door opens to reveal a boy, who, unnervingly, could barely be eighteen, at the oldest.

He looks at me and I look at him.

It's like a scene from some old VHS someone had once shown me, only with a baroque bourgeois setting.

The chimes' echoes end and he still hasn't uttered one word. He looks at me but as if he's affecting an indifference over a deep apathy, as if I am irrelevant. "*Tell him*." Hadn't she implied that this establishment restricts whom it admits? Perhaps it's members only. Perhaps its rooms are all occupied. Perhaps, I feel my face burn, it's my age. I may be younger than those to whom this house conventionally caters, though I had seen kids my age slipping in and out from curtains in the rld.

Eventually this boy butler performs several seemingly choreographed steps to allow me into a vestibule. Next he locks the thick front door and opens its slenderer glass companion, itself backed by a full velvet curtain. Through this we enter a larger, marginally brighter hall.

Here I get a good, if muted, look at him. His dull fair hair contributes to his adolescent appearance, as does his flat as a board body and his slim but long nose, which looks minutely tilted, as if it had once been broken and not quite properly fixed.

The dusk here, however, would shadow the best, or the worst, in anyone. Cramped wood paneling, busily carved, creeps darkly across the walls yielding every ten feet or so to dim antique-glass sconces or to Victorian globe lamps on tables. The half-light makes all it touches look morbid.

He leads me past a thick staircase into an enclosed wooden room, one that resembles the narrow parlor of a decaying Edwardian mansion. A taciturn walnut trim rings the high ceiling. The same velvet that had curtained the interior entry smothers one barely curved bay window.

In the wall opposite the entrance lurks a fireplace. A log pagoda flickers within it, secreting shadows. Peering through these, I flinch as I see a savagely civilized man sitting in an impossibly upright wingchair not five feet from the fire. He has dark hair, a trimmed beard, and a suit fit for a funeral. Instantly I feel the excruciating intensity of his gaze, of his fierce black eyes forcing me to look down. I focus on the thick carved legs underneath him, their claws resting on top of a thick Persian rug.

I look up. Next to him, on an old Chippendale-style stand, sits a china teacup and a saucer. The boy, I notice, has gone

Left alone I feel pinned and Prufrockian until I hear the man grate out, "Welcome. Welcome to The Beaumount House." He sounds as if he's speaking for the first time in years, his words falling out of his mouth as if from some primordial maw in a harsh yet in a relentlessly refined eastern accent.

Despite his timbre, his voice exudes an uncompromising promise of control. "I assume," he lets escape, "that you know what we do here, and that you wish to *associate* with us." My desires must be obvious, but he requires that I affirm them all the same. I try, yet under his gaze I feel as if I have fallen into arctic water and have, horrifically, forgotten how to swim.

"Yes, well, I'm looking for someone …" I peter out.

"We have *several* someones."

I hear this with relief.

"Yes," he says, as I nod, "but unfortunately," he shrugs, "we have no openings"—I expect him to say, "this evening"—"right now in our society. I am sorry," he folds his hands, "but no doubt you did not come all this way just for us."

I am surprisingly crestfallen. Not because I've come all this way but rather because I feel undeservedly rejected. Then one of my hands, almost of its own accord, makes its way to my pocket and clutches a crumpled piece of paper. "Gretta," I say, placing the subtlest emphasis on her name, "suggested that I come here."

He looks confused. Then his lips twist forward. "Gretta?" He taps his black clad knee. "Hmmm. You are American?" I nod. He frowns. "Yes. I am good with accents even if we do not get many *actual* Americans.—Fortunately," he says, "we do offer one-time 'passes' for foreigners. This entitles you to services for *one* evening. Additional *acquittements* depends upon who and what you want, how *unusual* your requests are, and other such requisitions."

I nod as if I understand.

"So," he says, his tone altering, becoming so obsequious that it's almost reassuring, "come closer. Tell me what you want. What you are *look*-ing for-"

I creep closer.

As I do, I catch a faint whiff of smoke or of mold. These odors could be coming from the fire but I sense that they are emanating from him, from his suit, as if it had been buried underground then dug up when he had wanted to wear it. Quite smoothly, he reaches down and I examine him. He is immaculate. I can't find a single speck of dirt on him. Straightening up, he places a leatherbound album of sorts on the stand set up next to him.

"We have," he says, "the choicest selection of any house in the city. We offer even one or two scions from very old, very fine Amsterdamian families and then of course myriad strong shoots from stock shrouded in obscurity. When one gives advanced notice, we can offer whatever race, whatever color, whatever size, whatever in fact, almost, one might want."

He has become a hieratic showman.

The "*rituél*," he tells me, as he opens his book, which holds polaroid after polaroid of young men, some smiling, some not, is that I might pick *three* models to see in person, although certain dispersements might be made if I want to see more. "Each subject," he says, "if he has not been re*serv*ed already for the evening, will be brought out and you can appreciate him from the neck up." I picture a six-foot-high fluctuation of floating heads. What he no doubt means is that I cannot see the men undressed. Then from these three I'll choose one. "*E pluribus unum*, as you say, yet *all* are *satis*factory, I assure you," he says, though I had not asked. "Still, as our good friend *le comte d'*—well, we are *very* dis*creet* here, so I cannot say, but is a dear old *gentle*man of very *compelling* tastes—as le comte delights to say, 'you must *choose* before you are *amused*.'" At this anecdote he smiles, and I'm reminded of the cracked faces of Hieronymus Bosch's medieval monks. "I am sure that you will find someone satisfactory and if you wish to try another, there is always tomorrow. Or even tonight."

"I thought you said—"

"Of course arrangements may always be made, depending upon your resources, and our other *obligations*."

As he speaks, I glance at the white framed photos, unsure whether to focus on what he's saying to avoid what I'm seeing or to focus on what I'm seeing to avoid what he's saying. Unfazed himself, he keeps turning pages, revealing image after image.

Some of the subjects look my age, many are older, a few look as young as the one who had opened the door. Each picture comes complete with a terse catechism of "attributes" underneath it. Some, he says, are here tonight, for others I would have to return.

Back and forth he asks and I answer questions.

Half the pictures are only vaguely alluring, or perhaps I mean only elusively erotic. They are all tinted with a general aura of nausea that must just stem from this situation. The proposition of the book is already absurd, so though I'd love to pour over each shoddy snapshot of a life caught in disarray I decide almost at random on three imprecisely appealing images—two look up at me angrily, one forlornly—all with strangely sensuous eyes, and all, he reports, are within my stated range.

A bell rings from somewhere at the front of the house—his eyes, I notice, blink at the sound—but his demeanor remains the same and no one appears until he himself has rung another subtler one.

The same boy from earlier, he calls him "Jonas," skulks in and receives a few inaudible, to me, words then leaves. All the while I watch for any sign of who could have come in, but I see no one and I hear no one. They are discrete.

Bracing myself, I tell myself that I will take a brief look at each boy who comes in and if and *only* if there is a mutual—I'll *insist* on this—a *mutual* attraction between us, will I proceed. One could argue of course that mutuality is not based on equivalent reciprocalities and that they have all already, perforce, shown interest. But I want chemistry not casuistry. I am not, after all, physically repulsive, so why should this be solely a *one-way* exchange of desire for dollars?

Footfalls sound softly and before I can entirely change my mind three boys, two of whom are right around my age and one a little older, have filed into the room. They are all, miraculously, almost as attractive as their pictures. "Ahso," says the emcee, "ma petite 'société joyeuse!'" None of them seem startled to see me, as if my age is not at all a surprise, before their half-shut eyes have fastened on to the floor. Is this some bizzare sign of respect? Or of fear? No one appears afraid. Obviously I had not asked for that, *and I would not want it*, though neither had I asked for my own hot self-disgust. Regardless, they each look, mercifully, much less terrified than I am, although they, of course, have done this before.

With their eyes on the floor I feel a bit freer to peer at them. This is the point, I suppose, of their downward gaze. Two look a little sulkier and, perhaps, a bit more ragged than in their picture and one looks a little more forlorn. I look away, and when I glance back they are one by one turning around. I'd not asked for that! I'd *never* have asked for that! But they do it as if on cue, as if it's a practiced procedure.

I'm so flustered that when one edges his eyes up, I immediately choose him. Yes and thank god for when they had come in, he'd appeared the most relieved, if still far from excited, to see me. He also looks the least, I guess you'd call it "professional." The other two, if more traditionally attractive, look a little too experienced, a little too strong, a little too intimidating. I suppose this makes my decision that much worse. I'm changing my mind when I realize that he's sending the first and the third ones away. He whispers a few words to the one who was in the middle, who then goes off too.

Next he reminds me of our earlier conversation and accepts the required remuneration. He also prods me for a "pourboire" for the boys, *it isn't contrived if it's noblesse oblige*, and in addition a credit card and a state ID. I'm reluctant to hand over the last two, for obvious reasons, but I'm too far in and too fraught or worked up or whatever to refuse. "Our rooms are old," he explains, "and the furniture is valuable. I am sure that you understand-" Scarcely glancing down, he slips what I hand him into an envelope from inside his stand.

All throughout our encounter, it strikes me, we have not touched. Not once.

Minutes later I'm following Jonas up a narrow flight of stairs. Beyond the first landing the house is drenched in a viscous near-absence of light. Dull sconces with frosted glass globes glimmer, letting off barely enough of a flare to see five feet ahead. It's just enough to glimpse Jonas who had reappeared in the first-floor salon to lead me up and into this twilight. Under our feet is a thick crimson carpet that devours any flush and blurs into the dark wood of the walls. Wrapped in the dusk is a scent, a faint intimation that someone has walked through here before, perhaps earlier in the evening, perhaps in an earlier era altogether, wearing a thick leathery cologne. Its decay constricts my chest. The air has grown too saturated with the weight of too much time and too many men and the hallway is too narrow to hold it. It crowds out every thought and every emotion, leaving only the entangling of hot wants and scorching anguishes. What I want is to turn around but the hall has tapered and my knees, bolstered only by my momentum, can't move save to step forward, staggering ...

    I want to ask Jonas a question. I want to keep my mind off of ... I want to ask him the way out but we have stopped next to a door. Here is where he will leave me. Here is where I am supposed to—and flushed with the time, with the place, and with some stupid conceit of sin, I look at him, I nod, and I enter in....

Chapter Ten

Once through the door I am struck, almost instantly, by the cold. The door has shut and there is an almost overwhelming absence of heat. A candle flickers in the corner. An actual candle. Is there even electricity here? Or gas? Next I notice that *he* is across the room. On the other side of the bed. Thank god he is still dressed and, squinting through the smoke, I am glad to guess again that he is right about my age.

Right now he's gripping the carved wood of an old footboard. He is striking. Not in an All American sense but ... He moves and I start, startled. He doesn't laugh. I'm drenched with gratitude. If he had, I would have *hated* him. But he looks as if he understands. Moving more slowly, he starts, despite the temperature, to take off his shirt. I reach out, possibly to stop him. I try to speak, not knowing what to say or even if he understands English. I stop. I had not asked—I know *nothing* about him. Unable to advance, I stand still. He stops too and stares, as if my continued reticence is curious. He goes on then silently until he is more undressed than anyone I have ever seen.

My first instinct is to devour him, to lick him from his hips to his armpits then—but my tongue is already too thick to move. An exquisite embarrassment that had started in my thighs works its way up and twists upside down in my stomach.

I am flustered. Why? It's not as though I've never seen another man naked, though even he hadn't ever been entirely unclothed, always a shirt, half-undone shorts, a jockstrap, even in the locker room—and he had been beautiful still, of course, but by the time I'd gotten to know him his body had given way to a soft cynical roundness and to a half self-condescending smile, both originating from an overpaid-for ease and too much alcohol.

This boy however has a tautness that fills out his thinness, giving his skin, his face, even his eyes an incandescent intensity. My own eyes, unaccustomed to the dark, have to enlarge to take in first his awkwardness, then his tenderness, now his timidity, now his assurance, all of which makes him unfairly, because so uncynically, alluring.

He smiles and in a painfully uncalculated twitch, like an anxious effigy, he brushes a strand of hair out of his eye. I can't but notice—though I try, I *swear* I try—as his arm raises how the hair on his head matches the three sparse patches around his armpits and abdomen.

He comes closer and touches me and time opens out, our tongues intertwining half- and half-not willingly in and out inevitably in to so many seconds, our atoms expanding and contracting, forming and transforming, until all is confusion, my hands on his skin, his hips:—until I am at one and the same time touching and fleeing him, hurting and healing him, am overpowered by and am proleptically overpowering him, the two of us dissipating into so many ex- and inexpedient alleys ...

Then it is all over and he withdraws. Shocked by the absence of his tongue, of his heat, I reach towards him greedily and kiss him, touching his sides, his neck, until my mind reaches in and I recall where I am, who he is, what I've just done and I start fumbling and blundering. Instinctively and no doubt too forcefully, I pull away.

A frown flickers through him. Surely he must be used to nervousness. He licks his lips. But perhaps I am unaccountable, such a forceful blend of desire and of guilt, of innocence and of remorse, not for whom but for how, so potent that I am now unable to move on my own.

Ever so slowly he comes again closer and impulsively I back

away for whether or not his quest is of his own accord, and surely to some degree it *must* be, is to me of the utmost import—

He's so near again now I can smell him. He slips nearer and nearer until his tongue touches mine and we are kissing. I can taste him. All of him. His tongue, his teeth, a million different molecules of his sweat and saliva. The grains of his tongue slide up against mine, shifting all that there is out of order, sending out so many lines of altering, of *altered* potentials such that no one could remember or explain or imagine which will be fulfilled and which have faded out already into an inert eternity.

I start away from him. It's too much. I don't want it. It's a lie. I *do*. Now more than ever but—

His eyes flash confusion and, I think, fear.

I get irrationally, and I know it, upset. If anyone should be scared …

He says words I can't catch. Partly the language, partly his low tone.

The words are gone and my ears thirst for the sicksweet grain of his voice.

Once more he murmurs, as if from afar and in a soft *vox voluntatis*. I move closer. I'm near enough now that I could breathe in from him.

"*You regret me.*"

His head hangs down and he turns, slightly. At this moment, if I dared, I could trace with a finger the wine-colored curve of his neck.

"You too wish for another …" he trails off.

It's not just his seraphic strain, wilted, but the sheer shock that he can speak English that takes me aback.

His accent is so thick that there's a chance that I had misheard him, so I ask him to repeat this. I do so hesitantly, as if I'm afraid for some reason to be too forceful.

He whispers again, still softer, as in the back of my head I rehear him.

"Me *too*? No!" I am jerked out of my self-centered reverie.

"You will tell Mermalain that you are 'unsatisfied'—"

"No, no, not at all." I get up and, in an unanticipated reversion of authority, I take charge. "That isn't it at all."

He had offered himself and I had rejected him. As, I guess, had someone else. Tonight?

Sitting down, if at a distance, I reassure him, my voice sounding as if it's coming from someone else's mouth and from an entirely different direction. I wet my lips with what might, only a moment ago, have been his spit.

"No, really, you don't understand, I won't complain. That isn't what I want. I don't want anyone else."

He has hunkered down, his forearms on his knees, his stomach protruding out unattractively.

I feel a faint stir that I hope might help—but no.

I slide over awkwardly to sit next to him.

Immediately he moves. I glimpse his cock, soft, shriveled, and raw. Its smallness makes me long to take it into my mouth, to make it grow. As if cold, he covers himself. He has only his hands and these are only just adequate. He is shivering. I grab his clothes for him. But as I do, I grow afraid, on account of what he has said, that this is the most intensely insensitive move I could have made. Moving stupidly, I put them back again.

Once more I want to touch him. I want to wrap my arms around him. I want to warm him, to kiss him. Most of all I want to return to him what I have taken. More. I want to be *with* him. But how can I, now? Regardless of roles, I have given up the right. I don't have the privilege, if I ever did, that his desire, however small or tentative, had at one time bestowed.

Needless to say, this is not how I'd hoped this would happen.

"This is not," I whisper, "what you think."

My voice sounds shaky but indulgent and gentle, even as without warning I now feel irritated, brutal, and breaking. Why should he be this upset? I was the one who had come all this way. What does he have to worry about really, save money? For an instant I think selfishly that this is it, though what does happen if some customer says that they are unsatisfied?

No doubt I'm overestimating my own importance but had he

not just said, "you *too*"? *Has* this happened before? My irritation alters. *Has someone been upset with him?* A desire to defend him floods through me.

I am an undaunted knight-errant.

My eyes, meanwhile, have narrowed over the crease between his crotch and his hands, bits of ivory composed around rose. Only now do I feel my body growing awkwardly interested.

What is *wrong* with me? Worse, what can I do? How can I console him, show him that I really *do* want him, without seeming like I'm some sort of sadist?

"Look," no, that's too commanding, "really, I only ever wanted to talk." Weak, and utterly incredible.

I have struck the first false note.

She had sent me here and without thinking I had come. My body had simply had—who knows what intentions.

He looks up at me in total bewilderment, his hands still guarding his groin.

"Come on," I prod, attempting to reestablish myself, "I mean, you've got to get a lot of men who just want to … and I'm not going to complain. I promise."

If I took off my clothes too perhaps it might help. But I can't find the right moment to move.

He slides towards me once more and, with my relief and my arousal interwoven, I put an arm around him.

At first he resists—then perhaps thinking better of it, he nestles closer. He leans his head on my shoulder, then he slowly unbuttons my shirt. A rush of joy floods through me, a miracle more than monstrous. Our movements remain awkward but he lets me come closer and closer, until we have both given in and it's over.

About a half hour after, when we'd decided that my leaving would no longer look conspicuous, he pushes a button. Jonas, he says, will soon appear and before I've finished putting on my shoes, he has arrived. Moving ruthlessly, he handed me my license and credit card, directed me out of the room and down the hall, away from the way I'd come, and all but shoved me down some stairs, and out into the snow.

This was, I'll learn later, a break from the rules. Only "the boys" use the back entrance, thus skirting the members who will, on occasion, wait out front, wanting, with a sort of sweet sick tenderness, not to go home alone. Going home with anyone, he had said, is *verboden*. *Immer*. Of course, for otherwise how could poor Mermalain make his money? Anyway, a "member" having just arrived up front, Jonas had taken a shortcut and that was why I'd ended up as I had. Outside.

Outside it is cold. So much so that my breath smokes as it stumbles out of my mouth. When I inhale, the air burns clean and cold. It's not dense as it had been in doors.

Looking around I see how while I was inside enough snow had fallen to cover the street. I reflect, vaguely, that this will make my return trip more difficult, slippery and spectral, as I make sustained efforts not to trip into a canal.

I laugh.

It echoes.

I am discomfited and I am glad that I am alone.

As I think this, as if from nowhere, though really from a nearby sidestreet, three figures turn towards me. They're covered scantly in light coats, hoodies, and tight jeans of the type that show that they're teenagers, likely young ones. I could ask them, I suppose, which way the Dam Square is. I wonder if they speak English.

As I consider this, one of them comes right up to me, his pale face right in front of me, speaking softly and quickly, his breath warm and repulsive, words that I can't understand. I shake my head to show my confusion. "*Kut.*" His intonation is wrong. How can Dutch sound so angry? Before I can blink, one has slipped behind me and has twisted both of my arms.

Someone's hand thrusts into my right pocket then into my left. Fingers fumble. From my periphery, a flash of silver. Now a too ironic intimacy. I'd laugh but my head is shoved against the snow, against the wall, against the road—

Gradually it strikes me (haha) that a cold wetness is burning my cheek. All around me I see a darkness, like when you close your eyes and you see a dull colored haze.

I try opening my eyes.

I am, it would seem, lying down.

Staying still, I listen. I hear no one near.

My face hurts but I am too tired to bring myself to move. This inability floods me with happiness. I can't now walk back to a place that I can't now quite remember.

A dull throb on my side works its way into my mind.

I inch my hand through the buttons of my jacket. I'm surprised to encounter a rapidly numbing warmth. It's not so bad. I withdraw my hand and, with an effort, bring it up to my eyes. Next I know I'm staring at my thumb and my forefinger, which are red. Three fat drops fall on to the snow. Unable to turn, I stare at them. They remind me of the full flush of his face....

My head hurts. Worse, I feel dizzy despite lying down.

My head moves on a hard surface. I am, nonetheless, sinking. All the while, my eyes are entranced by my body's last onanistic act, dissolving out there in the snow.

Sometime later someone shouts. Someone bends over me. It could be a seraph. Not one in a painting. Like one I have seen on the internet. Black, gold, and creamy. Manmade.

It goes away …

I was, of course, imagining it.

I am alone.

It's back and it has another one with it. Taller. A higher order. Transporting a tarnished glory. Alleluia.

They go off and I rest for a bit. The warm stickiness stays in my side. Hot yet cold. I am glad that it's there and at the same time I wish that it was not.

Someone is by my face. He has a long black cloak and he covers me. Then a gruff voice booms out. "Is alright. Has only *faint*ed!" Who has fainted? It can't be the orphaned angel, can it? I must be confused. I *am* confused. Why else would I have left him?

"Get him inside," the gruff voice whispers, "*now*. We get you inside."

My body moves. I taste snow. It tastes of rust, honey, and excrement. The tastes are indistinguishable. I feel nauseated, and high, then the light abdicates from everywhere.

Chapter Eleven

I am on fire. Someone has piled on too many sheets. I am swimming. I am suffocating in a sea of sheets.
Someone keeps saying "*is alright.*"
In my moments of lucidity, I doubt that this can be true.

When I wake up, I'm in a bed I don't remember climbing into. The sheets are tossed and turned and I am wrapped up into them. Above me there's a coldness. Below me there's the sourness of old sweat.
Next to me hovers a pair of eyes, soft, golden, brown, with more than a hint of hurt in them.
This makes me more confused than I am afraid.
I lick my lips, unsuccessfully, to ask where I am.
My voice rasps out in an inarticulate whisper. He shakes his head and says, "you are alright."
He hands me a glass of water and the awkwardness of the moment echoes from earlier in the evening. It is him. He is here, beside the bed.
"Mermalain was here," he says. "He said, 'he will be alright.' In army, he was a medic!"
At the name "Mermalain" the memory of where I am dislodges from the murkiness in the back of my mind. Words and images swim to the forefront, as if in a revelation. Is this then how revelations reveal themselves? Slow muddy repulsions then

understanding? Bits and pieces come back to me: three men, three kids, one holding my arms, one shoving me, hitting my head, one had, I remember, his hand in my pocket.

"My wallet!"

"Was next to you." He hands it to me. No cash, of course, but my license is still there. My credit cards had been in my right shoe right under my sock. He points to a side table. "Your cards are over there."

He pushes me back down. To rest. His arm has the force of one that could, on its own, hurt no one. Is this the same room where last night (tonight? I have lost track of time) I had been unable, unwilling—"my god, I must be out of my mind."

What if Mermalain had decided that he hadn't extracted enough from his one-time guest? What if he had sent some of his boys to—no, why bring *me* back? Too complicated, too—

I look at him. He's wearing jeans and a sweater, but with his twitching he looks like an anxious backbench angel.

"No, no. You are not now," he says, which can only mean that I once was. "Mermalain says that you were delirious, from your shock, from knife, from snow, but that now you are 'alright.'"

He keeps repeating "alright" as if having gotten hold of an English amulet he is afraid to release it. At the mere mention, however, of the word "knife" my body has tightened, stupidly trying to protect itself. A sharp stinging pain shoots splittingly, literally, up my right side. I reach down and brush, with infinite care, my hand against what feels like a bandage. Pulling it up I catch a brash whiff of an antiseptic. God, what could they have used for that here? I look at my hand. Rust and water.

When I again realize I am conscious, he is still here. Now curled in a chair at a distance.

I raise my head and he is next to me. Remembering my wallet, the cards, and that Mermalain was a medic I can't quite recall how I got to this room. His answer is hard to understand. Agitation has thickened his accent. I gather that Jonas had collected me and, cutting corners, had taken me out the back door of the townhouse. I had started in the direction of Warmoesstraat.

A half hour later, when no other clients had arrived, not for him at least (he implies this and I feel as if someone has kneed me in my stomach), and since the snow had made the chances of many more appearing unlikely, Mermalain had sent him home. Leaving through the same back door, he had found me in a drift with a small pool of "red" by my side.

I feel my face blanch. He takes my hand and says once more, maddeningly, "is alright. Although," he stops, and for a second he seems reluctant to continue, then he hurries, "Mermalain says you have lost blood. Perhaps liters."

He looks so sad, so distressed to see anyone in actual pain that I have a strong desire to be and I am actually ashamed that I am not the one consoling *him*. At the same time I feel a fear, a hot spurting jealousy, I have almost a *rage* that he might have felt equally distraught had this happened to anyone else. Clearly, I am still delirious.

This thought is reassuringly and distressingly confirmed when he puts his fingers to my forehead and he says, "you are burning." He gets up. "I will be right back. Do not move." I can hardly glance at my hand without passing out. I can't imagine what would happen if I had to heave up my whole body.

A minute or two later, perhaps half an hour, time is still indistinct, he comes back with Jonas and Mermalain. I recall hazily the latter insisting, though why should I have protested? that I be moved inside somewhere fast. In the back of my head I hear him pronounce harshly, "is minor wound," his fastidious grammar gone, "is no need to call *any*-one." Am I actually remembering this?

He juts towards me and brusquely snatches off the top bedsheet. Instead of burning I am now freezing. Probably because, as I'm made abruptly aware, I've been stripped of my shoes and my socks but also of my pants, my shirt, and my T-shirt. All I have on is my underwear. Uncovered, my flesh looks sickly, is riddled with weird looking goosebumps. I pull at the linen with a weak embarrassment. He clutches on to it, smirking, so sure that I won't win. He's right and I give in, frustrated almost to tears. He murmurs nastily, "this is not what we have not seen here, unh?"

He uncovers my wound, takes a look at it, then swipes it with water and what smells like alcohol. He shoves two pills at me, makes sure that I swallow them, then gets up to go, launching words at the others that I can't catch. His eyes next meet mine and we share an understanding: it is better for everyone if I stay here. He turns to the boys, nods disagreeably, and walks out, shutting the door behind him.

Jonas mutters a few more words to my protector, whose name I still don't know, before following his master.

My slim-shouldered guardian fumbles with the lock on the large old-fashioned doorhandle then returns to my side. Shyly but with an unhesitating circumspection, he pulls back the covers and cleans all around the bandage with the handtowel used before by Mermalain.

"No one," he whispers, "is allowed to sleep here. *Ever*. Tonight he lets you *and* me, so if you need help," he points to himself, "you will have it."

How generous. Mermalain wants me to feel that I haven't been mistreated. Due, I'm sure, entirely to the decency of his blackhole heart and not at all to fear of complications should I die, or try to run right to the police.

Still more evident, however, is how thoughtful, how sweet his—my benefactor's own anonymous attention must have been when I'd been out. Pillows surround my head and a water carafe waits by the bed.

His voice and his face, alternatingly timid and eager, make him almost unbearably alluring. With bewilderment I think how he must have sat by me, possibly for hours, in what from our previous perspective would have been a perversely pure vigil. Now I want desperately to touch him, and as if sensing this innate desire of mine, and perhaps, I allow myself to hope, even of his own, he comes over, and for a while he just sits holding my hand.

Next I know, before even opening my eyes, I'm overcome with a potpourris of confusion, fear, and exhilaration. This stems from feeling woozy and not quite remembering where I am. Overnight I might have escaped or have been transported or I might no longer exist as I once was. This half-playful half-frightening fancy creeps into the cracks between my consciousness and some decomposing dream I'm not done dreaming.

This time my existence, at least in some physical form, passes unquestioned thanks to the ache embedded in my side. It is then with a deep disquiet that my eyes open to an utterly darkened room. A voice, hazy as if just waking with me or on the edge of falling asleep itself, murmurs nearby. At some point, he must have crawled into bed with me, but even half-conscious I recognize at once who he is. Perhaps this is not so surprising considering our restrained earlier attentions. Now with me weak and with him exhausted, drives and desire override shame and scruples as the closeness of his face, closed into a gradual relief, sways me into an upheaval. Then we are kissing. His cheeks, with the barest hint of an unshaven sharpness, press into mine. Neither of us has brushed our teeth, but this proves one of those rare intimacies that get instinctively then eagerly embraced in moments of a rough fevered fervor. Having subsisted all evening in a strained and straining tension, each distanced from the other, our bodies join more naturally than I would have imagined. His skin is soft and hot, his stomach unsculpted muscle just covered with a layer of fat, his nipples jut out just enough for my lips to find without effort. He removes my teeth from him and he sinks until I feel him, wet and warm. After a while I pull him up and ignoring the pain in my side I slide down him until my tongue is in the middle of a sparse patch of hair. His cock is hard and small and it tastes of the sweetish sweat and the musk men make as they age. His balls are compact and almost entirely smooth. The odd hair or so brushes my fingertips. This excites me more than I'd have imagined. I'm pulled up and over and I sense more than see him arching above me. A cap clicks, foil rips, and a warm oil envelops me. There's a surprising, anxious push and then I am, to my elation, inside him. We rock clumsily together, me ignoring the zipper of pain in my side, until I feel a warm slickness seep on to my stomach and we both come, myself with an usually frantic excitement, with an ecstatic heat that hurts.

Keeping me inside him, he leans low and kisses me. Then he lifts himself off of me and lies back down. I feel euphoric even as much more of me now feels incredibly sore. He sighs and as I start to come down he turns on a small lamp that diffuses weakly through a thin yellowish shade. Following his eyes, I see an old-fashioned alarm clock, the kind with bells and hammers that asserts deadlines with willful arrogance and with an inevitable inaccuracy. "No one," he says, "will come until six. Then they will clean." So we have several hours before we have to be up and out of here. Or, I watch his face flinch, before *I* have to be. Because "we"? Why would he want to stay here, or anywhere, with me?

There's no way though that I want to go anywhere, not any time soon, and save for when he went to refill the water carafe, he has not abandoned me once. In our now orangish flush, I see his achingly pale chest. For once again he has taken off his shirt, his shy attempt, I suspect, to make me more comfortable, so that we might lie here talking at ease. The sight of his skin however reignites me, making me want to touch him, to kiss him, to caress hidden parts of him. He must feel the same because his fingers explore along my arm, along my left leg, along the line leading down to my abdomen.

But mostly we just talk. He seems intensely interested in the U.S. He asks about cafés and cars, about states and schools, about the sheer size of it, and I try to describe, to an extent, what it's like to live there. In return he tells me, perhaps still more obviously to an "extent," what it's like to live in Amsterdam. It could be an uncomfortable subject but he's at ease and funny about it: about the influx of foreign tourists, and I can imagine, to my own annoyance, only men; about the recent rise in immigrants; about wondering how people can have such nice apartments without hardly having to work; about the language difficulties. He has had, he says, no real schooling here so he has learned Dutch and some English from "*friends*" and from TV. He talks fairly freely and only occasionally does he seem to restrain himself or to avoid a topic.

Every so often he feeds me an aspirin or an old Vicodin or he picks up a coarse cloth to wash off my side. At one point he goes off to shower himself. Back in bed, he smells like ashes and honey and I try to keep in my mind that he is always actually him. Having intermittently glanced at the clock by our bed he announces at last that it's five fifty and that he has now to go find Mermalain or Jonas. I will not, I decide, ask why.

When he's out of the room, his presence, as if a shadow, remains somehow inside it. As if he's walking around a side of me that I simply can't see. Haphazardly, I wonder when my body will be healed. Already I sense that I could get up and move around, that I could fend for myself if I needed to, and I consider how amazing our ability is to reconstitute ourselves. Still more amazing, I think, the thought passing not unidly through my head, is that two people can exist in such an intimacy that it never once becomes necessary to know one another's name.

I am bothered though by the idea that if I had to ask for him, it would be difficult. If he has left, really left, I would never know how to find him. Not without Mermalain's good graces. Still, he's given no indication that he wants such an exchange of information. Does he know from experience that such details can be—what? Dangerous?

But who cares? After last night don't I know him as well as anyone? As anyone who knows him only from the cold light of day? More, surely, than someone who knows simply his name. So why not ask? Because he has not asked for mine. Because I am reluctant to take the first step. Because I know that I will lie.

I am wondering if all this is a game for him, if I am the same for him as some dirty-minded old aristocrat, when from outside the room, I hear a noise. The door opens and he comes in, smiling. He has an air of roseweeds and snow, of renewal and remembrance, of an unfinished Stravinskian phrase.

He slides back, clothed, into bed with me and holds my

hand. He seems happy. Why had I been worried? I wonder if my last fever had not briefly come back.

"Mermalain," he says, "is happy you spent night, and from what I told him he said you sound 'alright'"—had he *told* him what we had done? "and he hopes you realize, he said, 'the *generosity* of the establishment for helping you after *your* incident outside,' he wants me to stress '*after* your visit here.' But he also says, 'we must have the room.' Is how he ..." and again there is that catch, "is how we *all*—" no—that has to have been just between us and whatever he was going to say remains mercifully unfinished. "So I have said that I will clean the room." Earlier he had told me that "the boys" take turns cleaning the rooms, which are then assigned depending upon what sort of "ambiance" and "host" a client wants. Anyway with this promise to clean, he says that Mermalain has allotted us the room until four.

Suddenly I have a vision of him abandoning me while I go out into the cold ... of me, not that I have any charge to him, abandoning him to some deviant decadent. All while it is so warm here and the bed is so big, and it would be so easy to stay in it, to lie next to him, forever.

How on earth though can I be expected to walk back to my hostel when I have not once gotten out of bed all day? An anticipation, if only my own, crackles in the air. *What if I asked to stay here?* For the evening. This isn't a hotel. Mermalain has made that clear. But what if I paid—no, this is the fever, this would exhaust my funds. But what if I offered to pay for *him*, exclusive of the room? I know. I know how awful this sounds. But then Mermalain could make about double, and I could have him. *We* could have each *other*.

I explain the plan, but his head starts to shake.

But this is a good, this is a *great* plan! Mermalain could be satisfied, and millions and millions of times more importantly, the two of us could stay together.

So why does he look so unhappy? Why is there a fall in his eyes? Of couse, I've only known him here and here is where we have had our peace.

Unless I have been wrong?

My stomach sinks. I *have* been wrong. There's been no connection. No attachment. No intimacy. Just a bond made out of money.

"What's the matter?" I beg. Then too forcefully, to hide my timidity, I demand, "what's your name?"

It's a last ditch effort.

"What's your name?"

What does it matter? It could not tell me more or less about him than I know already. It could not increase our closeness, which I pray doesn't exist only inside my head. I would only start to think of him, start to recognize him, with the same words as everyone else.

Still, I ask, half-hoping that in the weary warmth of the room he will consent to remain an ephemeral half-identified hope. Simultaneously I want some sound to grab on to, to bring him back should I lose him.

"Janêk," he says, his voice wrapping around the word, around me, half-hiding us in a warm wet pant.

"I'm William." My response just slips out.

Of course, having instantly recognized his name, I nearly blurt out next, "I know your sister!" Or could there be two here with the same name as that thrown out by Vash? Janêk. John. It must be as common a name here as at home. Mercifully these words refuse to materialize, for bringing even the *idea* of her into the open risks upsetting our still overreaching accord. I let her slip into and under yet one more of our uneasily poised equanimities.

There is, after all, our more pressing issue. I want to ask him once more to accompany me. But I'm afraid now of how he will answer.

Eventually, of his own accord, he says, "you, William, will have to go soon," "*you*," not "*we*," I notice.

I start to move toward him and my side sears.

I try not to, but I can't help but wince.

"But ..."

I wait sulkily for him to ask, "but what" but he does not.

"Do you like me?"

"William," his eyes tear up, "yes."

His voice sounds so bruised that I want to believe it.

"If you like me then why can't you come with me?"

He sighs.

"But why? You were not happy last night, not before …" he points to my side, "to spend all those *guilters*. Mermalain, you know, has others."

I realize how foolish I've been. I've been churlish and morose while he's acted with the sort of awkwardness that ends up as grace. He has been honestly altruistic. When he had said "all those guilters" there had not been one note of desire or even of envy in his voice. There had been a genuine fear that I am only reluctantly, only halfheartedly attracted to him. To find someone, and particularly, I imagine, in his line of work, whom you might actually want to touch, only to find out that they don't want to touch you …

I can't stand the thought that I had hurt him. I hate it! I'm ready to spend any amount to show him that I *do* want him, that I want to spend time with him. He must have been burned, must have learned the dangers of taking too seriously any all-too-transitory overtures of trust.

But I'm not asking him to take me solely on trust.

I want to throw my arms around him, a too intense and a consequently too suspect response from which I am saved only by the simple chance that he is standing too far off. "Look, last night didn't go at all like either one of us had wanted. I … but we didn't know each other then."

"No, but how then now?"

How? How could he ask how?

Tears well up in my eyes. Of frustration. And I feel unwell. I am exhausted. I feel as if I have not slept in a hundred years and as if, on top of that, I have a thousand knives sticking out of my side, and now he, who could not have slept all that well either, looks as if someone, and there's no one else around but me, is about to hit him.

I want to laugh and to cry and to embrace him all at once.

"Janêk, please. For me. Go tell Mermalain that I want to spend one more night with you."

He looks at me and then leaves. I hope to find Mermalain.

Left alone, I find the room's intense warmth disorienting. It adds an inexorable lethargy. I want to feel settled. I want him. I would pay all that I have, on me, to stay with him.

After about ten minutes he reappears. "What did he say?"

I'm hopeful, almost arrogantly sure that he has agreed, if only to keep me happy, to prevent me from reporting what had happened, right outside his establishment, to the police.

"You are sure?" He asks this with an intense anxiety.

To answer, I hold out my hand. He takes it and I pull him down next to me, happy and ridiculously relieved. We lie back and he now seems happy himself. Pulling up his sweater, I kiss his stomach, tough and taut. I lick a mole three inches above his belt. He smiles and it reminds me that life isn't always awful. Hot tears rush to my eyes. How lucky I am. Those *thugs* could have ended this. Or forestalled it. His eyes stare back at me unaware. Of course he can have no conception of this close call. Of having to call home, of telling someone from there that I am here. This whole experience, supposed to be my one unaltruistic act, would have been ruined. Forever. As it is, all those assholes stole is enough cash to buy an overpriced Americano. I laugh and laugh.

Then, disdaining the tearing pain in my side, I throw my arms around him and I kiss him, slipping my tongue tenderly inside of his mouth.

An hour or so later we are out on the sidewalk. A dry powdery snow, I notice, has completely replaced the freezing slush from last night. This lightness covers the streets, nature presenting a blank canvas for a newer and a better beginning. Together we complete the bizarre quest of finding an ATM, taking out money, then returning to Beaumont House to deliver it to Mermalain, who had urbanely agreed to "release" Janêk temporarily from his duties on condition that I pay for "full services," minus room fees, upfront. Janêk will get his standard share for tonight when he returns for his next shift. I had agreed to it all. In response, our second exchange is cool, crisp, and business-like save that Mermalain seems, for once, almost suspiciously acquiescent.

And now I have him. Or, as I insist, he has himself. Walking back to our hostel I explain, fighting waves of revulsion, that the money is already spent. He can leave whenever he likes, or he can stay. Whatever he wants. I promise I won't complain and Mermalain, I suspect, won't really care. He has his money and he had not, I tell Janêk, seemed to have much liked me anyway.

Chapter Twelve

When we get to the hostel, I go directly to the receptionist—thank god it's one of the old geezers, not the kid from last night—and I announce, "I'll take a new room. A private one." Walking back it had occurred to me that using the dorm room was no longer an option. There were any number of reasons for this, not the least of which is that, already nervous myself, I'm burning to hurt, if not to kill, anyone who might insult Janêk. As such I'd decided that it'd be best if I sprung for a regular room.

With a mixture of panic and relief, I realize that this is the receptionist who does not speak English.

For a second he looks at me, then he glances at Janêk.

Already I am angry.

He grabs a pen and paper. He writes for a second then pushes the paper to me. It says 75 €.

No. I shake my head. No way.

"I came in a few nights ago and your friend offered me a room, a '*nice* room,' for *forty* Euros."

He looks confused.

I grab the paper and pen from him and write the number "40" alongside the euro "E."

"Look," I say, "this is what your friend told me and this is what I want."

He has the look now of a demented deer caught in headlights.

Taking the paper he writes "65" and looks back up at me, anxiously. What an arrangement! Beside me I feel Janêk shift. In the past 24 hours he has probably slept less, I know he has eaten less, than I have.

I write "50" and underline it, as fiercely and as politely as I can. He shrugs his shoulders and gives me a key.

Minutes later we are in the right "wing" of the hotel, locked in our room. I sit him on the bed. He looks a little woozy and I wonder if he might not be getting sick himself. Of course it's my fault that he has been up for days, but I can't help but be pleased at the chance that I might now get to nurse him.

For a minute or so he looks silently around the room. Normally I'd be annoyed by its cheap splendor, by its gaudy gold curtains and its stained chaise-lounge, but now I am happy with how impressed he seems by it.

"Lie down," I tell him. "Rest. I'm going to get my bag. I'll be right back."

When I return, he's still staring around and his persistence makes me review the room from what must be his perspective. I'm embarrassed now not because of its vulgarity but because it seems so showy. No wonder he seems sick. Who else could he possibly know, with the sole exception of Mermalain or of those aristocratic cockolds claimed by Mermalain as customers, who could plop down 50 euros an evening for a hotel room? and if you add in what I had already handed over at the Beaumont House, it all must seem excessive. As if I am flaunting in front of him what he could never have himself.

Well, I think, if you could put a price on him he would be worth it, and if he doesn't know that then so much the better that I do. While he is here, or at least while I am, I will take care of him and tomorrow I will just haggle the room back down to forty or forty-five while he is in the shower. To fight over money in front of him, and when he is obviously not feeling well, would be inexcusably coarse.

I put my clothes into drawers and on to hangers and he starts to look, mercifully, a little less stunned, even if he's not quite yet at ease. Finishing up, I drop down next to him and he shifts an inch away.

"Is just," he lets out, "so *much*. You," he looks around, "and this.

"We have some nice furniture at work, of course, but this looks just like how the count Arenovsky tells me he lives."

I was right, and to make matters worse, Arenovsky, he had told me late last night, was the client who had recently grumbled about him to Mermalain. The count is an erratic regular, of about eighty, he guesses, who had come to Beaumont House to celebrate "the golden jubilee" of his ascension to his title. Fifty years on, however, he was no longer quite able to "rise to the occasion," and after having done an unseemly amount of feeble groping, all the while bragging about his former estate, in a futile attempt, I imagine, to puff himself up, he had attributed his failure to the retainer closest to hand. Janêk had found out later that this had happened a few times before, but the other older boys had known to go ahead and bring the count off anyway as he had drippled limply on, while Janêk had simply sat there politely and listened.

Peering around, I reflect that I wouldn't be surprised if the count's apartment did look like this. Tiny rooms crowded with gold lamé curtains, chipped "antique" furniture with cigarette burns, valueless etchings, not so much flashy as fustily fourth- or fifth-rate. Of course Janêk can't see this. A bathroom of our own, even one with painted-over rust, seems luxurious to him. I hope, in fact, that the count's rooms are exactly like this. For he would know just how to rate them.

"And you … you won't have trouble? With all this ex-pense?"

The expense of spirits.

I draw him close and I kiss him. He puts his hand on my thigh. This alone excites me. I flex my groin and the bulge nudges his hand. He giggles and I kiss him again. On his lips, on his neck.

"I'm sorry if this reminds you of him. Of Arenovsky. But he's not here and I am, and I am not him. Here we can do whatever *you* want. I just wanted us to be alone. If only for a little while." Again I'm struck with a near-crippling guilt.

He nods.

"Good," I say, and smile, "and don't worry about me. I won't get in trouble, and neither will you. No one will know what we do or what we don't do. No one, I suppose, will even know that we are here."

The rest of the afternoon is easy. We grab food and settle in, but sleeping turns out to be rougher than I had expected. Early in the evening we had changed my bandages according to Mermalain's instructions then had lain down. At some point, however, I wake up with pain radiating from my side. "You have a fever," he says, his hand on my forehead, his voice sounding like a fuzzy lightweight liquor. My whole body aches but each dull throb of it is thwarted by the wonder of him simply existing, talking, walking nearby, or, far better, sitting half-undressed by my side.

He gets me another pain pill and after a while the heat in the room seems somewhat less suffocating. The sheets feel coldish and wet, as if I had pissed myself and not noticed until now, though when I subtly take my fingers to my nose I guess that I haven't. He has not run away, further evidence, and he wipes my body with a washcloth as if to wipe away sweat. Eventually, I think, my fever subsides and he slips into bed next to me, now utterly naked. Not, he says, because he thinks that I want *that*, but because the warmth in our room isn't all that strong and I am shivering. He wants, he says, to keep me comfortable. Currently I am in so many ways disgusting that there has to be more to this than … there has to be, not love but …

Regardless of his reasons, his very closeness comforts me. His nearness turns the remote winter of the room into home. Into some place homier than home. For though I'm used to the cold in Carlton, the coldness here blossoms and folds into his heat, extending and amplifying the iciness of any air not yet breathed by his body. As 3 a.m. approaches, any semblance of artifical heat has fled. But when I start to shiver, strangely, even curiously beneath the blankets, the blaze from his body keeps me from wondering whether I'll die in this ornamental hovel far from every place that I have ever known.

At some point during these distending, these innocent yet

guilt-ridden hours, evidence I suppose that I still have a fever, I tell him that I know his sister. I am terrified beyond reason to admit this and for this very reason, telling him seems so appealing. It's a test, perhaps. For him? For me? Instantly after I confess, I shrivel, emptied of bluster, for even in my haze I can feel how he convulses: I had been holding him—how he looks, how he backs away from me as if I am anathema. Still, I am confused. Why should this matter so much? Then in creeping waves, I understand. I *swear* to him that I had never known her in *that* way. In that role. I *swear* it and I watch him as he wonders whether to believe me.

"I'll tell you," I tell him, my franticness invading my voice, "how we met." I recount how she'd come up to me at a coffeehouse, the only one I've ever been in I say, and how we'd met up again the evening after and that she'd done little more than get me drunk and lecture to me about economics and about editing her father's essays.

His cheeks and his lower lip shudder. Okay. He has lived with her. Obsessed. Self-absorbed. This is exactly what would have happened on one of her few evenings off. He is unhappy that I know her but after he takes time to reflect, he'll remember, I'll remind him, that we had known each other long before we had known each other's names. My knowing her, he'll realize, is not a knowledge that is unendurable.

He sighs. I reach out for him and he snuggles closer.

His brown-gold head rests remotely against the sparse sandy strands on my chest. The brush of his hair in my lips leads me to want to come clean. Completely. "You know," I murmur, "I've come here, I think, to meet you. I'd not known that ... I'd not known that you were you until—I did not know your name or what you looked like ..." What I want to say, I guess, is *I have fallen in love with you,—I have only ever known you as you, but you are who I had hoped to meet.*

In the subsequent silence a pipe squeals dully somewhere along the right side of the room.

My side twinges and he moves his mouth towards my hip and he kisses it.

As so often in my life, I've been not only uneloquent, but broken, repetitive, and confusing. Set adrift, I'm not at all sure of what I've been saying. I'm not at all sure what he understands of it.

Without looking up, however, he lightly scratches my thigh.

"I am glad," he says and he has anchored us.

Together we lie here unmoving. We have reached an equilibrium. We are safe and so we are satisfied to continue stopping, sweating with unfinished exertions under the covers. I am glad I have told him. It may have been selfish but he has not fled and I am content that we are starting off honest, at least as close to honest as our circumstances can allow.

The next morning I wake up in near darkness. Naked and intertwined, I am comforted by an exhilarating excess of limbs. I recall with perhaps the first real relief of my life where I am, remembering to whom this extra head, these extra arms, this soft scrotum, and this tender strong stomach belong. His skin sticks softly to mine. I'm more content watching him, running my hand through his secret hair, simply breathing with him as he lies unawake than I have ever been at any other time in my life. This bliss promises to last forever, situated in dark silhouettes on the edge of consciousness, until he stretches and yawns, his body one arc of hot hard flesh.

Looking immaculate and confused, with traces of sleep and an awareness of unseen intimidations, he peels himself off of me and peers about him. Outside, from a nearby room, we hear a harsh angry knocking. These walls, our door, are too slim to protect us even from this. He shakes his head then looks at me, sighs, and smiles.

Motioning for me to stay put, he slips out from beneath the covers and heads to the bathroom. From the open door, I hear the faint sound of him pissing, one more warm wet intimacy. His shorts, I note with a glow, I can still feel with the tip of my toe, nestled at the bottom of the bed where he had abandoned them.

When he returns I risk saying, "Look—" trying to create a sense of composure, "what are you doing today?"

He looks up at me oddly, "what am I doing?"

I can see in his eyes that we both fear a repeat of yesterday. Still, I press on, "what are you doing today?"

"I go home. I sleep. Tonight ... I work."

I can see that he does not want to say this. But he does. He is honest, and why shouldn't he be? I know, after all, all too well what he does. Yet I also know him. He is not his sister, and what is right for her is obviously not right for him. He does this not because he enjoys it, but because untrained and uneducated it is what he can do, a circumstance of which Mermalain takes undue advantage. This is why he is ashamed and she is not.

"Look," I say, hearing myself from afar, rushing to get through this before I, before *he* can stop me, "why don't you hang out with me today ... *and* tonight, and I'll ... reimburse you," how horrible, "for your time and that way it will all be yours," meaning of course that he won't have to share even a little of what he earns with Mermalain.

"It's impossible," he says.

"Why?"

"If we do not show for work, he finds someone else to come in—and only those *so* often requested ever return—" there is an uncomfortable suspension of sound, "and when we work, we must work *only* at Beaumount House or we are gone 'ab-solutely.' If we meet, we must meet there."

Mermalain makes sure to get his, except that it is *not* his, not at all!

"That hardly seems—"

"Please, William."

"—fair."

"It is a *good* job."

Hearing my name on his lips fills me with an unexpected giddiness. But now the tension is so sharp that it cuts without either of us being able to stop it. It has grown too obvious too quickly how much we do not know, perhaps how much we never will know, about each other.

"He *protects* us," he says—*yes, like a pimp*—"he makes sure that we, that everyone stays safe. Please ..." there is a sour supplication in his voice. I can't deny what he's insisting and I can't but hurt him by pressing a point that must, I suspect, be right. So I back off.

"Fine," I say, frustrated, "so instead of you calling in sick, why don't I re-offer to 'rent' your services," am I intentionally getting revenge for him against himself? "as a sort of guide to Amsterdam. You know the city, and for each night you're out Mermalain would again all but double his profit. He'd have the free room *and* this way you would without a doubt be making him money."

In his eyes I see Count Arenovsky's retreating shadow.

"No. You know what I mean, and last time, remember, went better than either of us had expected. Really, I just want us to go out. I want to take you to a restaurant, to a movie, to a museum. I want us to have a ... I'm not sure what. But I want it to be outside. In the air, in the open ... well, not in the open, because it's winter ... but in a park or in a restaurant, but not there where you will be tempted—" *to remember everyone who is not me to be at Mermalain's or at Jonas's beck-and-call.*

"I want to take you out," I insist, "on a—to dinner."

He looks up at me with his perpetually surprised eyes.

"Is that alright?"

He watches me and I watch him debate himself. I understand, without him uttering a word, that he's afraid. He fears that should he leave Beaumont House, he won't be able to return. Not on the same terms. Neither on Mermalain's nor on mine, and his own terms, he suspects, are irrelevant to the both of us.

I can't, I know, make him promises.

I reach out for his hand, persisting only because I can tell that he wants to come with me, that he is ... interested.

"Please?"

I've never heard such a plaintive tone to my voice. I hadn't known that I was capable of it.

He sighs, a function that with him is as inevitable as breathing. I'm sure that he himself doesn't know how often he does it.

He nods, hesitantly, his consent.

He has agreed!

"It'll be fun," I cry, leaping up on the bed. "We'll talk to Mermalain, then—don't make plans with anyone, not with your friends, not with your roommate, alright?" Last night he had told me that he has a roommate, someone he'd worked with before the older boy had quit Beaumont House to go off on his own. He only likes him, he'd said, "a little." Now I wonder if he'd said this only because he'd sensed that I might get jealous.

"No plans," he says. Then he pulls me to a kneeling position, eye to eye with him, nose to nose, lip to lip. "I want to stay with you but …"

"But what?"

"But *you* must talk to Mermalain. If he thinks this is my idea, he will get angry." He shudders. "Tell him this is what *you* want, that I said 'no,' that I told you '*ab*-solutely not.' Remind him of money and how I will return to him after …" after what?

Neither of us knows.

He turns his hands up. It's an oddly familiar gesture. A helpless inversion of her self-assured shrug.

The meeting with Mermalain is messier than I had anticipated. When we arrive at Beaumont House around eleven am, we ring the back bell and it seems like a half hour before the door even opens. When it does, a bedraggled-looking Jonas—is he fucking Mermalain?— refuses to let us in. He capitulates only after I mention all the money that those in charge, for there has to be more to this conglomerate than Mermalain, will lose if he doesn't.

After he half shifts aside, he takes us to a room off to the left, to an old kitchen, and tells us to stay put. Looking around now, when Jonas isn't rushing me out and I'm not unconscious, I get a sense of the crudity of the back of the house. Peeling laminate and the fetid smell of rot counter the front's far more formal Edwardian elegance.

Eventually Jonas shuffles back in, looking not at all pleased to have returned. He waves at us then leads us out of the kitchen through a hallway and a door and into the more otiose public rooms, which themselves seem somewhat more moldering than I had remembered. Following too closely behind his ragged pajama-ed back I catch a whiff of rancid skin, an extension almost of the mildew smell, as if he has taken on, at an accelerated rate, the circumambient decay all around him.

As we approach the room where I had first talked to Mermalain, I step ahead only to have Jonas throw out an arm to block me and then point to the opposite room to the right. Practically pushing me that way, he shuts its double doors and I'm alone in a long parlor stuffed with ostentatious yet fraying furniture.

I wait, my back straight in an overstuffed chair, the coils of which I can feel pressing up through the cushion.

Then outside the door I hear a voice whispering rapidly, ruthlessly, in a language I cannot understand. It's not Dutch. Maybe it's Czech? Or Slovenian? Abruptly it switches to English, with an increase in volume.

"You will kindly tell *het goldtjeugd* that we are *unfortunately*," the voice is Jonas', I'm sure of it, "not a 'guide' agency." He twists this in an ironic citational fashion. "If he wants to return, he must come back in the evening, when the club is open, with an appointment."

The voice returns to its previous language and its harsh mutedness.

Then the door opens and Jonas is wholly within the room. Behind him I see Janêk with his face flushed. Not in anger, as one might expect, but with a deep embrassment. I could only understand about an eighth of what was said, but it had sounded as if he had been cruelly and unfairly chastised, like a child. He looks, however, as if he has been convinced that he is the worst of all ingrates.

He takes a few painstaking steps then drops dejectedly on to an ottoman, not two feet from the door, and yet more distant than in just time and in space from the bed in which we had spent our first crudely nuptial night.

"Jonas has reminded me," he finally says, "that if you wish to see me, you must come back *here*, at night."

Clearly, this was not *all* that the little toad had said, but I can tell that it is best not to press him.

Besides, I'm more interested in what Mermalain had said. I'm wondering now if Jonas had even talked to him.

"I want to speak to Mermalain," I tell Jonas.

He shakes his head. "He is not available."

"If he's in the house," I say, "then he is available and I want to talk to him."

"He is *not* available, I said—"

Footsteps fall outside and Mermalain himself appears. He glances at Janêk and then at me. Jonas he ignores entirely. His eyebrows raise but this is the only sign of surprise that he offers. I knew it! Jonas likely hadn't talked to him. That *shit*.

Standing, I give an unironic imitation of an old world bourgeois bow, an inch tilt at the waist, and I ask to speak to Mermalain alone. Still ignoring Jonas, despite the latter's obvious blanching, Mermalain accepts the situation and leads me into the other room. From here events go more as I had expected. Whatever else he may be or have been, Mermalain is now a businessman. He listens impassively to my request and afterwards we make arrangements. No boy is a surefire bet. But this plan allows Janêk to come close and since I'm not from here, there's no real risk that our liaison will culminate in a way that's not profitable for all involved.

This time Janêk waits at Beaumont House while I go alone to get cash. Hurrying along I wonder, despite myself, if I am ruining Janêk's 'career.' At least under Mermalain's protection. I wonder about all that an impotent count might offer and all that I cannot. I remember asking him earlier, "but do you *want* to go back?" and I remember giving him no time to answer.

I understand that Mermalain offers him some sort of safety. But how am I supposed to respond to this? By commiserating? 'I know how hard jobs are to come by if you can't really read'? Of course, he hasn't yet admitted this to me himself. Still, my mind has changed regarding Mermalain. On our way over, I had been angry. I'd hated that I'd have to haggle over what I've come to think of, inaccurately, I know, as my boyfriend's body. But I now see what he means when he says that Mermalain protects them. When we had shown up, Mermalain had looked at him meticulously, as if to make sure that I had not hurt him. Undoubtedly Mermalain is protecting his stock … but still.

But I know, I really do, that I am making him happy. So at the ATM I ignore the doubts telling me that this is wrong and that I cannot afford this. I distract myself with three quick calucations. He works, Mermalain had said, five nights a week. Using my personal credit card so that my father won't know, I take out a sufficient cash advance. Really, the quick equation runs once more through my head, this will take two years, at the most, to pay off. Hell, in two years, once I am employed, it'll take two days.

A half hour later, it's all over. He seems happy to be free from the house and Mermalain had seemed happy to have his money. I have, *we* have Mermalain's assurance that if Janêk returns to work the afternoon that I leave, he'll still have his job. Not counting the money, not even discreetly, Mermalain had shaken my hand, as if to seal a "gentleman's agreement." His cold touch, I had noted, had matched the funereal style of his suit. Then Janêk and I, one right after the other, had walked out the front door.

Chapter Thirteen

Back on the street we walk away from the Beaumont House then through and away from the rld.

"Are you cold?"

"No, ... are you?"

We've agreed, I guess, not to discuss what's just happened. It was a nasty necessity and the faster we forget about it, the faster we'll get back to the way that we've been. To the way, it feels, that we have always been.

At some point we find ourselves at the Dam Square.

Here he tells me that he needs to go get clean clothes and to water, he says, a plant that he keeps by his window.

Last night and this morning I'd lent him my toothbrush. But there are other intimacies, I know, that it's best not to share. He doesn't suggest that I should accompany him and for some reason—a fear of the daily details of his existence? of being immersed in a space all his own?—I don't ask to do so.

We make plans to meet up at a café. I suggest around two but he says that he had plans to help an uncle with some cleaning. I suspect that there's some money involved with this so I say that I understand, and I do because I remember Gretta telling me about their slumlord uncle. It must be the same man. I don't, however, mention that I've heard about him since it might unnerve him that I know bits about his life that he hasn't told me of himself, and we agree to look for each other around six, about when, I suppose, he'd normally show up at work.

On my own, I head back to the hotel to shower. Once in our room though, I stretch out on our bed. It's lifeless. Save that his pillow holds some of his scent. I can't not think of him and thinking of him makes me miss him. Makes me depressed. Why, I wonder, had I let him leave?

I laugh self-mockingly, *let him leave*, what a thought! I step into the shower. Risking my own happiness I had, in fact, reminded him that if he did not *want* to come back, he need not. His time, I'd said, is now his. These sentences had taken no more than three seconds to say. Then they were over. He had simply smiled and said, "I will meet you at the café at six. I promise."

Congratulating myself on my being generous—I hadn't even mentioned the amount I'd just spent, way over whatever pittance he might get from his uncle—I soap myself and let the suds' clean odor overcome the splotch of mold where the tub meets the wall.

Afterwards, I rebandage my side. Then sitting naked on the bed, I let my still moist skin and the lingering steam from the shower overwhelm me. I remember the heat of his presence here. Of our togetherness, of our intense simultaneity. My hours with Chad, with his roundness, with his sarcasm, with his films and his languid athletics, it had all been overripe. He had initiated me into an asymmetrical intimacy, one caught amid the past, the screen, and the present, and that time now seems mushy and amorphous, like the sunrays that bifurcate then blur together again, dancing across the surface of their pool. With Janêk, I can remember the precise movements of his lips when he had said "I *promise*" in the icy air.

He will meet me. I know he will. Right where he had suggested: at the café in the district, since he hadn't wanted to come to the hotel alone.

Anyway, now that I have made good headw—good progress, I should say, towards accomplishing what I'd come here for I might as well explore some more of the city. I might, in fact, forget that I'm missing him if I visit places that might not immediately appeal to him.

Out on the street though my mind goes back to him. Really, and I guess I might as well admit this, I had wanted him to break his promise to the old man—Gretta had said that he is a nasty old miser anyway—so as to spend the day with me. The potential consequences of this give me a brief anarchic pleasure. Say that he had stayed, made his uncle mad, and had gotten kicked out of his apartment. For if the old man owns Gretta's place, why couldn't he own Janêk's, too. I'd then of course be responsible for him. It would force us, at least for a little while, to move in together. We'd have to find some cute little garret apartment, no doubt right here in Amsterdam. I indulge, for a moment, the tortured euphoria of imagining what would happen after my father found out and cut off my allowance. I don't have a work visa but I could get some under-the-table job as a waiter or an English teacher. But really then, how could I protect him—and the idea of him supporting me ruins the fantasy—and without a degree or a job or "prospects" of any sort, what would I have, in the long-term, to offer to him?

Someday, I think—

"'*Sumday*,'" I hear her sneer, "is a treaty-term of capitalism. It is the Hymn of the Preconceivedly Saved."

Well, what am I supposed to do? Get myself disinherited? If that was what I was really fantasizing about I must still have the remnants of a fever.

Truth be told, I am feeling a bit off. I'm a bit short of breath and my eyes keep darting to people's hands. Outside and alone for the first sustained time since that night, I'm afraid, I realize, of getting stabbed again. A light crowd surrounds me, but its very sparseness might make it still easier for some thug to slip near me, to jab his knife in, then to run off again, unnoticed and unencumbered.

When Janêk had been with me I'd been distracted. Or perhaps I'd stayed strong to protect him. Now I make my body as small as possible and I swerve each time someone's path bites into mine. Rude Europeans and college-age Americans weave between sordid stoners, would-be-rich wastrels, and world-weary hippies wondering, I'd bet, why Eden in actuality is so much more sordid than in their daydreams.

By Dam Square I'm feeling a bit better. By the time I've reached the Museumplein, I am unusually exhausted but I am much more myself. Perhaps, I think, because the setting is not so unfamiliar. Uncrowded and cold, without a gauche affectation, the scene is a realist picturesque. People wander along sipping hot chocolates and in the middle of the park kids are wrapped in fur coats, no joke, or puffy jackets and are skating around on an ice-rink. If I don't look to the right or to the left, toward the gigantic brick Rijksmuseum or toward the shorter squatter Concertgebouw, and if I ignore the kiddy fur coats, I could be in Carlton.

Moving decisively now, I head to the Rijksmuseum. I've always found old art collections to be calming. The best act like giant alembics, filtering our most personal impressions not just through art but through the abstract cleanliness of stately hallways, wide-open rooms, and the manifold traces of other people's perceptions.

The Rijksmuseum has the added sedative of Dutch restraint. It's a rigid mixture of affluence, artifice, and industry, or maybe of empire, conquest, and escape. But on its surface, the museum is overwhelmingly reserved. It's impressive but not otiose with a main hall and a notable but not imposing staircase. Its walls quietly boast a multitude of black-clad burghers and a minimum of naked nymphs and rapacious Greek gods, though in reality the burghers were no doubt the more debauched, picking meat from between their teeth and biting gold in between mouthing obscenities. In these paintings the sole hints of such humanities are the faint red flecks around their noses, earlobes, and cheeks, veinities inherited by their staid present-day spectators, the balding men and the flower-fragranced women who weave chunkily around intermittent art students camped out in front of sketchboards. It's funny to watch each camp protest against, and occasionally sway after, sparse factions of blazered middle- and high-school students, many of whom exude the threatening sexuality of adolescents, boys still young enough to make flesh seem once again a sin, for old enthusiasts and for timid adult copyists alike, with their barely postpubescent scents spicing the imperious air until it has the odor of sex mixed inextricably with art.

I wish now that Janêk was here. His nose, his hair, the indents in his waist where his underwear presses into his skin, I feel a slight swell in my shorts, and his instinct to cut, however silently, through self-deception. A balance both to the dreary blandishments of asceticism and to the stilled lives of glut, to Rembrandt's self-portrait depicting the great painter dressed down absurdly as "St. Paul" or to a scene entitled *A Gallant Conversation*, more conniving than courteous as it gentrifies still one more bleeding between amour and money. This is the classic catch of Dutch painting, how its very discreetness shapes cruelties and pleasures so sadistic in their subtleties, so pitiless in their prosaic veracities that they outdo the excesses of even someone such as Bosch.

After a while, I come across a heartwarming canvas titled *A Winter Landscape with Skaters*. Both romantic and homey, its figures play precariously on a temporarily frozen river. I return to this painting several times, crisscrossing from room to room to discover some new entrancing aspect of it, some couple holding hands or a group of friends holding each other up, everyone alone yet in accord, even the animals, so that there's a joy to it despite the grey gloom of its sky.

There's a freshness to this landscape. Its natural coldness combines with the warmth of its humanity to make up for the building's other morbid strokes of gluttonous meat mongers and its few unenthusiastically crucified saints, Dutch martyrs reserved even in their agony, clearly sensing the futility of too much pain. Hence, I suppose, the look of well-bred reluctance on the face of a burgher making an offering. The patrons here are different from those other northern dogmatists, the Germans, zealous seekers of suffering, and not at all like those psychologically astute, sensually vivid apostles of the ecastatic Italian schools, where the artists capture both the unmistakeable guilt of an acolyte while the young man whom he is "adoring" can't help but look like the hustler-thief that he actually is, a kid trying no more than half-heartedly, half-mischeviously, to achieve the innocuous look of an angel of anguish, knowing full well that with his robust body he is incapable of being altered into an impotent manifestation of man's making.

Moving from painting to painting and room to room, centuries of European obsessions make me feel irrelevant and mercifully unremarkable until after about two hours, I get hungry and, in the end, a bit bored. Passing out of the museum and turning to the right, I slip by a cloddish sign advertising the *Heineken Experience* and then an immense graceless structure with its oversized forecourt filled with hundreds of swarming baseball-cap bearing tourists.

Soon I come to a differently bustling yet livelier bohemian square, one stuffed to overflowing with stalls selling almost whatever you might want, from bread to books to flowers to linen and lace.

After stopping at a food stall for a sandwich, I walk over to a small outdoor bookstore. I'm paging through a volume titled *The Tronies of Seventeenth-Century Amsterdam*, when a grained voice breaks through my browsing—"well, look who is *here*." I turn and am startled to see his face but grown taut and morphed into a female form.

Recovering from seeing Gretta's face compared to his, I smile. She smirks back, knowingly, as if despite her surprise, she had been thinking of me.

"I'd been hoping to see you soon," I say, and she smiles outright, "but I didn't want to barge in on you at night and I thought that during the day you 'worked.'"

"So I do. It's why I am here. M. Trébouché was an acquaintance of my father's and when he gets certain volumes, which every now and then he does, from Russia or from Germany, or from China in English, that he thinks might interest me, he saves them. I come once a month to see what he has."

Her eyes darken, "it's a neverending effort to replace what we lost when we left, and now, when good works come so few between and others can pay so much more for them," she nods to an approaching soft rotundity, "is, how do you say? an unattainable goal." She raises her voice, "Charléus! Come! I have asked and Trébouché has not one item under 200 guilders, but look who I have found."

"A most satis*fact*ory consolation," Charléus drawls, beaming at me obliquely, as if he is attempting to be coy. Sober, he flirts only slightly more subtly than when he's six sheets to the wind.

Turning back to her, he fishes out two hardbound books from a battered black bag. "No luck, unh? Well, I have found two *treasures*." He shows us one volume on eighteenth-century Meissen porcelain and another on Belgian *argenterie*.

"It's typical," she sneers to Charléus, "you are somehow satisfied, while I am disappointed on all levels. He will go home," she tells me, "and place these 'treasures' next to his flea-market faience," I hear a muted snort of dispute. "We will go. I am tired of looking at books that this *monger* will sell to the masses for pfennigs, while for me he holds back what no one wants, and charges hundreds."

Charléus demurely 'pooh-poohs' her suggestion that he himself could have any "mass" interest.

"No matter—Walk with us," she commands me, "perhaps you will make good this trip, no?"

She sticks her right hand around my arm.

If it were not for Charléus, and if she were not so anarchically older, we could look like a couple.

"So tell me," she says, interrupting our silence, "have you seen my wayward brother? Or did you decide on somebody else?"

"Mein *lie*bchen, did you … ?" Charléus acts playfully aghast, and she pinches me roguishly, an unusual attitude for her, although even her pinch packs a punch.

"I think he did," she announces, "for he has the look of a boy who has recently been '*contented*,' but who cannot now decide what to do with himself," she laughs. "Eh, *Charles*?"

Charléus turns to gawk at me, pruriently. I shudder to think of his imagination.

We walk on. "So *if* you saw him, how is he?"

Her question reeks of carelessness.

"Is *that* why you sent me to him? As a spy?"

She grunts in a guttural fashion all her own.

"In part. But also because you needed what not I—nor any other woman, no matter how *tawdry*—could offer you."

Once more I wonder if she, or anyone, has found out about my exploit with Vash.

"But the *best* gestures are those that help out more than one. The gesture that has only *one* goal is the selfish, is the *bourgeois* gesture, *n'est-ce pas?*"

"My dear," Charléus interjects, "you have no sense of propriety—"

"You have sense of little else," she retorts.

"Well?" she continues, turning back to me. She prods me but I don't respond. "Hunh. Perhaps even now is not doing his job. Cannot even do this right. He had better learn, not that you would be the one to teach him. No matter. Is not *your* job."—"I, of course," Charléus interrupts, "would be *happy* to—" she silences him with a look. "Still, he had better learn. The harpy who lives there does not know what is charity. You think me cruel," she grimaces, "no? But it took my work to get him even this. I 'entertained' de koppelaar's hunchback brother. A successful *avocat*, yes, with money to invest, *et à un bon frère, un bon frère*, and is good place. The troll makes sure that the boys are safe and he gives them good rooms, if a bit in 'inelegant disrepair,' but is better than the street, eh *Charles?* Even you only like to *find* them there. After this hunt, you take them home."

"No, no. You must not think this," he says to me, "only *occasionally*, is so much *easier*, you see." He smiles, silkily, "and at heart I am a philandropist."

"But why are you walking so stiffly," she stops and grabs my arm. "Surely Janchêk could not have—"

Briefly, I outline what had happened, with muted murmurs from Charléus when I get to the mugging, "and I just spent two hours walking around the Rijksmuseum. I suppose that's why it's aching again."

"That old *warehouse*," she declares, brushing over all else I'd told her, "that is what is bothering you. It gives everyone in it a constipation."

"You, of course," Charléus interjects, "would not be happy unless it had only portraits of solitary people suffering, or perhaps of soldiers having sex."

She laughs mirthlessly. "Ahzo? These are the *human* beauties, are they not?"

"You mean beatities?" He chuckles at his own imperfect pun.

She looks confused then barrels on. "So tell me, how is the Bowmont House? How is Mermalain?"

"Is her professional curiosity," Charléus tells me. "Is he still dressed for a funeral? I always assume, you know, it is for his own."

"He is a bit creepy."

"He spends all his time shut in that house," Charléus fairly hums. "In the back rooms though, he has some lovely carpets, and one fabulous forgerie of Vermeer's *Bei der Kupplerin*. He had a boy once who was the master's bait for an old Vichy art dealer."

"Yes," she interrupts Charléus, "but did he help you to decide what it was that you wanted?" she asks me. "Did you try your 'assortment'? I am curious. Or did you just ask for Janchêk straight away?"

This question is unconscionable. Even Charléus looks embarrassed, though this does not stop him from peering sideways at me, obscenely.

I refuse to answer. I'll not let them make fun of us. I'll not let them mock my choosing *him*, us choosing *each other*, by fate.

The question nonetheless hits hard, not so much on account of its invasiveness or its tactlessness but because in the past forty-eight hours I had forgotten my goal to experience as wide a *variety* of experiences, of 'types,' as possible.

She catches right at this and smiles, "well, I admit, I was not expecting *that* bunch to have been so distracting. But when you did not come round next night I guessed I might have been wrong. I had been expecting you."

This is one of the few openly affectionate overtures that she has made to me.

"I'd wanted to," I say, though this is not *strictly* true, "I'd been planning to, only this," I point to my side, "took me off my feet a little longer than I had anticipated."

Charléus snickers then we walk for a while in silence.

"Janêk, you know," I say, "you should know, he helped to take care of me."

"Ahso," Charléus sighs, "*Lanval a finalement trouvé son fée. Héllas, le fée disparaît toujours.*"

For a second she stops and peers at me and I realize that they do not know—because I have not told them—that my 'association' with Janêk, et al., is far from over.

She starts walking again and I wonder whether I should mention that I'd spent last night with him. Unasked for, unanalyzed, and simply accepted, this detail is an astonishing if unsettling jewel in my otherwise lackluster life, and knowing how she scrutinizes each word that comes out of my mouth, I realize that I've been afraid to mention its existence, that I've been terrified that she would intuit it and start picking apart what is beautiful, what is burning, and what is compassionate, dissecting and dissipating it, all in *her* terms of what is "*real*" and what is "*worthwhile*." Charléus, conversely, I know, couldn't care less beyond his lust for language and for images, capital for what real romance could never afford him.

All this anxiety is pointless, I discover, when she asks, with a bored half-interest, born more out of her sympathy with me, I suspect, than with him, "and where is he now?"

"At your uncle's," I say. Then, "we're actually going to meet up later, at a café. In the meantime, though, he said that your uncle had some work for him."

I feel myself doubly on guard now, refusing to surrender specifics and fighting my own urge to pry under his defenses, to ask her, in case there is even a chance that she might know, where he goes or who he sees during his days. To learn all that I can of him while I can.

It's not that I don't trust him. I do. But it's an odd situation. To know how someone tastes, how someone clenches when he comes, but to know so little else about him. It can takes months or even years to learn how someone equivocates.

We pause by a canal and it's Charléus who, as if sensing vaguely what I want, comes to my rescue, musing, "yes. The boy *does* sometimes still work for him, no?"

Silence.

Then in the guise of moving us on again, his fingers graze her elbow, prodding her into speech.

"Yes, so?" she begrudges, "is old man. He needs help lifting his lifetime of ill-gotten gains."

"But," she continues, "I am surprised he is seeing you at *café*. Should he not be at actual work? ... Not that it matters to me what he does, or whom, or even where. He knows that I cannot support him."

That she will not.

"Don't worry," I say, irritated, "*I* will take care of him."

"Of course she will not worry," Charléus assures us, "is *romance*, young limbs, young love, so all is alright!"

She laughs bitingly, her humor mordant. Then she turns silent. For now at least she's willing to let my claim stand uncontested, to let my words stand for what I will. All the same I can all but hear her calculating the statistics of our time together, of our survival. Charléus, meanwhile, looks on ahead smiling, nodding indulgently, with all the tranquility of an experienced gambler sitting out a hand.

If not, I think, for their cynical and self-preservational cruelty, wrapped up in their swath of a shared laissez-faire silence, I'd probably not have said one more word, it's too nice to at last have company while walking along the canals as evening arrives. But with Charléus exuding his enlightened aesthetic support— clearly he just likes to imagine Janêk and myself fucking—and with Gretta upholding her ironic need for an intellectually unequal social order, I can't resist insisting on my own chivalric intentions.

"I know it sounds stupid," I say, as her unspoken ridicule and his starry red eyes spur me to still greater absurdities, "but I *will* take care of him … for as long as I can"—she smiles—"and if you think I don't mean it," there's a newfound fervor in my voice, "then you don't know him. Not like I do. He won't *have* to rely on you. Not on your work, or on anyone else's."

The irony of course is that if he *were* here, I'd *never* have made such promises, not because I'd not have wanted to, but because I'd never have been able to say in front of him, and so fiercely, so many sweetly insulting words.

"*Yes!*" she exclaims, "*Yes!* and *there* you are right, my dear, and, as always, *de-spite* yourself. He will *not* depend on 'anyone else's' work. He will have to depend on his *own*. You may not have to, although you should. He will, however, forever and ever, and you should think of this before you help him to lose his job."

He will have to work.

"Hmm, and you think that I do not know him but that you do. From what? From one night? From two? I'll give you advice," her gifts are rarely long-awaited ones, "and I'll do this because I like you, because you are a 'friend' now, as much as anyone, but you and Janchêk are too much alike. I understand that this may not seem true but it is. Neither of you know what you want. But *you*, one day *you* will. You will not want what *I* want but still, you will know. Janchêk, pshh—Janchêk can barely *read!*" "My dear," Charléus protests softly, seeing poison in this admission that she no doubt overlooks, "and," she laughs, amazed, as if this is an innate inability for him, "what kind of life could you half with him? The Princetonian and the prostitute—besides," she whispers, "he does not even *like* whatever it is you are doing to him—"

"Gretta," Charléus interrupts.

"Oh it is not you," she shakes her head, "believe me, and I do not mean that he wants women. He does not. I could tell from before he was twelve. He is just, how you say? 'cold.'"

These are *not* the revelations that I had wanted, and they are making me angry. I keep thinking how he has been, and probably in more ways and on more levels than I can imagine, abandoned again and again.

"My dear," Charléus speaks up, "perhaps you are too harsh on the boy."

"These are not your 'Warmoesstraat rambles,' Sharlé," she retorts, "not your *jeux*. This is life ... such as it is–"

Not wanting to offend her but unable to bare this, I lash out, "actually, you're just showing how little you know about his life. He works right *off* of Warmoesstraat. He tends more hot than cold. So, I'd bet you know still less about what we are willing or are able to do."

"Oh, I know, I know," she says, becoming suddenly, aggravatingly agreeable, "but you see—no?—that his," she jerks her thumb towards Charléus, "Warmoesstraat is different from Beaumount House, and you know also perhaps, or perhaps not, that the bodies of boys are different. They betray in ways that those of women *rarely* will. Just because he—" she gestures her arm uncouthly upwards, "does not mean that his heart, much less his head, is in it, no matter where yours are. Eh, Charles?"

Charléus shakes his head, refusing to play in public a game that, on his own, he must enjoy all too well. Enough to worm his way into it, again and again.

"But do not worry," she says to me. Is she trying to console me? "He knows we are here, people like you and me, and even Charles, who more than any of us looks for 'love, limited,'" Charléus snorts indelicately, "although he pretends that he does not, and in some ways, you know, Janêk knows more about your place in all this than you do.

"Anyway, for now I have no time for this. I have an appointment with an old colleague soon and I must prepare. He has 'reclaimed' from his bank '*ein ton*,' were it not electronic, he says, of money to finance two unpublished pamphlets." At this she turns to me, "might your family's firm be interested?" Instantly I freeze, but she continues on facilely, "so I must go." She rewraps her coat while Charléus looks at me in a discomfortingly intrigued new light. In an uncharacteristic gesture of affection, her hand rises to my cheek. "I have ... let's call it 'missed' you. Come early this evening, and bring Janêk, if you like. If not, then not."

"Come, Charléus," she says, her tone changing, "*now* you may gossip to me about your friends." She has grabbed his arm and is pushing him past a break in the railing of the nearby all-too-exposed canal, his lavish if faintly-the-worse-for-wear black bag dangling lightly at his side.

Chapter Fourteen

An hour or so later I stand waiting in the late afternoon light outside the café at which Janêk had suggested we meet. Having peeked inside, I stay out front, willfully bracing the cold so as to not risk his missing me.

It's a typical rld café with one window and one obvious entry. From my perch near the door I listen uneasily to the low hum of the crowd. I can't help but glance at people's hands, at the frequent strains on their faces, at the clumsy sexual excitement as eyes trace this girl here, that man there, as pupils study that person for whom stock genders can't possibly apply, and I wonder when such categories might crack. Similar scenes must have played out on this street across centuries, creating layers upon layers of past lives in all but eternal accretions.

This has been an afternoon of accretions as after leaving Gretta and before arriving here I had meandered once again around the old arteries of the outer rld. Edging into the more open and more openly affluent Jordaan I had wondered how this distict's old inhabitants, its butchers and bakers and tailors—recalled now by only a few antique stone advertisements—had interacted with their nearby neighbors. Had still work-soiled apprentices run wild to the bars and red-lit windows before being shut-in at night? Whom had their eyes lingered on and whose eyes had lingered on them? Surely under some laborers' smocks there had been both more and less than others had expected. Yet how different they all must have been from the Jordaan's present day denizens, the city's aesthetic elite living side-by-side with executives and would-be bohemian bankers, each modern-day guildsmember palpably clean and giving off the unmistakable stink of sleeping soundly in safely chic beds. A haut-bourgeois so content that even its children, parentally apprenticed, oozed an aura of being well cared for and rich, as they exuded their undoubted ascendency.

As if to emphasize this, I'd seen a governess pushing a blue velvet baby carriage. She had been clad starkly in a black worsted wool coat and had worn her flaxen hair twisted so severely and so ruthlessly high on her head that it had seemed an imitation of the minor crown that she must hope one day to have in heaven. Three exquisite children had trailed behind her, all in an orderly alignment, and all in what had looked like cashmere. I had noticed them because a ray from the sinking sun had flared, for an instant, off the top of the middle one's head, advancing him an aureole. *My god,* I had thought, *what this one will one day be able to do,* though right now he must be too young to know it. Already though he and his two rigid sisters had secreted an arrogance, if one that *that* governess, that protestantly proud lieutenant, could still hold in line, such that they would not dare to deviate, save perhaps for a millimeter or two within their permitted rebellious parameters. Their governess had seemed so sure of them that she had stared rigidly ahead, not looking back once, as if she had known, not from a motherly instinct or from any other distorted trust, but from her own work in raising *these* children, at least, right, that if any child should run off, it should not be one of hers. By all accounts, of course, her certainty had seemed safe, save for one brief moment when the middle one, who I really think now is an inchoate modern-day de Sade, had stepped out a bit too far and had stared just a bit too long when he had turned his head to look at me ... But kids can be curious. Regardless, save for that, he and his sisters, as if by an unarticulated agreement, had allowed her to lead them right back, I imagine, to their father, to their mother, and to their dinner at home *à leur table.*

A hand on my shoulder causes me to turn and I see his flushed face. How different from that other aureoled angel. Had he hurried? Inflamed with a rush of relief, my first instinct is to kiss him, to push my tongue up against his, to make up for my ebbing hope that he'd show, for the swelling certainty that I'd never see him again. He has however, and in the most considerable way, come.

He looks cold though so without stopping to touch him I get up and head inside. After getting drinks, a coffee for me and a hot chocolate for him, we make our way towards a table. Soon we're seated, arms and elbows to others, with strings of colored lights swaying over us, giving the air an electric looseness, a sense of expectation. This morning, even before I'd met Gretta, our interactions, his and mine, had seemed heavy. Not burdensome but stiff and formal after our nights of cloistered caring. Then after I'd talked with her, after I'd been so *insistent*, my thoughts of him had gotten, well, 'weightier' isn't the right word but forceful in a way that I hadn't expected. Now whatever we have between us feels lighter, as if it's ready to be refined. To be enjoyed.

"Well, cheers ..."

Awkwardly, after he hesitates, we clink cups.

"How did today go?"

"W h a t?"

"With your uncle?"

"It was fine." He shrugs.

"What did you two do?"

"I moved boxes and helped to clean."

I wait for him to elaborate, but he does not.

Not wanting to pry, I start to ramble on about my wanderings, pausing every so often to give him a chance to jump in, but he sits silent. I describe for him the ice skaters outside the Concertgebouw and those in the "Winter Landscape." He listens, I think, but he fails to offer an opinion or to intervene at all.

It's hard to converse with him when he gives me so little to work with ...

He must be tired. Of course I've walked miles today myself. Still, I suppose there's a difference between galavanting about and lugging around other people's junk.

I stretch.

"So what," I try to gossip, "do you think was in all those boxes?"

"Books," he says, with utter certainty.

If what she has told me is true, there's an irony here that's hard to surpass.

"Then we cleared out an apartment where someone had died."

"Oh."

"An old man. From Estonia."

By now the heaviness between us has returned. The backs of passersby, the shifts of tourists' shoulders, the grossly staring men—where, after all, has he chosen to meet me?—the separation of hours and the distance of incalculable experiences have come in between us.

"Did any of the books look good?"

At last I've hit on a naturally evolving topic. I'm sure that what she'd said isn't true, that she had exaggerated. Next I'll ask him what he likes to read. Ask what his favorite books are. What he likes about them. The best way to clear up misconceptions is to ask right around them.

"I ..." he seems confused, "no, I think that they were account books. He has apartments. Rents. He puts his numbers in them."

I hear her laughing, 'my uncle, at least, has *his* favorites.'

He looks somewhat sad, and exhausted. This is not going as I'd expected.

Had he not slept well? When I'd asked this morning, he'd said that he had. But he had not. Not really. I know it. He has bags under his eyes. I'll not ask again. He might say he doesn't want to come back and the idea of sleeping in that room by myself makes my flesh creep.

"Are you okay?" he asks. He looks up at me.

Concern pours, unexpectedly, out of his eyes.

"Of course," I answer, taken aback, "why wouldn't I be?"

He shrugs. "You did not sleep last night. Twice you sat up. You said words I could not understand."

Is he repenting *his* inability to untangle *my* nightmarish mumblings?

"No, no," I assure him. "I talk in my sleep sometimes, I think, when I've been sick. But I feel fine."

Actually, I'm a bit surprised. Other than my mother, and perhaps Gwen, no one's ever really worried about me.

For a while we just sit quietly, enjoying, I hope, each other's company, even if he does look like he's trying not to topple over.

"Look," I say, trying to keep up his energy, even if by irking him, "I saw your sister this afternoon—*purely*," I stress, "by accident. We were at the same book stall, and she suggested that we stop by. I think she wants us to, well, to be friendly. We don't have any particular plans, so I thought …"

I can see in his eyes that he will say no.

But all he does is shake his head, ambivalently.

"Are you hungry? We could grab a bite to eat. I had a sandwich earlier, so I'm not exactly ravenous, but …"

"No. My uncle gave me a late lunch. It was pretty un-eatable," he smiles, "but I ate it."

We laugh, though I'm not sure why.

"We could take a walk. I'd hate to see a movie when we've got the city, though I would if you wanted to, or we could grab an actual drink somewhere," he grimaces and I get the sense that he doesn't drink. That or it's exactly as she'd said. He's being polite but he doesn't really want any of this. Not with me. Perhaps not with anyone.

"You want to head home. To your own home."

"No," he perks up, shaking his head, "no."

"Besides," he says faintly, "I cannot. I told my roommate—he works, sometimes, from our apartment—that the room was his tonight. I thought," he sinks, "that you would want me to stay at your room tonight, not at mine," he trails off.

These words, him simply saying that he had assumed, even intended to spend the night with me, are the sweetest, the safest sounds that I have ever heard.

"You do," he starts, "still want me to come back with you? Later?"

He looks at me, oddly scared yet with affection.

There's a hell of a lot in that "later." Has this been the reason for his standoffishness? Some fear that *I* might have changed *my* mind? That we might talk and eat and walk and then, at the end, I'd say that on second thought I'd sleep on my own? Only, he might have supposed, to go out to find someone else?

Cruelly, perhaps, I savor his want of my want before I rush to reassure him.

"Of course!"

Brushing a sandy forelock out of his eye, he smiles shyly.

I smile back at him.

Then his smile fades and he looks away again. With this gesture, a light goes out.

I look up, then say, "how about we grab some food then go back to the hotel room, to *our* hotel room, so we'll both be fresh for whatever we want to do tomorrow. You don't need to go work for your uncle again, do you?"

With what looks like relief he shakes his head "no."

"Good," I say, "let's go," and I reach out and interlock my left hand with his tired and yielding right one.

Chapter Fifteen

An hour or so after I'm back out on the street. On my way to Gretta's.

We'd eaten and then he had insisted that I go, saying that he'd take a shower then go to sleep but that he wanted me to go if I wanted to see her. Like her, perhaps, he sees me as an intermediary. He had made me promise though that afterwards, I'd return right back to our room, to him.

This was, he had said, what he had wanted.

First, however, I'd gone back to the hotel with him because he'd been worried that the receptionist would not let him in, even with my key. He had thought, for some reason, that they would embarrass him then toss him out on the street. So when we get there, I make a show of asking some new clerk to put *both* our names (so far as we know them, the Hotel Royal Holland not requiring identification) on their guestlist for that room. So it really is, I insist, his room as much as it is mine, and if some bellhop bothers him, I say, slipping him, against his objection, some euros, he should just tip them. A good tip can generally go a long way to getting what you want.

His dignity at any price.

So it would seem.

Halfway to Gretta's, however, I consider abandoning my plans and going back to be with him. But if he wants to enjoy a shower and some sleep on his own, I shouldn't surprise him. There is, moreover, a sweetly sensual, nerve-tingling anticipation in knowing that he'll be sleeping in a bed to which I myself will soon return.

I remember too that I'd told Gretta that I'd try to meet her. It wouldn't be right to keep her waiting.

I *have* missed seeing her and I'd like to keep whatever embers of an intimacy we have still burning. Walking quickly now I wonder whether she'll be relieved or upset that I'm not bringing her brother. Regardless, she'll just act indifferent.

Whatever her response, I'll wind up back with him.

Back with Janêk's back. Back with Janêk's front. The thought of him sleeping, of his too sweetly solid flesh, of his flesh and blood body curled up in our bed, anchors itself in my mind. Whatever happens, whatever we do, whatever we say, whomever she has me meet, we will enjoy ourselves, and then I will return to him.

A few tingling hours later the cold whips against my face as I make my way back to the hotel. I'm a bit drunker than when I had arrived but I appreciate the paradoxic logic as I move both forward and in reverse.

Three or so hours ago I had found myself struck, for the fourth if not for the fifth time, by the decrepitude of the alley outside her apartment. By its darkness. By its odor. By its deadendedness. It's dizzying, particularly tonight when it all seems so firmly interfused with him. This is where after school (had he gone to school?) he had come home. This is where in his free time (had he had free time?) he would have played (had he had friends? had he frolicked with them amongst the broken beer bottles and the cast-off condoms?).

A half hour later I had been in her living room laughing as she had imitated a "colleague," a German banker, whom she had met with that afternoon. He had called three hours early, disrupting her work. But today alone he had given her thirteen thousand euros for the next few installments of Herr Professor's *gesamtgelehrsamkeit*. The first pamphlet of which will be entitled:

"On the Importance of Interstitial Communication between Minor Experimental Communes."

To be followed shortly by

"On the Importance of Interstitial Communication within Minor Experimental Communes."

To be followed shortly by

"Late Thoughts on Interstitial Communication and Experimental Communes."

He had promised, she says, more money tomorrow.

With part of this rich man's penance, she's going to purchase vinyl covers to make the volumes sturdier. She shows me an old report. It's bound in a thin green cardboard and on its first page is typed *"the importince of urban agriculture in the modern era."* In smudged block letters is what looks like a name, her father's?, when I lean in for a closer look, Melek Fische?, she pulls it away. This is the "first work," she says, that she had produced on her own. Now no more mistakes, no more missprinted words, no more unpleasant covers to get stained and bent.

If her "colleague," moreover, really comes in with the second installment she's also going to get, at long last, a computer, although only, she's adamant, so that she can save her work electronically instead of on the thousands of typed up pieces of paper, which she stores, at present, around the apartment.

"Ooomph," she gets up, "I will show you." She looks unstable, though she has hardly had enough alcohol, so far as I have seen, to knock her over. "I stayed up late last night," she explains, "correcting *plusieurs proofs* for him to see *why* we need technology. 'How would your bank function,' I asked him, "if you had no computers?' I will tell you. He and his fat friends would at last have to get off their asses for a reason other than to get a new drink or to stick themselves into something! Though," she laughs, "soon he will have to get someone, ugh, to do even this for him. He will have to embezzle a private plane to come visit. As it is, he can barely fit into his seat." She laughs. "Also, he always stays in some *historical*, although of course *luxury*, hotel—and you know how buildings are here. Every time, hallways for him get more and more narrow so that his obese bottom can barely fit through them." She imitates his huge cumbersome body trying to negotiate her own hallway and she laughs so hard that, as we walk into her bedroom, she has tears in her eyes.

I've never met the man before but I'm laughing at him too, snickering at his inordinate appetite, at his dining lightly at chic restaurants then sneaking out later to gorge at grease pits, at his over eager oily voice heftily-heavily asking her to ask him why he can't get an erection ... until I see the mess all around us.

Inside her bedroom there is, without a doubt, a bed. One six feet by four feet at the most and no more than a foot off the floor and it is surrounded, drowned really by piles and piles and piles, four feet, five feet, six feet ceiling-high stacks of books and notepads and papers, repositories of what look like bluebooks and journals of all sorts bound in cloth and in cardboard, and more shoved in boxes, like in an overcrowded armory, many in languages that I can't even begin to recognize. More, certainly, than one person could have had time in one lifetime to learn.

Dusty and dry, the room smells like some lost Alexandrian attic devoted solely to some, really to *one* insane sort of knowledge.

She cackles, not quite steadily, then grabs my arm and drags me next door. It's more of the same only a little less organized. She points to four locked trunks in a corner, "is where goes what is finished." Next to these is a child's dresser. I feel a wave of recognition. Did this used to be Janêk's room?

"No," she says, without my asking. "He slept in the front room. I slept here, when I was a girl. After I took the next apartment to make money, we kept this," she gestures, "as a work-room." I shudder, trying not to wonder what it must have been like for him, sleeping each night on that decrepit couch. And had he known that his sister was turning tricks next door?

We walk back to the kitchen.

I see now how even the corners by the fridge, by the sink, are stuffed with foxed spiral-bound notebooks.

She pours two new drinks.

"*Prost*," she says, raising her glass to me.

We clink glasses and I take a long sip. After that tour, I welcome the drink. Whatever is in it, it's clear and it smells to high heaven. Evidently I'm no longer a guest who warrants the especial prunish port. Rather I'm a ... what? A friend of the family? "*Now*," she continues, "you see why the good Herr Habtgier must help us." She shakes her head, "There is so much to do and the firm that publishes this, that distributes this work cannot always 'foot,' you say? the first bill."

"Well, why not just publish the best bits?" I ask, trying to sound sensible. "I mean," I find myself backtracking as I see her face, "I mean, I'm sure that *all* of it are the best bits. But surely *some* parts must be more important than others? Why not publish the passages that would undo Herr Halbiger, Herr Halbigburton, or whomever, and his banker friends as soon as possible then be done with it?"

"Is impossible," she sighs.

"But why?" I ask.

"It just is—"

"But why?" I interrupt, "I don't understand—"

"It is not *for* you to understand," she snaps. "*It is the way it is. There is a system!* Is a *total system* for regeneration *before* and *after* revolution. *This* is why. *This* is why— ... and I had promised him."

"A 'revolution'? Where? In Russia, again? Here? Or in the States? Or in England? Believe me, if it's not happened yet it's not going to ... besides, I thought that you said that your father's plan—with its no-military rule—wouldn't even work, so why not start fresh? Or like I said, edit down what you've got to the still—to the ultra-relevant bits, and be done with it."

179

She snorts.

"Come. Enough. Look around. You should know that the States and England are hardly all, and you who have been in *college* for how many years and do not know what you will do? I should take advice from you? Besides, as you should know, *sometimes the work itself is the reward.*"

Now that, for her, is a cop-out answer. But her mood has turned so crotchety that I leave it alone.

She turns and pulls us out of the kitchen and into the living room where night after night he would have slept.

An hour later, she has had a few drinks and, to keep her company, I have had a few too. A recording of a Shostakovich quartet quavers in the background.

"So, William," she says, waving her cigarette, "where *is* Janchêk? Did you not 'meet up' with him?"

"Of course I did. Just like we had said, at the café."

"Hmm, at Het Oude Kluizenaar?"

I nod, wondering how she had guessed.

"He has his habits. He used to work, you know, almost across the street. Before I got him his job." She smokes. "Last month I saw him walking out from there and I wondered if he was still with Mermalain, who does not, you know, like his boys escorting 'extra' on the side." She looks at me, slyly.

"Well, considering the arrangement we made, his time with me could *not* be called 'on the side.'"

I can see that she's interested but she restrains herself. Perhaps she supposes that I wouldn't answer questions. Perhaps it's just her usual reticence regarding her brother.

"Anyway, we didn't stay there."

"Ahso?" Her eyebrows shift up.

"Not for long. No. We went back to my room, and since he was tired from helping your uncle I came out alone."

"Well, at least you seem to be taking a more '*raisonable*' view of this since this afternoon. It's no use getting caught up, you know, in what, by nature, must be temporary. Charléus says I am cruel," she pauses, "but of course his *rapports* last only an hour, at most, and most of this is taken up with his little lectures to im-press ..."

I laugh, then feel guilty recalling all Charléus' live-and-let-live kindnesses. "Well, reasonableness is a matter of perspective, isn't it?"

"Of course," she smiles, "but it's important not to let 'perspective' get out of hand. Janchêk, like any of Charléus' tools, is no more Greek statue than he is a lost little boy. Do not exaggerate or you will lose track of what is accurate, even Charléus knows this—for himself."

She gets up and disappears into the kitchen. When she returns, she sets down what she calls "Jenever" and two glasses. "It's a Dutch drink," she says. It looks clean and clear, like what she had poured us before, but this smells like a hundred broken pine-needles. Ones so fresh that their scent is painful. "I bring this out only when I have what to celebrate. So, to next volume! Prost."

We clink glasses.

Silently, I dedicate my drink to Janêk. To us. I take a sip. An alpine forest, distilled, trips all along my tongue. I swallow. She raises her glass again. "To sacrifice and to sexcess." She drinks, this time without offering to cheers me. Right. So what, I wonder, exactly *is* her success? She works with all but dead books in which she has no interest. What, moreover, has been *her* sacrifice? She lives her life as she wants, while her brother—

"One day *you*," she interrupts this thought, "will make some great act, no? Or maybe I am wrong. You will just give money to stop your conscious. If so, remember my work."

She must be getting drunk. Sober she never imputes good intentions to others.

"I hope to give to charity," I say, taking a sip, "but I hope too to work someday at something worthwhile."

"So do not 'hope'! Hope works with doubt and doubt will kill it."

"Alright then. Absolutely. I will. Still, I fail to see why you don't want me to help out your brother. I fail to see why you refuse to let him help you. So, he can't read Russian. But couldn't he help in other ways? Couldn't you send him out for books or for coffee or let him recopy your work? Wouldn't that free up some of your time? Then he could have some success, too. Why don't you share some of Herr Habtgier's money with him, to get him started?" Why should she alone, after all, profit from his sacrifices for his father?

"I have told you," she retorts, "I do not care at all what you do with Janchêk. Not at all, and the reason I do not 'share' this money, and I know what you think, believe me, is because this money goes *only* and *all*-ways to the work. I never take one cent beyond what I need to subsist. Already Janchêk could eat better than I do, *if* he wanted to. I am *not, I am not* one of those *imposter 'academics,'*" she spits, "who sits and studies in order to go home to big house and five cars and fancy wines. I do not buy stocks and bonds to *jail* my mind to companies to underpay and pimp and *rape* to bring me *profit!*"

For a second I simply stare at her. I think then of the business professor whose "History of Accounting" seminar I'd taken as a freshman "fuck you" to my father. Eschewing practicalities, his course had offered sections on topics such as "accounting and courtiers" and "data entry and ecclesiasticism." He had worn Patek Phillipe watches and sedate Italian suits, bought no doubt from writing books and essays that few would ever read. Those that he'd assigned to us were all password protected and he had taught, I think, just one class a term. But, I find myself wanting to redeem him. He had incited us, all twelve of us, to read and to *think* about Marx and Farolfi and Fra Pacioli and whomever else, names I can't even remember, and it was probably half because he'd dressed up that he'd been able to do it. For better or worse, it's easier to take someone seriously who looks like they are successful. A maxim not entirely unrelated to her desire to clad her father's volumes in vinyl, though she'd no doubt kill me for the correlation.

The professor, I now recall, had even had a section on "economic entity assumptions and peasant revolutions" but so I far as I can remember I hadn't heard him once mention her father, or the communication problems of minor communes. Perhaps because she has kept holed up in this apartment, 're-editing' or 'translating,' whatever 'genius' he had hoped to send out of it. Perhaps I wouldn't have heard of him anyway. It's hard to imagine that Professor Steele, with his Charvet ties, would have been interested in some minor Russian revolutionary. Perhaps this is what her father had intended all along. Perhaps he'd been afraid he'd been wrong. Or worse, irrelevant. Was that why he'd made her promise, again and again, to finish what he had not, knowing that she'd end up refusing to let out all but snatches of it for fear of relinquishing some long festering failure, as much her own now as anyone else's?

Granted, even the most minute points of history—and most of her father's ideas, as she herself has admitted, obliquely, are by now no more than this—ought to be recorded somewhere. But to what extent and at what price to be paid by the present? With what tax to be extorted from tomorrow?

She smiles. "You think, I know, that I am vicious and that this process causes Janchêk pain. But my dear, what you must understand, what he understands, is that work, for our family, has all-ways come first. This is not new. We work for after the 'revolution,'" this being one of those words, I've noticed, that she only ever says with a sneer, "while your father and your family play for profit: your cars, your clothes, your vacations to Amsterdam … to buy more, even when all of you have already enough. So now we have to balance this out. Balance out your and Herr Habtgier's over-industrialized senses of self. We have to think of the others," she hiccups, "that will come after us in their *cradles*," her voice gets high here and she, of all people, preparing for babies sounds ridiculous. "My father, myself, my mother, and Janêk too, have sacrificed ourselves to the future."

She tilts her head up and sips her drink and I can't but wonder once more how much of this act is for her own self pleasure, for her own seductive sense of self-righteousness. I mean, her even *contemplating* a cradle seems so utterly out of character.

"But children," I latch on to an idea at the edge of my brain, "don't they go against your whole grain?" She looks at me, her glance askew. "I mean isn't a love of babies and all that no more than an engrained sort of self-interest?" Sensing now that I've got her, I get excited. "I would argue, of course, that it's a self-interest of a good kind. I mean, isn't it children that make parents, most parents want to 'sacrifice,' as you'd say, for the future? To save? To invest? To make more money? Which makes the world go forward instead of in retreat? Should not *that*, and *exactly* that, be what makes you want to help your brother, so that he doesn't have to—"

She shakes her head, amused.

"No," she smile, "and you have missed, once more, my point. You and I are talking about two different *types* of 'self-interest,' as you call it. Yours vests for you, you and those whom you consider yours, as if it's some kind of kinetic property moving from one generation to the next, each claim to it appearing to increase with each passing, when it is actually diminishing. As if it is in your name—"

"Our property *is* in our name!" I interrupt.

"Psssdt," she says, waving her hand, and then pouring me more vodka, "you *know* that this is not what I mean—but, you see?" she starts excitedly, "this is why he wanted it all, *all* of his work to be read, so that willful semantic missed-stakes are less easy. *Legally* property is in your name, to be sure, and *this* is what must be changed. But not just this law, but what is behind this law, what makes us want to make this law. What capitalizes on cupidity, on feudalism, which allows some to claim from their family property for which they themselves have not worked or have not paid an honest price but which they take control of anyway because of their name. Then after not so many years, this family, with no skills, of no actual help to society but with ridiculous amounts of wealth and 'education' and primping and preening thinks that it is smarter than everyone else. *This* is the self-interest that must change. Self-interest itself, the very nature of exchange, must change. We must come upon a self-interested *independence* ..."

"Except that parents work so that they can support their children and their children work so that they can support their children. This is human nature. This is how society succeeds!"

"Nature! Still we misuse this word. It's nature for some animals to eat their young. It's nature to shit on ourselves," she snaps. "Babies and old people do it everyday. But it's also nature to learn. To persuade ourselves to curb our excesses and appetites. You of everyone should know this. Ahzo, we must make each appetite useful. You see this too, of course, but all the same you think too narrowly *and* too fantastically. Desires must be worthwhile but not just for producing children or families or farms. Is everyone you know so close to their family? No. Too often family means simply a myopically extended self-interest."

Can she not see her own hypocrisy?

"Well," she says, "what you refuse to understand is that to go forward, we must go back. To rebuild, we must destroy. Must think larger! Why should we choose modern nuclear families at the expense, at the hunger, at the *cold*, at the *ignorance* of everyone else? Think of this! How this holds humanity *back*! The child that could one day discover new energies, new cures for cancers, she sleeps in the street. In a foreign nation. The tabloidist's daughter chooses one out of any number of freshly plumped mattresses on which to rest her empty head. All this 'loyalty' ends nowhere but in a stagnant *cesspool* of token aristocratic intentions. Eminence but not *attainment*. No. The individual—including you, William—must be liberated from all institutions, from all societies, from all religions, from all states. But *also*, and this is where my father was incorrect, from all minor communities, including all families and all friends—and, by proximity, from love—from, as much as possible, any identities that demand *limiting* loyalties, that allow others to turn into the parasites of *any* sized empire. We must be loyal to what *proves* to be right, but only as long as it is useful. Then no more. The only way for the individual to *love* humanity, William, is to detach from every other individual. To be entirely, to be absolutely, to be radically independent."

She looks, for the first time, so flushed and so alive that I almost, although this might, I know, be the effect of the alcohol, agree with her.

"Good!" she sighs, as if I had nodded or had smiled or had somehow given some false gesture of assent.

An hour later, I've stumbled out from her alley. It's dark and, against the cold, the heat trapped by my coat feels heavy. I'm no longer afraid, I tell myself, that someone will stab me. If they do, I trip on a curb, hiccupping, I no doubt deserve it.

No, now is no time for self-loathing. I have to get all the way home. After a few hours the sheer force of her ... personality must rub off.

It strikes me that I am quite drunk.

I consider this as I turn a corner. One vodka. Two jenevers. *Four* vodkas. More.

Somehow I must make sure to miss the Wormoesstraat and those side streets that have all the women too skinny and too scabbed to rent the windows, and the men in the trench coats. If I end up there, I might *end* up there. Not quite the end that I'm after. *Mutatis mutandis.*

I look up at the open sky. Even Damrak Straat would be an eclogue after that alley. But here the street stretches out dark and unencumbered. The sky mirrors it, a canvas clear and unobscured, up above. I take a deep breath and, for a stretching second, it sobers me. Right until I bump into a bollard. A small one. Rusted and puny.

If I fell into a canal, where would I wake?

I walk on. Past the state of drunkness when I am excited, when I want to go anywhere—

I try to imagine him at home. At the hotel. An anchor. I am anchorless. I am ami-less—Home is where the hurt is. Taking him outside Amsterdam is unthinkable. I try to think it and I slip on someone else's, I hope, vomit. Right on the sidewalk. It's disgusting the lengths to which some people will let themselves go.

Sensing he shouldn't see me like this, I stop at a still open kiosk and buy the cheapest toothbrush and toothpaste that I can find then backtrack to a pay toilet I'd seen off a side street.

A turnstile eats fifty cents then lets me into an empty room. Inside it three buzzing fluorescent tubes flicker and flounder but fail even to fail. If the refusal to replace the bulbs is to project an antisepticity, it's an intension betrayed. Brief blurs reveal greyish piss-yellow tiles, while the insincere smell of a not-so-fresh disinfectant gives the filthiness of it all away.

Back in our room, I feel exhausted and excruciatingly sober. His curved body rests asleep in our bed. I strip, my nakedness becoming unexpectedly febrile, then I crawl in next to him. He stirs and he touches me, his fingers soft and adaptable in a way that I had forgotten. Hazily, I realize that I'd been avoiding this all night. Was I afraid that we would not reconnect? But here we are, and softly and slowly we kiss.

Chapter Sixteen

I wake up and we're both here.
    Not in bed, which is odd. But a warmth presses round us and I am happy.
    He is here and I am happy.
    My hand is on his stomach.
    It's not yesterday, when he had, without warning, run off.
    His eyes are closed. His arms wrap around me.
    Had we not agreed … ?
    Yet here we are.
    I look around.
    I see unsanitary tiles.
    This feels right yet I am not sure how we got here.
    The room spews a fetid heat. Had someone drugged us?
    No one else is around. It's just us.
    I lean over him.
    I overpower him.
    Why are we doing this? Why are we doing this when we had agreed that we wouldn't?
    My hand is on his wrist.
    His head is on the floor.
    An invisible, intractable touch. Herr Habtgier's hand.
    It's filthy.
    It's unreal. Yet I can *smell* the smell of disinfectant. Of ethylene. Of apples.
    The sweet sourness of sweat from his armpits.

I am shivering.
Why are we *here*?
This is not where this should happen …
My hand is on his throat.
This is not *how* this should happen.
Skin to skin.
His torso rises up, unwillingly willing.
His thighs wrap round my waist.
I scream but I am silent.
This is not fair!
This is *not* how I had wanted this to happen!
He has to *know*. He has to *understand*. Can't he see that I am resisting? Why does he not fight back? *He has to know that this is not how I wanted this to happen!*
His face preserves an impassive acceptance.
I am desperate but I can't say so and, as I continue, I suffocate.

Next I know, it's morning. A pale orange clashes against the curtain's garish gold. My head hurts. Partly from last night's alcohol and partly from what feels like crying. I put a finger to my cheek. It's dry but gritty. I must have been crying. The reason rests just out of reach. Blocked by too much jenever and by my mind's own obstinence. By its own abstinence. I look at the boy, at the man lying next to me, hoping that I have not woken him. He's sleeping peacefully and I am filled with an intense desire to touch him. To talk to him. My eyes, unable to stop, drift down his torso to the blanket-covered crest of his abdomen. Longing for him, shattered scraps of a nightmare come back to me. Fitfully at first then several at a time. These memories could not be mine. How *could* I, even in a *dream*? His head on tile. My body burning. A bit of bile rushes up. I close my mouth and I grit my teeth. My muscles clench. He is so beautiful that I am unable to move. My whole self refuses to disturb him.

He looks so peaceful that I am more ashamed than I have ever been. Much more so than when I was with Vash.

This is, though, a provoking paralysis.

I start to rationalize: I was asleep, we were asleep, the violence, whatever it was, was all in my head. For a while I sit blindly, staring without seeing, assessing a distant prospect. When I turn back, his eyes are open and he has been watching me. As a lover? As a victim? He is inscrutable. I fidget, flitting my eyes back and forth from him, fearing any sign of a just accusation. Had I shouted while I dreamt? Had he heard me? Can he tell how sorry I am? Surely he can see that I have been sweating, that I am flushed, that … he yawns then he is holding my hand and he is smiling.

Whatever the root of the dream, his smile crushes it. It is over if not forgotten and, as if all is forgiven, we start kissing. The blue blanket comes down and his mouth is on me and mine is on him. After we have filled each other with waves of a warm wet elation, he sighs. He is happy and he is satisfied, and for now that is all that might matter.

When at last we have cleaned off and dressed, we venture out. In the cold sunshine, I still feel the warm aftereffects of our sex. Showering with him, utterly naked, slippery and shiny, had made me happier than I have ever been before, and we had both gotten off again. Outside, our intimacy doesn't dissipate. It deepens. This is our first full day, our first full morning without me struggling or him having other 'obligations.' We can go wherever we want. We can do and see whatever we want. We can spend as much time together as we want. Simply walking down the street is a new joy. I grab his hand to draw his attention to some sharp sight of the city, to a stone bridge, to a stoop, to a stunningly bright, for winter, flowerpot the likes of which he has no doubt seen three thousand times before but which to me, with him next to me, seems the second most wonderful sight in the world.

He is tolerant and each time I point out yet another window box he pretends to be interested, a process that brings us both, I think, a genuine joy. Simultaneously, I sense that such subtle touches to our surroundings leave him if not quite cold then indifferent, as if he is not so sure that they are important.

As the day slips past we walk on without either of us being sure who is leading whom so that at times the city seems to draw us on of its own accord until oddly enough, at the end of the afternoon, we find ourselves on the outskirts of the district.

He grimaces, "I never thought of it as having '*outskirts*' at all."

To lighten the mood I pronounce a few street names to see how close I've been to getting them correct. This proves a great success. As if despite himself, he laughs and I laugh hearing him laugh. "Don't mock me," I say, "but how are these?" and I rattle off a few more that I can remember, "*die Niezel*; *die Nieumarkt*; *die Sint Jansstrrat*; and ... *die Amstel*, am I right?" I try again: "*die Amstel*" and both of us double up at the awkward ways in which my lips wrap around the foreign phonemes. He admits that he has trouble, too. I beg him to say the names for me, jumping around him, undignified, until he does so. He says them slowly and swiftly but with assurance. Unsurprisingly, I suppose, as he has had occasion to practice them. I feel a short sharp pain. I ask him to repeat them. He smiles sheepishly then consents, allowing his breath to linger over the soft "ie"s and to clip the Dutch "t"s to their sweet rich shortness. It all flows unaffectedly off of his tongue. I kiss him. He tastes warm and wet in the stumbling sunshine. He seems surprised.

"You speak Dutch beautifully," I say. He shrugs.

"I prefer," he says, "to hear you."

Encouraged, I go on eagerly, mock-pedantically "Well, one can always walk by *die Singel* to *die Jordaan*—"

"*die Jor–daan*."

"—right, *die Jor–daan*. Then you can make your way up one of *die Voorburgvals*, either *neue* or *ooude*, to find yourself, say, by *die Paternosterdrag* or *die Oudekerkspelen*," in off-kilter words I describe his world and he laughs, if with the tiniest catch to his voice, and he says "really, you have a wonderful memory."

"It's alright," I admit, and go on, "and if you're in this area perhaps you might see one of the most beautiful boys in all of

Amsterdam. In all of Europe. Who certainly surpasses any of those in the United States."

"Typical American. You leave out Asia, Africa, the Middle East. Even I know."

I laugh. "Now you sound like your sister, save that even she takes time to take a compliment."

He pushes me and smiles.

I pull him to me and kiss him. He kisses me back.

The warmth of his mouth feels nice amidst the threat of winter rain.

For the rest of the day we walk around, occasionally stopping for a coffee and a snack until the light fades and a passive chill turns into an overeager cold. Perversely, the inclement weather emphasizes the beauty of the buildings, their strange solidity shining through a mist that threatens to consolidate into snow. Even with the aggressive aroma of weed and all the trite sex shops, it's easy to see how their old ornate roofs can lure in even the chastest of tourists, if only in passing. Even now tardy churchgroups hurry past increasingly less cautious reprobates and the dim neon signs, progressively twitching on, blazing luridly in the declining light, to stare up at the dignity of the seventeenth-century gables and garrets, the ambience of which makes just seeing sin seem safe on one's way home.

Or seem safe through its embodiment in art. At one point, on a whim of mine, we walk into the coldness of the Oude Kerk, right before its closing. The Kerk is a wonderful old wood-and-brick monstrosity set down smack in the heart of the old rld. In 1306, I read on a sign, some bishop dedicated it to Saint Niklaas, the patron saint of the city. The honor feels a little worn out, as Niklaas has not done much for anyone around here lately. Even so, as we walk around the nave, we fall into a semi-respectful silence, the kind that massive man-made structures seem to insist on. The solemnity isn't overbearing though as the echo of footfalls wafts down from the rafters, undoing any stifling of sounds, as if the church itself, made up of wordly materials, refuses to take its sacrosanctity too seriously.

This refusal offers the perfect seriocomic atmosphere for the inelegant act of staring up at plainly painted ceilings and then, with eyes aimed a little less loftily, at windows that are, to be honest, unimpressive. Much of the stained glass here has been interspersed with wide swaths of an unexcitingly sober transparency, a disingenuous element for a religious institution. I remember reading that the Kerk's caretakers had stuck these sections in after the original glass had been destroyed during the Iconoclasm, one of the sadistically destructive spasms of the Reformation.

The best churches, I think, the ones I feel most spiritual in, are those that had resisted any ascetic nonsense and rejoiced in the art inspired by a human piety. In such fortresses of faith, the windows are integral. Framed by dark stone, their icy elegies play out, reimagining eclogic landscapes as the pastorals that they once were, idylls and agonies interspersed, wherein the apostles and the saints shimmer back into shepherds and fishermen, students and artisans, imperfect individuals working for some earthly Eden before they had been coerced into an inhumane sense of salvation, when belaboring over an incarnate organ, aesthetics and theology could be intermingled such that a sensible faith in one could bleed over into the other.

Unfortunately, I suppose, submerged in this transubstantiation, art got enthralled through an unworthy transfusion, and with all the priests and the prelates of the new religion seemingly dominating their unwitting adversaries, they subordinated art openly to their atrocities. They degraded and demeaned art, adorning it with their artificial ideologies until it all began to crack under the weight of an aureate aura and inspired the backlash against false idols. This breakdown, of course, only implied that any religious victory was solely a temporary one. For after a while, the innate honesty of art, which almost everyone had been ignoring, reared its reflective head and re-earned its existence, owning up to its imperfections and all the gold-plated pictures and overwrought windows began to reveal dirt, sweat, heat, and humanity, throwing off any too frigid dogmata. Next, having been kicked out of its adopted home, uneasy art made its way into the outside world, back into streets, into public parks, and now even onto computer screens. If you think about these after-effects of the Iconoclasts and their ilk, it makes the blandness of this church almost beautiful.

Both of us, I think, sense some version of this as our eyes shift towards a supporting pillar of the building. The Kerk's famous grand organ rests flush up against the tower wall. Broad and thick, its countless limbs and appendages reach to the rafters lamenting, beseeching mutely to be enjoyed for what they are, a musical marvel, rather than what they were, arms of oppression, now set to sounding this moment in silence.

We continue on, the soft thuds of our footfalls echoing anonymously until each is held on its own as if in suspension or in a celestially slow transition through the obscure ice in the air, frozen particles no longer kept out by the weight of the walls though not yet able to establish a stronghold within them.

Gradually we move from the windows and the nave to the stalls. The air feels warmer here and the sights are earthier. Together we inspect the carved misericords. These have fanciful, often funny caricatures of common sense advice: don't drink too much; beware of avarice; don't bare your buttocks to a woman with a whip, though for some, I'd bet, this last serves more as an inspiration than as a warning. We show each other the individually chiseled exempla of monsters and mortals and when he asks what I think they were for, I explain that they sustained the countless sins of distracted saints.

As we walk out, he says, "I have never been in there before—but this church, I think, is a little like Beaumount House. Both lure people with promises that all know that they can't keep."

He says this without any hint of irony or of bitterness. Without thinking, I ask if his family had been religious.

He looks at me as if I am out of my mind, then he asks, reasonably I suppose, "you *have* met Gretta, right?"

For a second, he holds his face so deadpan that I wonder if he is serious.

Then he shakes his head and laughs.

He is mocking me and I am relieved.

"Okay, definitely not Gretta but what about yourself?"

He shrugs.

"Not necessarily now," I add, "but what about when you were a kid? Did you go to church? Celebrate Christmas? Get presents?"

"No." Once more he is smiling and shaking his head, though this time a bit sadly. "Sometimes my father's friends, if visiting Amsterdam in winter, would slip some small present into our pockets. Gretta always gave hers up though, always, after they had left so I had to do the same. Once I tried to hide one but our father took it and then made me also give up an orange I had gotten at school. We were too comfortable for that, he said."

How nice it is when people take their theories so seriously.

I ask him what his father did with them, the presents. He told me that he made them give their gifts to the "less fortunate" kids in their building, though having visited their apartment, I have a hard time imagining who that might have been. Each present had been left outside random doors at odd hours so that no one would think that they were rich enough to stockpile such stuff themselves, and then rob them. Also, he said, and more importantly, his father had not wanted anyone to feel forced into the abject position of having to say 'thank you' because his children had been more fortunate than theirs. "This was what he called 'tzdaka,'" he says, a charity that is more than charity, that is also a system of fairness. To me, this sounds like a contradiction in terms. Particularly considering where they had lived. Where she lives now.

How unsettling it must have been, I think, to have had Christmas in that dingy front room, where, he tells me, they had never had a tree, had never strung lights, had never acknowledged that one day of the year could or even *should* be different from any other. Although, he recalls, as if from the shadows of his childhood, that their second year in Amsterdam his father had felt an uncharacteristic nostalgia, for better or worse, for all that they had left and they had greeted, mutedly, the new year with a small cake, one they had distributed duplicates of to their neighbors. The following year, with a retaliation of intransigent reasoning, Gretta had induced him to abandon even this.

The result was that year after year all that had pervaded their apartment was a severe sense of sameness, an ever-present remembrance that every day is equal and the (self-)righteousness of knowing that people must not share with or remember each other on one day only but on all days. A single afternoon of prescribed charity or goodwill, his father had said, cannot make amends for three hundred and sixty-four other noons weighted with oppressions. It was not, he says, until he had arrived at Beaumont House that he had experienced what Christmas could be. Each year there the boys decorate the House and receive small gifts from Mermalain followed by a few cheap trinkets from select "members" Mermalain invites to a small party. Afterwards, throughout the rest of season, he says, he intermittently receives extra tips.

Then in a rare admission that he has any memory at all of a life before Amsterdam, he recalls how one winter, towards the end of his mother's last illness, when she had been at her worst, coughing and shivering and weakened to the point where she could barely be helped off the couch, her sister and her sister's husband, a tall thin man with a wispy brown beard, both all but strangers, had come over each evening for a week to light frail but beautiful candles, one candle smoldering an additional one each evening. They had put these in front of a window but had hid them behind two thick curtains. He remembers this, he says, because each evening his aunt had sent him running out into the street to see if he could see the lights. He can still feel the shock, he tells me, that would hit him as he would jump out hurriedly to stand staring up at the snow swirling past the curtained glass, through which not once, he says, could he see so much as a flicker.

He would then run back up and into the apartment to report, just in time to hear the thin man concluding a half-agitating, half-soothing chant, which they had never once waited for him to start. He would have liked to have heard it through once, he says, but he hadn't asked because the whole week the adults had acted conspicuously rushed. Their tension had increased with each additional visit, and each additional candle, until it was almost unbearable, he says, on the final night, when all the stems in the candelabra were lit.

This dreamlike culmination had coincided, unfortunately, with one of the rare evenings when his father had come home early, before the candles had burnt out and the wax had been flicked up with a knife, with an unspoken understanding that none of this would ever be mentioned by anyone.

He remembers his father's shadow surprising everyone from the doorway. He remembers how everyone had stared at it. How Gretta, his only daughter, had not said one word, but had stood stock still next to their mother, her impossible stiffness only stressing her intolerable treachery. Then together, in an unlikely unity, they had watched as with his short yet thick black beard shaking he had blown out the candles, one by one. Whispering as he had done so, so that he seemed all the more intense, "*he*—has not helped us—*he* has *never* helped us—*we* must *help* our selves—"

Their aunt's husband had never returned and it was the first and the last time that they had practiced, even obliquely, a religious rite in their household.

I stay silent.

The story has a strange power, partly from Janêk having channelled, albeit briefly, his father's voice and partly from it being made up of revulsion, of beauty, and of respect all at once. For as hard or as awful as their father must have been, it's hard to fault someone for the sin of self-sufficiency.

Chapter Seventeen

The shoulders of the sky relax into the abdomen of the afternoon, and he and I drift along the ever more genteel canals of the Jordaan. By now I find the Jordaan strangely familiar though he says that he rarely ventures here himself. This district's residents and its café patrons tend to stare at him, shifting their eyes after he has noticed them, only to visually urge him away again—he just knows that this happens, he insists—after he has looked off. He makes them uneasy, he says, as if they see him and know how he spends his nights. This is paranoid, I tell him, but privately I suspect that he's right. Against these burnished brown canal homes and solid white windowsills he is as beautiful as ever but the cheap fabric of his just-too-tight shirt and his slightly too longish blonde hair and perhaps even the brief sheen to his skin, which suggests some ever present sexsweat, all stand out. The Jordaanians no doubt dislike too public signs of those sins, both romantic and mercantile, that underpin their haute-bourgeois sophistrications.

Considering the unfairness of this, I grab his hand as we walk past it all and on occasion I lean into him to remind him that I am here. Together we peer into cracks and up into windows. Pointing out two or three silhouettes I wonder what their lives are like and soon we're creating stories for framed figures: here's a resetter of old jewels who uses paste to enhance his children's inheritance; there's the slim son of a banker who sells his sweaty jockstraps over the internet; there's an exhibitionist (his idea);

there's an ill-placed prude; these are a suitmaker *and* a dressmaker, good-naturedly at odds with each other having just discovered that they share one unaccountably elegant client. This window, I project, holds a couplet, two twenty-two-year-olds about to have a child; this next holds heaven, two old men who after a tough life together have decided just to enjoy each other's company.

He puts one arm around my waist.

What's nice, I think, not wanting to expose the idea to the open where it could corrode, is that this is just the two of us. Ambling around. As equals. With a naked sense of normalcy. Both of us subtly deferring, content to follow each other's unspoken whims and uninterrogated urges. As we walk along, I love to catch glimpses of him. I love to remember what he looks like beneath his coat, beneath his shirt, how warm his balls are between his legs. I catch the scent of his breath and I recall how it quickens when he's about to erupt, and it's on account of this that I don't feel in any way lost or astray.

Like myself, he never once asks where we're going. Instead he, who with such great care has told me so little about his life, dodging my now hasty, now timid inquiries, asks allusively about my own, wondering obliquely if when I travel I generally travel "like this," wandering about, without any immediate aim. "Well," I say, "I've only ever travelled with my parents, really, and it was rarely—it was never like this. We never just wandered around, enjoying ourselves. We were always rushed. We always had some predetermined destination, generally some lobby that my mother, my brothers, and I would sit in while my father went up to run some business meeting, and whenever we would walk, my father would always shove his way up front."

"Right," he says, I think in sympathy, since their father too had been intolerable, until he adds, "but this is his *job*, to do this. The father."

I laugh. He's so honestly, so uninhibitedly patriarchal. I can only imagine what *she* would say.

"Of course not. That's only the way that some men, well most, I suppose, think that it should be because it suits them. A few,"

I blush, "don't care to be in control. But he, *my* father I mean, *has* to, he *has* to be in charge. *Always.* So in his world, there's not much room for anyone else. Not up front. When we were kids, he would take off sometimes, after his breakfast but while we were still eating ours, without a word, without wondering where we wanted to go or what we wanted to see. He would just get up and go, expecting us, swept up by our mother, of course, to fall in after him. Instantly.

"Always, and regardless of whether or not we were in a city that he'd been in before, and he had traveled a lot before we were born, he would sit down at the hotel room desk before breakfast to memorize maps. I can still see him sitting there with a cup of coffee and two or three maps, forcing the rest of us to wait for him." It gives me a rush, I admit, to bash him like this. Perhaps because I can still see everyone forced to sit stock still, my mother, Sean, even Donny, who before he got sick could barely restrain himself from bouncing around, irritatingly, granted, on the beds, everyone afraid to move, everyone ravenous, until he had finished obsessively committing to memory every single last one of our routes. Being methodical is fine, for sure. What was so awful was his attitude. Even the best of intentions can be undone by overdoing and this is inevitably what happens with him.

"I remember the times too when after breakfast my father would set off for meetings and my brothers would go back to sleep and I'd go out just with my mother. I was the only one interested in walking with her to obscure monuments. She would reminisce then, gossiping about her days spent studying '*la belle epoque*,' recalling anecdotes about Mallarmé, Valéry, or Wilde. She'd speak of them almost as if she had known them herself. These were memories leftover from when she had been working on a dissertation at Harvard, before she had met and married my father, had been swept away from any life anywhere near as exciting. Afterwards she'd had, I guess, solitary moments snatched up during their whirlwind 'tours' of the commercialized capitals of culture. She'd wander then for hours alone through the cities whose literary landscapes she had studied. Once, only to me, and only with the strictest of confidences, she had admitted that before she'd had us and had had to start worrying on her own about medicines, toothbrushes, and underwear, on the evenings before flying off, she would take out and reread bits of her all but finished dissertation."

After a while, he says, perhaps to sympathize, "my father was the same, or similar, though not with maps. With books. He always brought books to the table … and we could not talk at meals. He and Gretta would read and read and read. Always read. Only read. Some people, I think, just do not like to waste time—" is he defending his father now, I wonder, or mine? Then he adds, in a whisper, "all the time," and despite himself what had started out, I think, as an excuse has turned into an indictment.

He seems suddenly sad. Well, why shouldn't he be? It's a bleak picture, him sitting there, meal after meal, with no one to talk to and no one, if it was true what Gretta had told me, even trying to teach him the family pastime.

"Well, at least for your father it was learning," I say, trying to twist this, to make him feel better. "For mine it was, and it still is, business. He studied his maps to figure out how to be at meetings on time. We'd be in these fascinating foreign cities and we'd hardly get to see them because he didn't have time and he didn't want us to have fun when he wasn't with us. He'd even lock his maps in his desk," inevitably some heavily polished, reflective affair, "and warn us all, including my mother, that we were not, under any circumstances, to disturb them. He'd say that they were with 'important papers' and that we were not to put 'our sticky little hands' on them." I can recall seeing him, when I was twelve, spank the daylights out of Sean, who had been eleven, because he had seen him touching some shiny reprint—not even an original—of a book he was pushing.

"But, he took you with him?" his voice cuts in, interrupting my memory. Is there a *longing* in it?

"Yes. Sometimes. I guess a lot of the time. But then he'd ignore us. Even when he'd agree to go sightseeing, you could tell that he was thinking about business. Or if it was someplace that he had not been for a while," like Trieste or Geneva or the one time that he had taken us to Wales, "he'd try mostly, it seemed, to remember what life had been like before he'd been married and had kids who slowed him down.

"Of course packing up and moving with all four of us, especially after my youngest brother got sick, wasn't ever easy. But I remember him swooping out of brass-edged elevators expecting us to be already ready. He'd be out of wherever we were waiting in seconds, picking up his pace to keep up front, everyone else having to hurry behind him, my mother all but dragging Donny. This formation was his favourite. I think because it allowed him to pretend that he was alone, without anyone being able to accuse him of abandoning his paternal post. It was our responsibility, *ours alone*, he'd insist, to keep up, to hustle through the streets of strange cities, through the catacombs of unaccustomed corners. In a way it's kind of incredible that not one of us, not even stupid Sean, ever wandered off. Not that this was ever for fear of getting lost, though at the age of eight who wants to get lost in Aberystwyth; but of what he would do to us if we got lost, and then we got found. My father is not a physical man, but he had and he still has his 'ways'"—

In fact, I laugh, a little harshly, understanding at last that it's not so ironic that my father, as irreligious and as unaesthetic as he is, should admire all those cathedrals, one after another, where he has to navigate thru pointed chapels and cramped crypts, viscerally working against others' wills, almost as much as his meetings, which, I know, he never actually enjoys but which he appreciates, respecting what they enable: namely his capacity to outperform *his* father, to outscheme *his* brothers, to exert *his* influence over everyone else's around him.

"My father, too," he adds in, "had his 'ways.'"

My mind turns to him but I stay quiet. I hope, once again, to avoid questions that raise intimacies that he's not told me of himself. I want him to be the one to tie his past to our present.

But when he sidesteps this, I risk callousness to ask, "what were his 'ways'? My father's almost always revolve around work.

He's forever preparing us to take over our business. Did your dad force you to work for him? Not, I mean, like for Mermalain, but by—" I trail off.

He smiles slightly and he shakes his head, "no," then he shakes his head harder, as if to clear away a memory. "No. He never needed this. He had Gretta, and by time I was born he had already taught her what he wanted …" he trails off and we walk on in silence. Surprisingly, it's not an uncomfortable one, as he appears to be neither angry nor even bitter that he had been left out of their 'great work.' He seems simply sad that he had not had much of anyone's company.

"I do not think," he goes on in the same contemplative tone, "that he, that they wanted me. I was a mistake. I—" I protest, but he shakes his head "no"—not unhappily, only honestly—so I stop. It's insulting, I suppose, to claim to know someone's parents, particularly when I've never met them, better than they do. Besides, we both seem to know, if from different angles—mine from Gretta, his from his own experience—that what he had said is probably true. "He was, my father, busy when I was born. He had already other 'obligations,'" he says this like a word he knows all too well. "He used to be a professor, at a university, then later, he had no time to teach *any*one, anymore. My mother I remember mostly as being sick. But so as long as I was quiet or outside, I never bothered them, I think—" again I shake my head, unwilling to imply, even by omission, that I can imagine anyone whom his presence might "bother." "But it is true and perhaps it was better this way. For all of us."

He spreads his fingers out across my hand and he smiles. I reflect back angrily to what she had said of him, that he is not, not really, all that intelligent. How wrong she is. It's not at all that he's not intelligent. It's simply that he has, for his whole life, been ignored.

The irony of this, of course, is staggering.

To let him know that I, at least, am paying attention, I squeeze back his hand, and we walk on so tightly intertwined that we are all but inextricable.

* * *

After a while I realize that we've entered a new part of the city, which he says is called the "Oud-Zuid." "You know," I say, thinking outloud, "this feels an awful lot like a much older Carl—" I've blurted this out before I can do much more than change the ending, "sberg," like the beer.

This is, of course, what he would ask about next. I could have told him about New York or Baltimore or Boston. But, and almost as if he's in a hurry, he asks about "Carlsberg," a place I'm not sure even exists in New Hampshire outside of a can. Not that it matters, because I draw all that I describe from Carlton, which itself could be any affluent New England town not on the coast. So with near perfect impressions, though without revealing any distinguishing particularities, say the architectural irregularities of our eighteenth-century meeting-house townhall, I outline the town's austere ostentations, its puritanical impurities. I describe its white clapboard houses, safe in the summer and warm in the winter, and the little lake and the rip-off yet tourist-free icecream shops and the park gazebos and the Christian country clubs.

I try to convey how it all *seems* so calm with all of its insincere restraints and how it is in fact the quaint restraint of where we are now, after all the excesses of the rld and the air of the Oude Kerk, that reminds me of it. Incongruously I recall the museum that I had gone to on my second, or was it my third? night in Amsterdam. I think of the mannequins and how they must have as much dust on them as there is on the faded gold lamé lining in the window of the Carlton sweet shop, and it strikes me that rather than being tantalizing, both displays are only exhausting.

While I've been letting him glimpse, in a round about way, into my past, we've wandered through the Oud-Zuid, and I decide that with its over two centuries of haut-bourgeois swagger, with its European *chic*, it can't truly be comparable to Carlton. I start to say this only to notice that he has moved so far to my right that I could barely reach out and touch him whereas before we had been walking almost arm-to-hand. It's a metonymic distance that encompasses my having grown up where I had and his having grown up as an indigent immigrant in the rld.

This separateness, however, I suspect, is only temporary and indeed as we leave behind the kept-up brick houses and the cleanish smelling canals, the decreasing propriety, I observe anxiously, unencumbers him, and as he slips closer to me we experience still another shift, an indistinct upsurge in the atmosphere, the sort that you know exists because the air takes on a strange liquidity, a near visibility that makes you feel both in it and under it. The strands of ether around us have become faintly detectable, intermittently accentuated thanks to the cold sun cutting across them, slicing through them in soft serrations, producing a hyperreal feeling of expectation, a nonchalant elation, allowing me to think that today is no less than an allegory of our lives and that we will be alright so long as we end it together

Now the sun slinks down and I am grateful for its impending exit. Red streaks emerge off the horizon and dawdle there, obstinantly resisting the dusk that, in the end, they will embrace. He brushes against me and I rage silently at the world's reluctance to turn upside down, at the cold fire continuing to distill *what* is *as* it is. I long for it to disappear and to drag the rest of this irrational world down with it.

At last the sun has retreated almost entirely, slinking off the edges of buildings and into the canals. Its haze brushes across people's faces and it gives his skin, in particular, a soft golden hue, just barely stubbled. For the first time I find myself admitting consciously how incredibly, how incontestably sexy he is. I whisper this to him and in between us, flanked by our shadows flickering, I see him smiling, shyly at first, and then blushingly, as if he's trying out a new idea.

The last vestiges of light fade out, stretching the silhouettes of buildings and of people into an impossible oblivion, turning the city into an animated mausoleum, really a moving museum, composed not of marble but of bricks and of flesh and of blood. I recall for him what I had read, it seems like ages ago now, burrowed in my bed in my apartment, how the land had evolved from marshes into a settlement, from a settlement into a city, how it had transformed from intrepid maritime trade, spawning exquisite indulgences and stomach-churning exploitations, into what it is today and how he, how *we* are now planting ourselves into its streets, into its history, into its very aura until there's a part of us that will blossom in all of the horror, the hope, and the humanity that is Amsterdam.

    As I depict all this, weaving in what I see around us, he adjusts or amends, a barge becoming a houseboat, a canal a gracht, a café a coffeeshop, for all roads lead to the rld, at least for us, and I recognize once again its outskirts with only the faintest hint of a ruby-red glow amidst the dirty signs of the shops, and still we walk on bringing the refinements of the city into a wonderful relief, details that now flicker and dance across the plum brown of the final flight of the hour with its low ochre beams twisting across the curves of the rusting wrought-iron fences, lingering on so many small stoops with so many flowerpots warily waiting out the winter, while the sunset's last lights recede out into the waterway, reflecting in one final film the muted meaning of our day … and it is all of it so beautiful.

Chapter Eighteen

When I wake the next moring, I do so slowly and disconcertedly. I blink my eyes against a dark impressionism, focus, and see that the sun has grown just strong enough to slip between the curtains. Even its faint advent shames their brazen goldness. After a sequence of semi-incomprehensible jumbles it hits me that this marks my twenty-first day, my third week in Amsterdam.

Turning my head, I find his face next to mine. Drool falls from his lower lip and I reach out my finger to catch just a bit of it. It's calming that it tastes familiar. The rest I let dry unevenly on the sheets. Between this and his sleep-tousled hair, and how many men have seen his *sleep*-tousled hair? I find him impossible to resist. I want to be with him. I also want him to rest. I want to watch him and to love him. I want him to be happy and healthy and whole.

I slide down and he sighs. I hold my breath ... he does not wake. After a while, I feel him moving above me. I look up. His eyes are open. He reaches out to hold my hand. We lie here, letting the normality of the moment drift on, blending into this day, and the day before and the day before.

The past week has been a dream. We've done little more than drift around, sporadically sightseeing, drinking coffee at cafés, taking plenty of time in the mornings and the afternoons to make love. Then we've gone out to grab dinner or just to walk around.

Last night, for a change, we'd sat on a blanket on the floor and had played a boardgame that I had bought at a sketchy convenience store. Our frequent disagreements over what the rules meant had served as a natural excuse for wrestling in between turns. When it had gotten late he had gone out on his own, he had insisted on this, for food. He'd brought back what he called "*snert*," a spicy mixture of peas and frequently meat, which hating the thought of caged animals he won't eat, and "*patats*," which are like "*french fries*," he had explained, proud to be able to toss out an American idiom. He had wanted, he had said, for me to try traditional Dutch street-food. He must have gotten it from some side-street vendor. Certainly not one from Damrak Straat, for it had all tasted fairly fresh.

Sitting on the blanket, we had spread out the food and had a picnic. I'd been touched and bit embarrassed that he had gone out of his way, that he had spent his money on me, despite my having tried to hand him cash. He had so ardently refused it that I had stopped when I had seen he was getting honestly angry. After the meal, he had gone to the bathroom and I had licked clean and hid his plastic fork then stole a pair of his underwear, which he had left folded under a chair, so that I'd remember all this. His warmth, his hands, the way he had looked in his jeans, the way he had looked out of them, so that I would remember that all this had *in fact* existed.

Our indolence spread from that late night picnic, save for a magnificent half-hour or so, into the late morning, and we didn't get out of bed until ten. We took a slow shower and we luxuriated in our unhurried intimacy.

By eleven, we are out on the street. I feel exhilarated and yet exhausted from our aubadic excesses, from misbelieving in our everlasting easiness.

At which point I imagine, but only imagine, that he turns to me and says, "you remember, I have to go back tonight …"

I close my eyes then reopen them.

It's a cold but beautiful day and the architectural atrocities of Damrak Straat stretch out in front of us. I had known of course. On some level. When I leave he will have to go back. It was why I want to give him nights to remember. It's why we were so lazy last night. It was why this morning I had sucked him off so slowly. Nonetheless, part of me wonders, *why* recall a return? Why bring it up at all? My blood rises, but lethargically so. I want to be selfish. I want to fly into a rage.

So I steel myself and say, "I want to go some place special today. So we'll both remember it."

He nods.

"How about the van Gogh museum?" It's cliché but sentimentality can be cold and mechanical as much as hot and excessive.

"You've probably been there before. On a school trip or some such. But I'd like to visit it. What do you think?"

Not a word.

Sometimes talking to him is like talking to a screensaver. Or to a two year old.

"Have you been before?"

He shakes his head "no," but offers no follow up.

"Do you *want* to go?"

He nods his head "yes."

Good. "Great, we can see it for the first time together. I hear it's supposed to be beautiful."

He smiles.

He is beautiful.

Flushed with the unexpected success of this suggestion I get inspired, "and tonight, I'd like to take you to dinner. On a date. On a *real* one."

I say this breathlessly, ecstatically, the words rushing out of my mouth. I turn to him and grab his hand. "Where do you want to go? Anywhere in the city. Somewhere you haven't been before." Is that rude, I wonder? But where all could he have been, untreated, if, as he says, he saves all he can? "Somewhere we can make 'our restaurant.'"

He looks confused. Likely he doesn't understand the expression. I laugh, though only due to the sheer joy of thinking that I can offer *him* a new experience. No doubt he thinks I am being silly.

All the same, he plays along.

"How about somewhere outside the district," he suggests,

"but not too far from it." As much as he dislikes, and for obvious reasons I suppose, that part of the city, he clearly distrusts any place too far beyond it.

"Of course," I say, noticing how my voice sounds high pitched and happy. My body has filled with an optimistic energy, an anticipation stemming from my feet, branching in my stomach, and flowering in my brain.

After this we bounce from museum to museum, starting off at the gorgeous glass-and-steel structure dedicated to the world's most-beloved posthumously reprieved psychotic post-impressionist. Janêk himself seems pleased that he recognizes several of the canvases. I had half expected this. First because he's smarter than he says he is, and second because the rld practically seethes with *Starry Nights* and *French Café Terraces*. He had thought, he tells me, that they were by someone named "van *Gokh*" rather than "van *Go*." I'm glad I refrain from correcting him because seconds later this is precisely how I hear a tour guide pronounce the madman's name.

A bit beautifully, what really draws Janêk is not the surprisingly shiny originals of the rld's imitations but the painter's calmer japonaiseries. So instead of gawking at the manic luminaries of van Gogh's night visions, we spend most of our time in front of the beautifully blue *Almond Blossoms* and the red *Flowering Plum Tree*. His absorption in the artist's exoticism enflames mine in his own and so with an intertwined acuity we admire the slender tranquilly twisted trees and the vague white wisps of willows and Geisha gowns, images that other visitors scarcely peep at in their drive to locate the star-studs, those oozing orgies of oil that they can boast to their friends that they've seen, if only through the crude screens of their cameras, which flatten all the heavily textured tableaux.

After the van Gogh we duck into the nearby Stedelijk. At first its abstractions offer a reprieve from the storied intensity of what we've just seen. As we move through though he grows jittery and I do too. The bold golds and severe silvers, gored reds and metallic greens grow openly aggressive. Sympathy seems scarce here, as if it'd been abandoned for a coldly considered sensuality, a late-twentieth-century obsession with concrete heads and unambiguous bodies, the cruelty of a barely controlled construction.

Outside we walk until we see a bold green sign with bright white letters. The "*Heineken Experience.*" In my state of mind it's an *objet d'art* as a beautiful ball-capped god struts past it and we both, I notice, peer after him until a swarm of fat American frat boys and a distinct sort of Eurotrash flush into focus behind him, all fusing together to form their own genre of post-abstract art.

As we get closer, moving past the Heineken Experience, the crowd blurs differently again until a large man with a mustache and a hat proclaiming his allegiance to the caricaturized beast of some sports team smashes into him. My him. Instead of apologizing, the bully acts irate. His body flushes while his body shrinks. I grab his arm, and he flinches until he realizes who it is that's touching him, while the man mercifully huffs off.

Violence and protection, affection and anger, so often so confused in the context of touch.

The city grows cold again, the time grows late, and we have not yet had lunch. Finding a nearby *eetcafé* we order cheese sandwiches and I get a local beer. It's fun to hear him speak Dutch, particularly after I had to point to what I want. My beer comes. He must not have realized I had ordered it, for he stares at the glass.

"What?" I ask, feeling foolish. But I am not his sister.

Eventually he's willing to talk again and our conversation grows light and easy. Someone brings our food and we concentrate on eating. The server comes around again and I order "een meer," pointing to my glass, "een klein," a small one.

When we leave the *eetcafé* it's with the pleasant feeling of having rested and of having food in our bellies. I feel mine sloshing around agreeably with the last bits of lager. It's warmed up a bit and a ray of sunshine brushes torpidly against my cheek. Despite his renewed surliness, the city has never seemed so fresh and so accommodating.

I spot a pale yellow flyer inviting people to a quartet concert tonight at the *Noorderkerk*. Pointing to it, I suggest that we go.

He nods silently but in agreement.

As we walk my eyes flit between the sidewalk and his face. He looks upset. He's still thinking, I suspect, about that beer. I like that a decision that I've made can irritate him. It means that he has expectations for me.

He leads the way as I consider this until I see that we're once again in front of the Heineken Experience. Here though he starts across the street, away from the flat factory yard and towards an old rock wall.

"I want to show you," he says, "my favorite place in Amsterdam."

So he isn't mad, or he is and he isn't. Either way I exult in my relief.

We turn round a bend and I see a gate opening discreetly into a garden. I half-hope that we're headed into it but whether we are or not I have abandoned control to him. With the sun and the trees and with him just in front of me, his back for once tall and firm, and not at all tentative, and with him not mad at me after all, or not too too much, I follow him feeling contented.

We slip quickly through the tall metal arch that forms the garden's gate. A few steps in and we're already cut off from the clamor of clanging cars and the catcalls of traders and tourists. What's left is the seraphatic stillness of an unexpectedly private public park.

Looking around, I see stretching out before me acre after acre of a yellowish-greenish, occasionally coffee-colored grass, invisible only a few seconds ago but now stretching inevitably forward, conjoining, until it's hemmed in to the right and to the left by winding walkways and paths. A thick far-reaching ivy stretches out in swathes, ascending out of short savage shrubs to cover the park's walls. The sun plays on the ground, bathing it in a muted multiplicity, beaming and scowling in and out of widening arboreal arms so that the half-cold heat and the undetached shadows mutter to each other, animating the whole underpainted picture, the entire urban eclogue.

I can see why he likes this. It has a sparse balance, a dully aching beauty. In spring and summer it must be magnificent, with colorful tulips, roses, and picnic-ers. But bared to its elements, its primary benefit is its repose. A few scattered couples sit here or there and one or two old men wander around on their own.

"It is quiet here," he says, "in winter. People come, but—" he juts out his hand towards brown grass, "is all that they see, so they go. They do not know that there is this rest."

With him holding my hand, he leads us off the path and on to the lawn. He sits and I follow him. The grass is rough, like little knives sticking into my hands though these retreat as I settle into them.

In front of us sleeps an earthy, iridescently dull lake. A derelict gazebo daydreams out in it, off-center and empty. This would all appear desolate save that both his gaze and mine meet somewhere in the middle, mingling as we watch the bronze-like light fade across the ripples of the water.

I glance at him. The tinge of fire on his cheek makes him look like some shaky seraph in denim.

In a vision, I see him falling away from me, into the water, unable to swim. I'm on the shore, enamored, yet I am powerless to go in and save him. I see him sinking.

Earlier the sky had been clear. Several darkish clouds now skirt toward us. Heralding them are a few fragile flakes of snow. Typically, I had read, it doesn't snow in Amsterdam. This and the events of a week ago are anomalies. But here it is and here we are and, as if for the first time, though by now it is certainly not, I am amazed to find him sitting beside me. Flesh and blood and bone, breathing and thinking and capable of getting hurt, or even of just catching cold. I see him shiver. His coat is not as thick as mine, so I offer him my scarf. He's staring at the water and doesn't notice. I wrap it around him. I want to kiss him but I don't. So I sit back down.

I look out over the lake and some associative synapse fires. I find myself recalling, "I read once online about a party," and I wonder why I'm telling him this, for compared to what he does it will only sound, well, *amateurish*, "called an 'underwear party.' Usually, I'd read, these take place at some undisclosed location, at some guy's house or at an apartment … But all those who went to this one—kids mostly about our age—jumped into a fountain in New York City's Central Park in the summer. They did it, they said later, because it was hot and the water was going to waste;—anyway, for whatever reason they leapt in and started splashing, for a quarter of an hour or so, and then they lifted one another out, laughing, their limbs soaked and slippery. The catch was, they had held this party in the afternoon, so they were noticed. Two policemen saw them, although only after, when they were already out but were still covered with a telltale sheen to their skin, in their soaking wet underwear, and with plastered hair, surrounded on all sides by middle-aged men and a few women—and they were arrested."

We sit back and watch the lake, watching its shiny muddy surface blinking up at us, opaquely.

The sun wanes and shadows extend all around us.

The snowflakes are gone but the wind sends the water to the shore in lackluster laps.

A bird chirps. Another answers. The footfalls of an intruder come close then fade away. The resonance of the story dissipates.

"I think," he starts timidly, as if he must first arrange his words, "that you are like Gretta. Not in all ways. But you both have, how do you say? too much *romantika*, too many books, too much history. You have too much to think when you wake up. You cannot," he sighs, "just go. Eating, shopping, sex, walking in a park. These can be fun on their own, and this is alright. You need not critique them or compare them to enjoy them. It's the fault," he says, bitterly now, "of your *univers*ity."

"I'm not sure," I say, "that I know what you mean." My voice sounds cold, as if it's coming from outside myself.

Each of us looks in front of us. I try to ignore him. To retreat into myself. Abruptly the world is too obscure. Too hard to understand. Too avernal. Rudely or refinedly I focus on the drab ripples lapping the shore. They create an all too nice, perhaps for him an all too irrelevant, reality, each ripple eroding the existence of some manmade restraint.

"Stories," I say softly, "records, histories, these are not just weights or ruins. She focuses on what they show us is wrong. Fine. But they can also show us what's right, or what should be. They add energy, attraction even to what's around us. Wouldn't it be better to know what this water hides beneath it than to see, from only one angle, its surface? Or what it has held? Or whose hearts it has cradled, rocking one body into another? From another angle, I like it better because it reminds me of those boys at that fountain. I like it best because I'm by it with you and its history now intersects with ours. But imagine if we knew just a bit about everyone who has walked around it? Stories. Pictures. Paintings. They provide a prism," would he know the word prism? "that turns parks into paradises, night-cafés into quests, that links the past to the present and extends it in ink or in oils. Stories, histories, art," I say, excited now, "are how we make meaning—"

"No," he interjects, interrupting me, for I think the first time ever, "is how *you* make meaning—"

I'd gotten carried away. The softstark sound of his voice jerks me back to where I am.

I wait a second, then say, "fine, how do *you* make meaning?"

He shrugs. "I just do. I walk. Mornings after work, I sleep. When I wake, I walk. I look at people. I learn 'who is who'"—he sounds like an owl and I smile—"the *vreemdelingen*, the *allochtonen* in Biljmer, where I sleep, everyday Amsterdammers in de Vatergrafsmeer, the *kosmopolieten* and the *snobs* in de Pijp and near here, and the Americans, and occasionally the English and the German, in de Vallen. I hear them. I learn '*ther ack-cents*,'" he's trying out his American one, I think, so I laugh, "and their clothes. And once a year, in the summer, I go to the countryside for some time away from Beaumount House ... this is pretty, but expensive and I feel not so welcome. When I am here though, I do not imagine what is not. I have done this only with you, and this I think is not so good.

"But," he murmurs, now almost under his breath, looking out at the lake and, I suspect, ignoring me, "when I go to bed, I dream before I sleep. Not awake, not asleep, but no more Beaumount House. No more smelly old men."

My throat convulses. I bow my head and I try, discreetly, to smell myself.

I'm not sly enough and he catches me. He laughs and he shakes his head. I smile back, shyly. The tension breaks. He leans forward and, for an instant, he rests his head on my shoulder. Thankfully, when I'd sniffed it, my wool coat had held only a hint of Amsterdam, of its twin traces of pot and the possibilities that linger *in perpetuum* in the rld.

I rest my cheek on his head. "What if I sent you books. Would you read them?"

"I would try, but—"

He picks his head up, stretches his legs, and sighs.

"But what?"

"But this has happened before. Not for me, but for others. Someone will say, 'I will write to you' or 'I will call for you,' or 'not after this trip but after the next, I will invite you to—' I know that this isn't what you meant, but all this, it never works out."

He looks ridiculously attractive. Desperately I want his head to return to my shoulder, so I resist pointing out that I'd never mentioned an invitation to anywhere beyond Amsterdam. A breeze twists and turns, and it carries his scent. It's faint but it's strong enough to remind me that by my side is a living breathing being who I want to be with so badly that it's as agonizing as it is exciting to admit that he exists on his own.

"Really though, despite what people think, Beaumount is not our beginning or our end. The boys, too, like the clients, they come and go. To other houses. To other careers. To other lives entirely. Sometimes, when I start to sleep, I think of one place someone once told me about. By a sea. Where it is hot in the day and warm at night and the sun is so sweet it never burns. Where there is not so much rain and not so much worry. Where people work and rest outside. Even in winter."

He relates all this with an oddly impassive detachment, "and when the sun shines at noon it is so warm that you need not even wear clothes," I wonder who has told him about this, "so that all the boys, and there are so many of them, right round our age, take them off and—just as you said—go swimming. Together. Everyone lifting everyone up in the sun, their chests shining so bright that you can see them brown and hot, and after this they catch fresh fish each one helping the others and they cook them on a fire in sand smelling of pine and of grass floating sweet and smooth and curling and they drink only what they want when they want it water or fresh wine and after they lay down and the wind runs through them wild drying their toes and the salt and the sand until they cannot take it and run to go wash themselves not five meters out to the sea

he pauses as if to contemplate the arid fertility of this eden and when anyone is tired or old they simply sit down at the edge of the sand enjoying the touch of the wind and the hunger for the dinner that they know the boys are cooking them and when everyone has eaten they sit sleepy and satisfied listening to the sounds from the boys making music and dancing on the sand with the shells made of memories from nights long ago and the thousands of lights of stars shining deep into the sea until even the last movements are done and the next day everyone wakes up and it begins all over again forever and ever until it is done

he blinks. his face has grown long and serious. does he suspect that, even if this place does exist, he will never sleep there?

"Of course I know that there is no place like this, that it is a 'lie'. It was a dream told by one boy in the house late at night, that an old 'member' had told him and he was drunk and probably high and he had been 'pretend' beaten by our 'Baronette von Pregnintz,' and of course I see their life here. I see the boys drunk or with weed. *He* says '*no drugs*' but weed is alright. I see boys crazy from coca. So I save money. I save one euro for every five I make so one day I will sail somewhere, to Sydney, to South Beach," he nods as if to say, 'I know these places,' and I hear their names slipping off the decrepit lips of some debauched old decadent ...

He tapers off now and sits still, and I am left on my own, with the sham sentimentalities with which I have, without thinking, enveloped him—"I will write to you ..."

He sits solidly here, however, and utterly without resentment. He knows that his island is unreal but he has nonetheless been enacting a long-range plan. Free from prepackaged paths (oh, poor me, I know) with a career, a wife and kids, he's working not to set himself free, no one can do that, but to run off, out of sight. I, of course, of all people, should sympathize. Still this makes me hot, jittery, and almost *angry*. It's absurd, but I *am*—I am angry. For this is the most that he has shared with me, the most that he has told me about what goes on in his head, and he has not once suggested, not even *intimated* that I would be one of the sunswept boys on his beach. In his daydream he exists utterly alone while I, like a fool, like I am always the fool, have been weaving his way hard into mine.

We sit next to each other, a hand's breadth away, yet already we're living diverging lives.

I am as good as alone again, and yet I want–no, I *resent* his independence! I want him to want me. I want him to want me to rescue him. I feel a lust filled with self-loathing, for in order for me to save him, his mind has to be here. But how in good conscience can I even attempt to tempt it back? So I sit here stupidly, watching him daydream at a distance with open eyes.

After a bitter perpetuity, he twitches and his hand, at first just barely, grazes my knee.

He smiles wanly. Cymbals do not crash and lightning does not strike. I can tell that he's alright and that he does not need me. Not to save him. Not now and probably not ever. But he is glad, I suspect, that I am here, and for now that will have to be enough.

Chapter Nineteen

When we leave the park we decide to go to his sister's.
Of course I'd been there just last night but it feels as if it's been years. It actually has been years since he's visited. But I want him to come and he consents. He feels bad, I suspect, for having left me behind in the grass.
I am excited to see them meet. And it will be helpful, in a few days, to know that he is not alone in the city. I half-hope too that being with someone else might alleviate, if only for a little while, the intensity of our being alone together. Since she runs roughshod over others' anxieties, she will at least be a distraction.
With an awkwardly artificial offhand manner, I ask when he had last seen her.
He can't remember, he says, but it was in some café in the district, not at the apartment. I know this, of course, because she had told me.
"Well, she always asks about you—"
He glances at me in a way that makes me jump tracks, "but we can leave whenever you want. Just give me some sort of sign and we're off."
We walk on in silence.
"But how do you know," he asks, "that she will be at home? And that she will not be ..."
"Working?"
"No," he says and he looks at me squeamishly.
"Oh! No. No, no, no."

Tonight, she had told me, would be an "evening at home" but not a "working" one, in any sense of the word. Just yesterday she had sent to press a series of paternal pamphlets critiquing how states fund militarism over medicine. They are small, she had said, and seemingly scandalous, so they should sell.

Regardless, we are on our way.

By the time we reach her apartment though, I too am reluctant to go up. As if rebelling against the lethargy of the park, I am now charged with energy and vaguely lightheaded. It's the result of having hurried here, of growing hot in the cold only to be thrust into the fetid air imprisoned within these walls.

It is also of course from being here with him. From seeing— well, I can't say 'from seeing him where he was raised'—but from seeing him where he had grown up. It's disconcerting. I feel as if I am peeping, depravedly, into some place I should not. Probably because he would never, I know, have taken me here on his own.

This makes me a voyeur. This is voyeuristic.

It's creepy and at the same time it's *inflaming*, though it's not satisfying one half of one zillionth of my desire to know all about him. I want to know each millimeter of him, about each crevice, about each hair from the time he was born until now, about each atom inside of him. As a start, I reach out and I hold his hand. I want to keep on as I crave the heat of his body back in our hotel room. I consider how I have kissed him, how I have touched and I have tasted him, from his armpits to between his toes to the knotted hole behind him, how I have slept alongside him, and this thought fills me with an elation so great that even the piles of rotting wrappers, of burned-out cigarette butts, of broken bottles, and of all the indignant refuse, that none of it can corrupt our happiness.

As we walk up the steps, I wonder what memory each one must hold for him. From the hallway, we hear a faint flood of music. A door opens and it leaks out over us. My god, this is surreal. Then there she is and there's the shock of seeing one's lover's face contorted and aged on someone else's skull.

She welcomes us into the apartment, moreso me, I notice, than him. There's a slight flush to her china-doll cheeks. I don't think from alcohol. As we move in she announces that this evening an old school acquaintance will be passing through and so she has beer. Presumably, I imagine, to show off, in the most slighting of ways, Amsterdam. She offers us one. I nod. He declines. She goes out and brings back two dark ambers in pint glasses.

All the while, with the weight of her books in the back, she seems to be both showing off and denying him his few hereditary rights.

We sit down and I suspect that they will have an abundance to catch up on, shared stories of their past, their present, family members, how I met each one of them. This imprecise surplus though seems to overwhelm them. My skin crawls with excitement, which turns to an uneasy itching as, watching their awfully mirrored images, I sense that the whole meeting might erupt into one unquenchable emptiness. With little eye contact, we all sit silently, waiting for I don't know what.

After staring at us for a while, she settles into her armchair and opens a window. Inching closer to the sill, she lights a cigarette. He crouches, his knees almost to his elbows, next to me. I watch awkwardly as they avoid each other's eyes. She smokes and examines her nails, all chewed up and ugly. He doesn't look anywhere but at his feet. Is he afraid of dredging up more memories? Could they really be all that bad? For the first time it strikes me that they could be and that my bringing him here was a mistake. All the while a cello holds a note out over us, alone, until a piano cuts it in half. He flinches. What right did I have to—

"So what," she asks, her voice going off like a gun, "have you two been doing?"

She asks only me, it seems, ignoring him.

Taking advantage of her opening to relieve some of the tension, I report that we'd been to the van Gokh museum and then to the Stedelijk and then to the park. "Tonight," I say, "we're going to a concert at the—" I turn to him, "how do you say it?"

"De *Noorderkerk*." His voice sounds high and close, as if it's an echo without an original.

I take a sip of beer. In the stifling warmth of the apartment the wetness increases my shakiness, threatening to turn it into giddiness.

"A concert. Of course. But Janchêk, will it not be wasted, so much, on you? So many sad sounds? Will you not run from the room? Will you not *cry*?"

Her tone is so biting that it's as if she had whipped him.

I expect his face to fall. But he simply sits still as if he's immune.

"Why would you say that?" I ask. She smiles and she shifts in her chair. Someone should defend him, as it's clear that he won't fight for himself. "Why would it be wasted on him? 'So many sounds,' 'so many sad sounds.' You think that he won't understand them all? No one hears every note, so—"

"I do, I hear every note—"

"Fine, whatever," I am not willing to argue this, "but why would he cry?" She treats him as if he's still a baby. If everyone has always treated him like this then it's a miracle that he has grown up at all—and he has.

I look at him. He looks as if he wants to disappear into the couch cushion.

Immediately I regret the question.

She however takes it up with relish, as if she enjoys torturing him and maligning me.

"It's certainly not because of the music. No. Is because someone—some cousin I think, no Janchêk? That boy whose penis you touched?—played Tchaikovsky at our mother's funeral and since then—" she shrugs, "he has cried whenever he has heard strings."

I must be looking at her oddly because she specifies, "no, not *modern* work, such as this, not Shostakovich. Funny, is it not? Look at him: it upsets him but he can hold it in, and not *street* sounds, like your 'rap' or your '*pop*,'" she smacks her lips.

As usual, she makes sweeping indistinctions. My "rap" and my "pop" because I am American, and because she has not advanced into the twenty-first century. But now that the opportunity of forcing some academic or aesthetic point on her has presented itself, I am no longer all that interested.

Other affairs have taken over.

I turn to him, getting down on my knees, my blood racing. "Look. I didn't know. How could I have?" when so often you won't give me one *clue*! I grab his hands. "Of course we won't go tonight. We'll go somewhere else. Somewhere—"

"*No*," he interrupts, whispering, "it is all right."

"Of course you should go," she says. "It is *good* for him and it is good for you, too. You will see him in a new light."

I jump up.

"I don't care what the light is," I tell him, "so long as you're in it," he smiles. My heart fills, as if to bursting, with warmth, "and I bet this concert will be worth it. Just imagine that the music is for dancing, slow or fast, everyone together, with exquisite movements," I mimic a minuet, pulling him up with me, "which is, originally, what most of it was for anyway."

For an overflowing instant he's up with me, my arms are around him, his head is nestling into my neck, no longer a passive automaton. I can smell his skin. His eyes look flushed and feverish. His hands are on my waist and we move. Then he's pulling away again, falling back down to the couch.

"—no, no, it is not true," I hear a voice say, "not all music is meant for this, for fun," she spits.

She's mocking me, switching her attack from him to me and through me to him, cruel psychological circuits, made worse because she is, as almost always, right.

"but what *we'll* hear will be—"

"Of course, if you only hear half of it! Your brains—"

"We'll hear half with our ears and half with our hearts!"

Behind me I hear him giggle, a tense half-laugh.

"That is *facile*," she snaps, "and you know it. I will not speak to you if you speak like a child."

I smile demurely, shifting from one foot to another, full of anxious energy. I hate her making fun of him; I love her arrogance. I hate his refusal to confront her; I love his tender mind in his pliant body.

I'm not sure if it's the friction of my feelings or the heat in her apartment, but I'm getting increasingly warm, and more than a little on edge.

I think back to his laugh.

Despite its tension, it lifts me up. I feel as if I am floating. As if the buoyancy of the beer and the slump-swing of his voice have elevated my body beyond its use. I start bouncing *childishly* around, trying not to get my energy out but to use it up. Leaning back to him, I kiss him. He blushes, quickeningly. Leave it to me, I think, to pick the one shy prost—anyway for the first time I have an amorous *raison d'avancer*: I am his shining chivalric, his obscure-errant, his *amour* armed only with my philosophy of the future, my future philosophy, which I will use to rescue him:—

"'*Mon bel ami, tout vien de nous,*'" I whisper.

He looks back at me and whispers, "what?"

"It doesn't matter," I say, jumping up, "whether we hear half a piece or all of it, the art is in the attempt!"

Stepping out of my way she shoots me a withering glance. "The art is *not* in 'the *attempt*,' and again, you should know this. The art is in the use."

I jump over to the cabinet.

"Do not touch this!" she shouts as I put my hand on its door, "it is fragile. You are an overexcited clumsy American and you will *break* it!"

"Come on, the 'art is in our *ab*-use'!"

His laughter bubbles out again, a little louder this time, and a touch deliriously.

It's the heat. The apartment is becoming a hotbox.

"The music, at least, is not so breakable. Should we turn it up?"

My hand moves to the volume.

"No!" she snaps and I jump, involuntarily this time, "and sit *down*. It is impossible to *think* with you *hop*-ping all over the place."

Stunned, I stare at her, then I jump forward again with more energy than ever, brushing my hand across her collection, "alright," I say, "what we need is a record with a little more 'oomph,' with an 'al-leg-ro,' you know …"

"No! There you go again," now she's shouting at me, over me, over the music, and the situation has become almost hysterical. "It is not '*what we need*,' '*what we need, what we need,*' *music* is not a *need*." Now she's deriding me, making frustrated fun of me, while remaining, as always, inelegantly articulate. "This is your willful disorder, you mistake your *wants* for your *needs*."

Alright, so says the woman who can't function without a record on and as much vodka as oxygen in her circulatory system. The line between wants and needs is not always so strong.

I look at Janêk and at last, as if having held my breath for hours, I'm in desperate need, a *real* need, of fresh air. Dodging around her table and almost knocking over my beer, "*William*" I hear her shout, I throw up her window and I thrust my head through it. I take a deep breath and … I choke.

I cough and my chest burns.

All the pent-up tension of living for weeks under a strange sky shivers through me.

She shakes her head, half-amused, half-irritated-beyond-belief, "are you on *coke*?"

Heading back towards him, I drain the rest of my beer and wipe my mouth.

"No."

"Well, *what* has gotten into you?"

I look at Janêk.

"I am in love," I answer, then laugh, struck still on the edge of absurdity.

"Ehhh," she turns her head away, exasperated.

I am bemused and standing still. Half-hearing the record, I feel every limb, every inch of my body tingling. I feel tendons and sinews, blood and bones, my healing stab wound, I feel my molecular extravagances in harmony with the objects around me, with her cigarettes, with the wretched couch, with the rotting fruit in her fridge, with the books in the bedroom. I stand still destilling this, feeling Gretta, feeling Janêk, feeling the eccentric old woman stretched out on her couch, her dirty mane entangled, her heart st—no, her hand moves. Outside I hear the wind and the sounds of the streets, whispering with the music.

As flushed as I had been, I now feel drained.

"It's all a myth, a modern day myth, an earthly allegory, people living, going on, making money, work, romance ... these are all merely myths."

"These are not 'merely myths,' *William*," she sneers, my name become one long tone on her tongue, "what people go through, how they live, what my father wrote. This is all not only an 'allegory.' It may not seem real—"

"of course"

"to *you*! But it is— ... in parts."

She points an exceedingly long finger at me, extending it until I can see its too short tooth-hewn nail. "Some 'stories' *comme* '*histoires*,' no?—are not just words—of course, sit down—which are not real, their ideas, even, are *perhaps* not real, even if someone believes them. But facts, actions, these are flesh-and-blood and *are* real *andyouareafoolifyouthinkthattheyarenot!*"

She pauses.

Beside me, he shifts uncomfortably.

As always, there is the music.

"Well, who knows," I say dejectedly, as she scoffs, "and if they *are* real, they're still just a half-written reality, even if only in our heads. What I did, what you do, what I think of you, what you think of me, most depressingly what we'll remember about what we did and said in ten years' time. They're just feelings that end up, when you reflect on them, in the stories that we tell to ourselves and to each other. Who we are or were, who we were with and where and when, and what it's all worth. It's all of it just words that can be rewritten, re-remembered, pulled apart, and spliced together again."

It's sad because even if I imagine a port-winey sort of elegiac alchemy, my existence here only a year from now could have become somewhat suspect. Worse, someone, anyone, say Janêk, could rewrite our present to usher in a newer, 'truer' aurean age, one in which I was simply a step that had just been stepped past.

"Haven't you said, for instance, that some parts of your father's work are archaic? Or even wrong? That he had overaccounted for collectivity and underestimated individuality? Well, why don't you revise that? Revive it. Use your 'stochastic' second-sight."

I mean well and I look up to see her agree, to see her uninhibited ecstasy, as freed from the cello line a viola reaches its apex overhead.

I turn to him and smile, as if to say 'see? I can create an accord.'

But there is only a scratching.

Gretta gets up and restarts the record.

Returning she says, and more calmly, I think, than either he or I had expected, "someday, I suspect, I will.—But," and here her voice raises, "first we must finish the tasks at hand, and for this we cannot 'rethink' someone else's ideas. Not how you mean. We would have no certainty, no *honesty* at all." She says this with the barren heaviness of a Sisyphus, not giving an inch for dissent.

Certainty? I am confused. Definite facts and interpretations, these, I agree, we must remember, and as *exactingly* as we are able; but to refine again and again so much exegetic minutiae evokes the incestuous floridity of a reactionary renaissance.

Desperately I want to reveal, to revel in her heterodoxy, in her regressiveness, in her selfless selfishness—as she so often reviles mine—to rate her own oaths as absolute. But she puts forth her front so forcefully that I forbear from inquiring into its weaknesses.

The look on his face moreover warns me not to continue. From the back of my mind, I recall what he had suggested about her father's work, about the onus it was on her, its overarching encumbrance.

I picture an old man who, by his end, could not have been more than two bright eyes, having his breakfast, his intentions infusing their apartment like his overcrowded tea strainer, excessively steeped. I see him pull some book off a shelf, handing it to her with a shaky solemnity, passing a single scratched piece of paper, his hands trembling, the quivering bend in his arm insisting to her that *es muss sein*. It would have been an agony even to be one's self in such a saturation.

It must have been excruciating, and still she stagnates. What an irony. With that all her education, with all her ideas, she is unable to act, constrained by one undying wish of the dead. She is sterile.

Deflated, she and I finish our beer, studiously avoiding any final subject of substance. She offers one last drink, I decline, then he and I take off for our concert.

Chapter Twenty

By the time we reach the Noorderkerk, the sky is already turning to dusk. As we approach, I see the shadows thrown out by a thick, obliquely Greek-inspired edifice, a sturdy structure prepared to withstand a staid apocalypse.

A filtered light emanates from inside it.

Its coolness offers an odd opposition to my mood. Unable to help it, though I try, I am irritated. He has lived in Amsterdam for almost eighteen years, and still we had gotten off-track *twice*. Of course I was leading us ... but I am *always* leading us because he doesn't know where any place is. He didn't know where the van Gogh museum was or where the Lindengracht was. Then he didn't know where the Noorderkerk was. It's as if the red-light district and wherever it is that he lives are the only two places that exist for him here. No wonder he is still turning tr—

Well, who cares? We are here.

Thankfully, people are still arriving and a line trickles slowly through the door, everyone moving with an orderly, if occasionally quavering, correctness. Undersized old ladies in middle-class fur coats hang off the arms of carelessly coiffed men. More people my–*our* age in couples or in groups of fours or fives than I have ever seen at a concert in the U.S. amble in talking and laughing.

The ecclesiastical insides are obstinately bland. The red brick exterior has morphed into an unassaulting yet severe white, an atonement for the extravagant accusations of its medieval antecedents. Here sin is hardly taken into account with the scarcely curved sinews of the ceiling dulling impenitent souls. Should any look up at its stunted height, its stark wooden bounds would dampen any attempt at awe, or conversation. If the Noorderkerk were the seat of someone's soul, it would be that of some cold, narrowmindedly clean burgomeister.

Suddenly, what an unexpected coincidence! I see Charléus grasping the shoulder of a skinny young man in corduroy. He takes off his hat and—he turns out to be someone else. Gradually, Janêk and I, we, wind a tacitly restrained path to two of the hard wooden seats set up temporarily, I suppose, in view of a modest organ. Both of us admire its narrow magnificence, its gold-accented yet vaguely democratic demeanor. He nudges me and I'm not sure whether I want to smile or whether I am still annoyed. I look over and I catch him staring off into space. It was an accident. His knee is shaking back and forth in its unkempt khaki. For an instant, I am disgusted. His whole body comes across as awkward and infantile and it exudes the sickly-sweet smell of piss. I shudder and I force myself to reassess this. It is, after all, a body I have covered in kisses, and he is here for me.

I elbow him, gently.

"What is it," I ask, forcing myself to look at him.

He shakes his head and a single tawny lock falls over his left eye. He pushes it back. He is, he signals, alright.

What's worrying him?

I constrain myself to sit still, silent but by his side.

His leg has stopped shaking. But it soon starts up again. I put my hand on it, ignoring the odd difficulty of this, and I whisper once again, "*What's wrong?*"

He shakes his head.

"Why won't you tell me?" There's an edge to my voice, which I instantly regret.

An older woman to our right peers at us out of the corner of her eye. I glare back. Her eyes turn towards a painting of, who else? St. Sebastian. Most Dutch, according to my guidebook, are "tolerant" of "alternative lifestyles." The two of us simply sitting here, our collared shirts peeking out over our sweaters, could not possibly offer much, to Amsterdamians, of an actual "alternative." This woman however has an air of abstem–no of obstinacy about her, with her puffed-up and faded flaxen hair, which no one could imagine crushing against a pillow. She has condescendingly arched eyebrows and just a little too much fat spilling out of her jacket. She sits in her chair like a sixties-ish lady-in-waiting, settled in her role by the weight of inherited jewelry, a sure sign that no bona fide care for comfort could ever be uppermost in her mind.

When her eyes shift away from us, my own move to the man sitting next to her. He must be her husband. He looks about sixty-five or seventy and is paunchy but well-put together. Cool and unruffled, he seems deceptively sanitary with a fresh silk handkerchief folded loosely into his breast pocket. A pillar to aspire to. Then I see his eyes flicker towards us. No, not towards *us* but towards *him*. His nostrils twitch. Extorting eyes run over Janêk's face and his midsection with an awful familiarity. Immediately I suspect he knows him. Professionally. I get hot and I feel my face flush. My clothes feel too tight. She couldn't possibly know Janêk but a lifetime of neglect could explain why she's so collectedly irate ...

Well, I am too. For all too quickly it's hard not to imagine that many if not most of the men in the room have had him, or are now leering at him, including some of the knife-blade bodied boys who came in with girls and are obviously on dates. One mottled man, whose sloppy suit strains to bursting, has leaned behind his wife to stare at him twice. He's clearly not the caliber of the Beaumonde clientel. But a part of him looks like he'd hand over the family farm just to touch him; another part looks like he'd commit untold atrocities afterward so that he could return to just sitting still.

Next I realize, Janêk has left, his program abandoned on his seat and he's walking, really all but running back up the aisle.

For a second, I sit still. Waiting to deflate, and in the midst of my frustration I detect a forgotten feeling. Self-loathing.

When I finally catch up with him he's disappearing through a small empty corridor. Around a corner, I cut him off against a wall. Behind us, in the lobby, the final stragglers mill on towards their seats.

I'm not sure if he knows why I've been irritated or why for the past hour I've been unable to look at him. Then again perhaps his flight had not been related to me at all.

He looks at me and in his eyes, which by now I have learned to read with an absurd precision, I see sadness and desertion, and, above all, strength. My need for him gives me a knot in my abdomen.

He holds himself excruciating still, as if both warning me off and inviting me in, and without thinking and before I can stop myself, my hands are on his face and I am kissing him and kissing him and kissing him. His hands move to my waist and I feel him fumble, as if he's unsure of what precisely he should do with me.

Grabbing his arm I pull him through a door, into an empty classroom. Turning the lock on the knob I close us off and we're plunged into darkness. On the other side of the far wall the instruments tune up and the music starts, and as it plays, I use my mouth, my spit, and my will to make love to him as best I can ...

L'Éternel retour

Chapter Twenty-One

The next few days go by like a flood and we spend all of them together. We go to his park, we eat, we explore, and in between stops we return hurriedly to our hotel. Once we take a day trip to Delft and we spend an entire morning walking along the canals. We eat cheese sandwiches and we drink Belgian beer for lunch. Even he has one. He gets slightly tipsy and he laughs a lot. Afterwards, we walk around in the sun then we find a secluded area in a park. The next day we rent bikes and we ride them around the outskirts of Amsterdam. Once, when it rains, we see a movie. We hold hands the entire time. When it's over, we run back to our room.

Twice, late at night, we visit Gretta. In an unspoken deference to him, we meet outside her apartment. We sit in cafés, drinking coffees or hot chocolates, once a pot-milkshake, which he flatly refuses to share, while she sips cheap jenever. Walking to and from cut-rate but not uncomfortable hole-in-the-wall koffiehuisen, she talks to me of the district, of the women, sometimes men, she has met, many of them foreigners who, unlike her, had fled west with scarcely any secondary education at all—"and this," she says, waving her hand, "is what greets them. They hear 'opportunity!' 'smart city!' 'clean streets!' But they, even those who have degrees, end up in the slums. Still," she muses, "it is better *here* than elsewhere …~"

On other nights, when he, for whatever reason, has to return to his flat, though he always comes back to the hotel to sleep, she teaches me how to watch the city. Not like a tourist, whose eyes glaze over with guidebook reports, or like a vacationer, who invests a scene with daydreams, but like a refined flâneur. She shows me how, at the peak hours in the rld, it's more revealing to watch not the red-lighted windows but the shadowy dartings around them. To spot who flashes through a dull door directly before a flimsy but opaque curtain shoots across a nearby pane, or to catch who sneaks out as an adjacent curtain draws back, or, more edifying still, to stick around long enough to map the adjustments in the faces of those who go in and slip out, or who return night after night until business or adventure takes them to newer cities and to other unforeseeable undertakings. She also knows, and tells me, how to find the oddest side streets, those just off once fine cultural mainlines, housing bona fide curiousity shops selling not plastic potleaves or keychains but memory books and pale picture-postcards, shops long since closed when we walk by at night but which he and I return to during the day.

On my first night out, of course, I had suspected, I had hoped that all this was here but I had been too distracted to see it, too wrapped up with what might take place the next night then the next night then the next ...

It made it easier then and it makes it easier now that there are relatively few judgments passed here, that there's an easy familiarity with almost all that one would want to sell or to buy or to rent. As I'd understood back in Princeton, Amsterdam has been peddling, roughly or with refinement, the same wares since before the thirteenth century, which is not to discount the change in human hopes and in primordial pathologies since then. Still, there's cold and hot comfort alike in precedent and in an onslaught of history, and I remember how she'd lectured me once, unwarrantedly, "do not damn the night here. Every evening, as the Jews calculate it, is the beginning of a new day, so every sunset is a moment of rebirth."

Birth or death, who knows, but walking to her apartment one night, on my own, I consider for the first time that returning to the U.S. will be a rebirth, of sorts. For myself. It's not a nice thought. But it's one that I had.

I take a left and seeing a bottle cap that says "Stella," I kick it out of a gutter and, unintentionally, into a wall. It bounces back.

My gaze follows it and to my right I see a man's face, shadowed by a fedora, peering out at me through a filigreed cage, like a bizarre outdoor shower stall. A public pissoir. Taking advantage of his being occupied, I hurry on, less angry now because half-grossed out, if also half-excited.

Walking in the dusk, I don't feel unsafe, exactly. I never have. But a charcoaled half-light cloaks the city and as with my first evening here life feels sort of surreal. It's in this atmosphere that I can see my head cracking against the moss-covered bank of a canal, my coat growing heavy with the dark urine-drenched water while some thug, his hands having relieved my pants pocket, runs off with my wallet.

Peering over a railing, I smell a grimey moldiness. I see my corpse floating in the greenish waterway, bloated. My head is cold. Water surrounds it. It's depressing and incandescent. But peaceful.

By now I've wandered somehow into an area that seems shabby even for the rld. It's not as trash-filled as her alley but the tenements are equivalently dilapidated and they too look like they were designed to be rather than slowly grew into being slums. One difference is that these lack even the dubious grace of neighbors that must once have been merchant mansions. Another is that the people around here are without even a simulated interest in sex, much less its income. They just look hard and angry and hopeless, save perhaps for that one old man at a streetcorner up ahead munching his lower lip.

Unfortunately, he must have caught me looking at him for he's shuffling over. I try to sidestep him, nodding as I walk past. This is actually all I can do since I can't understand one *word* of what he's mumbling. His meaning becomes clear enough though when he sticks out his hand. It's curled inwards like a claw, grasping and empty. He shuffles surprisingly fast to stay in front of me.

237

Normally, I'm not hardhearted but by this point I'm almost out of money myself, and I had not budgeted for beggars. So I shake my head and say "no."

All of a sudden it's as if a mini-devil has broken loose. I don't know if it's the foreign sound of what I'd said or the shaking of my head but he has gone fullout berserk, jabbering, shaking his finger at me, and jerking closer and closer. Now he's *laughing* at me, in a frenzy.

"Hey!" I snap, "stop. *Stop* it!" He's making me angry. He's drawing attention to us, plus I hate it when people laugh for no reason. He's crazy. Still, I *hate* it. I **hate** it. Then just as suddenly as he'd started, he's stopped.

He's stopped laughing but his face has started to contort. Twisting. I back away from him. Now he looks angry. He appears to be mimicking both of us, at once, mouthing "*stop, stop.*" His lips are speckled with spit, his gums look rotted. A bit frightened now, I grab into my pocket and toss him a coin. His claw catches it with a mechanical if spasmodic dexterity. At least, I think half-hysterically, this has proved profitable for someone.

I keep moving. He, thank god, stays put, as if his feet have stuck to the pavement, right where he had caught my coin. Ignoring my better judgment, I look back. I see no sign of appreciation or even self-satisfaction. He's simply standing still, turning the coin over and over, as if he's not quite sure what it is.

Another night walking around, Janêk asleep in the hotel room, I stop off at a twenty-four-hour internet café. Ostensibly I need to check my email but to be honest I've been wanting to see one of these places up close. I find them fascinating, and at the same time creepy. They're such public places for such personal purposes, emails, dating websites, whatever. Narrow shops with lean electric feeds plugged into humming, buzzing little boxes, all set up in lines. What, I wonder, could all those people possibly be looking up after midnight? Bills, plane or train tickets, sure. But what about those spending not a few minutes but hours in front of some screen. Some of them pour over computer codes—codes, well, I guess for what you'd think, hidden drugs, hidden money—or is it simply me that forces all I that see into judgments, malodorous with morality. No, it's the way of the world, of people who sit in liquid green lights in beige spray-can-cleaned spaces, and those who are curious about them.

Well, much like whatever goes on in those rooms, my last days in Amsterdam are a bit of a blur. I worry about the hotel bill, then I look at him lying naked and next to me. My last night, Gretta invites us over. She has boiled pasta and chicken, which he picks around. Together, she and I get tipsy on white wine. Even he has two or three unenthusiastic sips. Before I know it's happened, she's snapped a Polaroid picture of him and myself together, then one more. She takes them, I suspect, because she knows that they'll make me uneasy, and they do. She places them on a fresh pile of frayed books but when I look to take them later they're gone. Soon after, we kiss and say our goodbyes. He goes to the bathroom, comes back, and we leave ...

epilogue

I found the above account a month ago. It had been locked in a trunk between two VHS porns and a copy of *Le Roman de la Rose*. I must have stuck it there after college. This would have been in my "in between" stage, after I'd returned to Carlton but before I'd moved to New York for a job marketing infotainment for a profitable publisher. I'd gotten the job—not to boast, because I know why I'd been offered it—before I'd even graduated, and while I hated the idea of selling out, the salary, if not great, was enough to lure me into a life where I could continue to work with books, of a sort.

Not surprisingly, I suppose, recalling my time in Amsterdam had sparked an elegy for abandoned ideals. Remembering Janêk had jarred me to the extent, almost, that the apple must have Adam. When the fruit is also a seed it's hard to perceive it as sweet. What seed is sweet? What can sound appetizing when you've been told you're already in eden?

In a way, I was in an eden, if a narcoleptic one. By the time I got to New York for work, my mother had moved to L.A. and the few imported Princetonians I knew drudged nowhere near the city's literary lights or their outlets, while I went nowhere near their finance firms. With a gift from my father, given half out of pride and half to remind me where I would forever derive most of my income, I had purchased an adequate condo. This allowed for a façade of freedom, if one in which I felt compelled to earn more and more money. Rather than enjoy the city, I spent my time pushing online mass market ads, quickly written and quickly sold, a dizzying swing from reading whatever I'd wanted mixed with syllabi on the visionary histories of Saint Augustine, Hildegard of Bingen, or Nietzsche. Still, the people in my division were smart and funny and quick to catch on to good tactics. We all got along, mostly, and I got promoted. When I redesigned a presale system for online social media, I got promoted again, and got to start working with acquisitions. My psyche had shrunk but by this time I was earning a salary that would allow most people to live if not comfortably than not uncomfortably even in Manhattan.

It was soon after this that I'd visited my bank. There I'd arranged to have a percentage, a fairly sizable one, of my trust income sent to a firm not connected with my family. From there, a broker reinvests the money, precisely how or in what I'm not sure. Then a month or so after this, I'd hired a private investigator to track down those whom I had remembered from Amsterdam. Initially, I had wanted to know all about them, how and what they were doing, but by the time he'd gotten back to me I no longer wanted to know. The money anyway, sufficiently enough to stay under any international radars, goes to them. Forty percent to her, sixty to him. It will be this way for the rest of our lives. I'd fixed it, against the advice of the attorney involved, so that I can't change it. It's entirely out of my and my family's hands, until I am dead.

Callous. I suppose that this may sound callous. It occurs to me that when I was twenty, I would have thought it was. Six years, however, have passed since then and I'd been so racked with guilt or who knows what that some nights I could barely sleep. Now I sleep fine. I worry only that by thinking and rethinking my memories will grow stale. So I remember them only when I must. When I can't sleep, when I am lonely, when I wonder if I will ever find anyone to love. I hope that they can sleep and I hope that she is not lonely. I am honestly unsure as to whether or not I hope that they know that the money comes from me. In a way it does and in a way it does not.

Last night, I had dinner with my old roommate, Stephen. Surprisingly, he had treated. He was in town working on some new high-rise on the Upper East Side and, he dropped, sleeping with two women (maybe more) two subway stops apart. He is ineluctably the same, only more intense, more concentrated. After we ate we went to my place so that he could see a sketch I'd just bought, a profile of an old street in Amsterdam. In the cab, I'd tried to hint at what I had done and he had told me, bluntly, that people lived the way that they did for a reason and that I shouldn't mess with them. In my condo, he had glanced at the sketch, then he had fucked me till I had come on his chest. Afterward he had advised me not to tell anyone else what I had told him and to stop payments on my arrangement. "When you're O. G. New England rich," he had said, "no deal is non-annullable."

For all his success, Stephen still has little sense of American hierarchies of morality.

What I had not shown him, and I am glad that I had not, was the book I'd received two days ago in the mail. For the past four years, I have on five occasions received slim packages with no return address from somewhere in Amsterdam. I can tell by the stamp. Inside is always a brand new edition in vinyl of a work with a title along the lines of *Agricultural Anonymity and Small Aggregate Farms* or *The Import of Monetary Reserves for Rural Čiastkový*. At first I'd tried to read them but as I have never interacted with cattle or hoarded pre-revolutionary rubles the twisting articles were impossible to follow. Mainly, I found myself wondering why anyone had written them.

The latest one I'd set, for some perverse reason, on my coffee table. When I sit on my neo-Corbusier couch in my fifteenth-floor condo—I'd moved when I'd shot up from our pop academics to our tweenstar "memoirs" division—its flimsy cover stares up at me. It announces *After Industrialism: A Statistical Evaluation of its Aftereffekts* by Melek Fischer. I can only hope that she, nameless here, must be nearing the end of this.

Sometimes I can't help but wonder, have I saved him? The bank assures me that their accounts are emptied and that each of them alone can access their funds. This doesn't, of course, mean that they are alright but it does mean that they won't starve. I hope that one day she will use her fair share to live, for better or worse, for herself. He ... late at night, when I'm feeling less jealous, I hope that he has at last found his island.

Truly, though, I know that even having given up part of my inheritance, never honestly my own, that this will never have been enough. I had abandoned him. Leaving him outside that hotel, irritated because they had added a seventy euro "service" charge, had been hard. Then getting on that plane, without him, that—that had been the ultimate infidelity.

I will remain guilty of that for life. But guilt, like the moon in the morning, or an interest in endnotes, wanes and I'm left wondering if, as I live on, I forfeit the right even to reach out to him. Stephen, I think, is flat-out wrong. The right advance is to put myself out. To do just, in fact, as I have done. To let him know that I am thinking of him then to allow him to decide what to do. No doubt this is courage of the most pusillanimous sort ... but it is also love, insofar as it involves all the pushings and the pullings, the twistings and the turnings that lead both to my desire for him and to all my inadequate intentions. I know of course that these will never suffice. But I will continue to pay my penance, hoping that, having once held him up, we will end up holding each other.

TELL THE WORLD THIS BOOK WAS		
GOOD	BAD	SO-SO

about the author

David Deutsch studied medieval literature early in his career and now writes cultural studies of British literature, classical music, and queer American poetry and prose. In his own fiction, he prefers to take a break from historical subjects so as to explore actions and events that never quite happened but that have moral resonances within contemporary gay life. At present, he is working on a monograph on twenty-first-century American gay painting and a second novel set in New York and Oxford that focuses on modern classical music and genetics.

CPSIA information can be obtained
at www.ICGtesting.com
Printed in the USA
JSHW022043090321
12395JS00001B/23